SPANISH PIECES OF EIGHT

RICK GLAZE

SCREENSHOT
PUBLISHERS

ScreenShot Publishers
Nashville, Tennessee
650-492-0920
Ricksbooks@rickglaze.com

This book is a work of fiction. Names, characters, places, and incidents are the product of the author's imagination or are used fictitiously. Any resemblance to actual events, locales, facilities, or persons, living or dead, is coincidental.

The scanning, uploading, and distribution of this book without permission is a theft of the author's intellectual property. Permission may be obtained by contacting Ricksbooks@RickGlaze.com.

Cover Design: The Books Covered Team
Map Illustration: Scott Simpson
Editing: Stephanie Parent / Stephanie Reents
Line Edit: Peggy Thompkins
Formatting: Polgarus Studio

ISBN Paperback   978-1-7372951-6-7
ISBN Digital   978-1-7372951-5-0
ISBN Audio   978-1-7372951-7-4

Also by Rick Glaze

Novels:
The Purple River
Ralph & Murray

Silicon Cowboy (music CD)
Anegada Caribbean Breeze (music CD)

Visit Rick's website and listen to songs he wrote for main characters
Richard, Alice, and Jimmy.
www.RickGlaze.com

Contents

Preface

An important part of this story is to get a picture in your mind of the location and geography of this adventure. The map in these first few pages is a good way to keep up with the characters and their quest. I sailed into every place on the map first for my personal adventures, and then to gather impressions and details for the pages of this novel. But in 2017, the landscape changed and some of these places were destroyed. A devastating hurricane, named Irma, blew through the Caribbean island chain, before it crashed into the Florida coast. The Virgin Islands experienced a direct hit taking a terrible toll.

As you travel with me on this suspense-filled escapade and squeeze by the rocks into the waters of North Sound near the tip of Virgin Gorda, enjoy your visit to the world-renowned Bitter End Yacht Club. Look out over the calm, morning waters of this breathtaking bay during your breakfast along with Jimmy, as he tries to unwind the seemingly un-solvable puzzle his dad engineered. Read it one more time, because it's the only time you'll see it. Irma reduced the Bitter End to splinters.

On a happy note, rebuilding is on-going, and life is returning to normal. Bathers, beach comers, and sailors are back. While sailing the Virgin Islands, I have a saying, "Each morning you leave the most beautiful place you've ever been, and each afternoon you sail into the most beautiful place you've ever been."

Read on and you'll see what I mean.

Character List

Richard Dennison, father, sailor, and Silicon Valley Entrepreneur

Samantha, waitress from Mississippi

Jennifer, meets Richard in a marina in San Francisco Bay

Children:
 Zach
 Alice, Andrew is her husband, Bev is her daughter, Branson is her son
 Maureen, Randy is her husband
 Jimmy

Bill Price, lawyer

Bruce, former employee of Richard's.

Prologue

"All those gold and silver coins would be in a bank safe deposit box if Richard hadn't died Friday morning. He finally agreed to abandon this treasure hunt trick and dig up his sunken fortune. When I reached the hospice at noon Friday with the trust amendment for his signature, they were wheeling him out under a sheet." Bill Price paused, pulling the phone receiver slightly away from his ear.

A voice crackled through his phone as he pressed it again to his ear. "We know it's buried on that postage-size island in the Caribbean, let's just go get it."

"Impossible. The trust is iron-clad. All the coins stay, and the treasure hunt begins."

"We've talked about this," the voice responded. "When we buried it, silver was thirty dollars an ounce and gold was three hundred dollars an ounce. Now silver is three hundred and gold is two thousand."

"I know full well its value is around five and a half million," Bill Price said.

"Richard didn't tell you?"

"Tell me what?"

"Bruce added to it over twenty years just to humor Richard, but mostly they undercounted it on purpose. It's at least a hundred million now."

1

1

The Trust

Zach Dennison turned into the entrance of the underground parking garage at 525 University Avenue in Palo Alto. His brand new 2017 dark blue Boxster convertible was shined to a mirror finish. He wore a maroon short-sleeve collared shirt with a Palo Alto Hills Country Club logo. After pulling into the first parking spot marked "clients of Price, Prince, McClather—2 hour limit," he reached for the key to shut off the engine and as his hand fell back to his lap, he sat still, his eyes fixed through the windshield onto the blank wall. A thousand things raced through his mind: his dad's recent death, the estate, the money, Jimmy, and the money again. After about a minute, he punched a button on the console to lift the ragtop of the two-seater. He sat quietly in the cozy bucket seat while the convertible top snuggled in against the rim of the windshield.

Arriving at the law office, his half-sister, Maureen, was waiting in the firm's large conference room. He greeted her and turned to see his younger sister, Alice, walk through the mahogany double doors and take a chair beside Maureen. Zach accepted a bottle of water from a young staffer.

He turned and looked through the floor-to-ceiling glass wall of the conference room just as his half-brother, Jimmy, walked into the reception area wearing off-white slacks, a pinstriped shirt, a navy tie, and black blazer. Jimmy looked like he just stepped off a yacht in Hyannis Port, totally out of his element here in workaday Silicon Valley, as he flashed his signature smile at the receptionist leading him into the conference room.

Jimmy walked straight over to Maureen. They began talking to each other, but their eyes were fixed on Zach. Alice stood alone wistfully staring through the picture window into the cubicles beyond. She looked up at Jimmy, flashing him a kinda toothy smile, red lips and the greenest cat-eyes in the room that turned hazel in the morning light. Her dark, almost jet-black hair rolled down along her cheeks and onto her shoulders, framing her long, ivory neck.

Zach was the middle son of the deceased. He had managed the businesses and portfolios for the family for a decade. Over the last few years their father slowly increased his responsibility, piling an onerous weight on his shoulders, and that stress combined with the sudden death of his wife, Debra, left him unwillingly at the helm when his father died. Now everyone in the room was dependent on him for something. Zach became the "go-to" guy for the siblings, including Jimmy's unrelenting need for spending money and his frequent creative ideas for new businesses with Dad's money. Maureen was levelheaded, and conducted her lifestyle in a prudent way. On the other hand, her husband, Randy, looked at the family assets as a smorgasbord of opportunity for "sure thing" investments. When the "promise of stem cell research" hysteria was the next best thing in California, Randy popped a half million dollars into an investment fund his law firm worked on. The result was happy scientists, interesting research, and intriguing academic papers, but no salable products and no money back. The only "promise" Randy got was Maureen's that if he did anything like that again, he'd be single. Maureen used her annual distributions from the family trust for several years to pay off the mortgage Randy took on the house for this "sure thing." It never sunk in with Randy that Maureen was already wealthy, so he could just cruise through life. Randy thought of himself as an entrepreneur in shining armor. His mission: slaying dragons and making lots of money, in a kind of 007 fashion.

Alice was the fourth child. She lived quietly on a foggy, rainy forty acres in the coastal mountain range between Silicon Valley and the Pacific Ocean. Alice's land was a combination of lush forest and wide-open, grassy knolls. She lived with her husband, Andrew, a daughter Bev, and a younger son, Branson. Alice made pottery and Andrew grew vegetables and wrote poetry. Unlike Randy, Andrew could read the tea leaves about the money, so he kept under the radar, made no waves, and started no businesses. A few years ago, he self-published a book of his poetry and managed to get some group to give him an award for it. He was now an "award-winning poet."

Alice and Zach had one thing in common that everybody knew but nobody talked about. They were, in common parlance, illegitimate children. Their father had not married their mother. This could have been a showstopper for any other family, socially embarrassing and legally sticky, but Richard Dennison never acknowledged any difference among *his* children. Any legal ramifications that hung other people up and created greed and envy were put to rest from the start. He made everybody aware that "his" meant his.

Zach looked up as Bill Price entered the room. The lawyer settled in, as everyone took a seat. He looked casual, but his light blue button-down shirt was crisp and the casual cut of his black slacks didn't detract from his professional demeanor. He carried only one document of about fifty pages, laid it on the polished mahogany table and looked up with a cautious smile. The cover was printed in bold, black letters:

Richard Dennison Trust and Last Will and Testament

He began reading, "Dear children. In this trust you will find the first clue leading to other clues that will take you to a treasure of extreme interest. As in our previous games, the precise nature of the treasure will only be revealed when found. I always thought about this game as the crowning jewel of our family adventures. Love, Dad."

Zach examined the stunned, sober faces as Bill Price finished reading and closed the summary page of the trust. Jimmy lifted his water bottle just short of his mouth but then slowly returned it to the table. He didn't appear to be breathing. His wide-open eyes stared at the mahogany-paneled wall behind Bill Price. Maureen dropped her right arm to an open handbag on the floor, shuffled her hand blindly into the purse for a few seconds, then pulled out a small green carton of chewing gum. She mindlessly flipped the top open and put the tab of gum on her tongue and began to chew. Alice didn't move a muscle. It was as if she melted into her seat, her loose-fitting cotton dress cascading over the chair to the gray carpet.

"Is this some kind of joke?" Jimmy's voice modulated to an octave above his normal range. "Our dad was self-centered and heartless, but not cruel. Somebody tell me this is his last trick and the real trust is in that stack, right, Mr. Price?"

Bill Price's eyes remained focused in that expected "attorney look" with the purpose of giving away no secrets, no ground, no answers. Then he slowly glanced at Zach, who gave a slight but detectable nod.

"It's no joke, Jim. Dad set it up this way on purpose, just like all the other games," Zach said.

"I have a life," Jimmy chortled. "I can't go on a wild goose chase. People count on me."

"Oh, you mean that herd of raggedy bloodsuckers that do whatever you want as long as you pay for it?" Maureen blurted.

5

Jimmy's lips slammed together and his cheeks filled with air ready to burst, behind his clenched teeth. His face turned red, looking ready to scream. Alice shifted, slightly, in her chair. None of the siblings jumped to Jimmy's defense, nor did they shower guilt on Maureen for her seemingly rude comment. Zach watched the bickering with little interest. Neither he nor Bill Price made any attempt to arbitrate, having both been defeated in that task many times, for many years.

"Zach, tell me there's a way to get around this. I know you've figured out a way," Jimmy pleaded.

"Bill wrote it. It's ironclad," Zach said.

"Well, give me a copy of the whole damn trust. I'll find a way," Jimmy said.

"It's not a public document, Jimmy," Zach said. "Nobody but the trustee can have a copy. That's the way Dad set it up. Look, I'm the trustee, and there is nothing in it but the two million allocation to each of us. The big money is tied up in the real estate portfolio. And this, whatever it turns out to be, is hidden and the trust doesn't say where it is. Bill doesn't know and I don't know. If you want it, you're going to have to find it just like the rest of us."

"Our next meeting is in a week on Tuesday at ten, right here," Bill Price said. "At that time, we can all look over the instructions and the first clue."

"Sorry, sailing in a regatta out of Chesapeake Bay next week. What is the alternate date?" Jimmy asked.

"The alternate is next Tuesday at ten," Bill Price answered.

"How am I going to tell my crew? They have been training for months and Christ, it's my boat!" Jimmy answered.

"Call 'em on the phone, Jimmy. That's how people do it," Maureen barked. "They call 'em on the phone."

2

Richard

Later that night Bill Price inched the door of his study closed. The kids were tucked in and his wife was reading in the den. He eased into his favorite leather chair and picked up a large brown envelope. The day Richard died, a nurse handed it to him at the hospice because there was a note with his name stuck on the front. She said he was holding it when he died. A spiral-bound notebook titled, "My Private Diary, Richard Dennison" was inside. He stared at the blue, near perfect cursive as he flipped through the pages. The haphazard, quick, on-the-go entries common in a diary were not there. This reminded him of memoirs or handwritten autobiographies he'd seen. With a slight curiosity he began reading.

A landlocked Tennessean, I was an unlikely candidate for a life on the water. There is no serious sailing in Tennessee. It's fishing and water-skiing territory. There's no water large enough for sailing big boats. Yet even though I traveled many miles all around the world and radically changed my lifestyle, it was a long time before I got my little hometown out of my head. People I'd meet and places I went seemed somehow temporary, or in a strange way only on the periphery of my big picture. I'd travel back to that little town sometimes every year, other times ten or twelve years elapsed between visits—always looking for a bookend for my life. After one visit in my late fifties, I knew I didn't have to go back anymore. Of course, I was sure of the reason for this sudden epiphany at the time but honestly, I don't really know what changed and I quit thinking about it years ago. I don't think there ever was a bookend for my life. There is, however, a story.

I have had a fun life. Some would call it colorful. I worked under the assumption that life was an adventure and all the worries and problems that slowed other people down, I just didn't think about. Not everybody liked that approach, but I never cared. I engineered a bit of adventure for my children—Jimmy, Maureen, Zach, and Alice. I think of it as kind of a character builder. I'll get to that later.

I bought my first boat in Oakland right after the IPO for Intermediate Microchip in 1981. The six-month lockup for option holders was over, and I sold stock worth $200,000. A four-year old, thirty-six-foot Catalina sloop popped up for sale, and I bought it and moved in, writing a check for the two months left on my lease of a two-bedroom walkup apartment in Mountain View here in Silicon Valley. I had never set foot on a sailboat, and for six months the Catalina, my guitar, and I just sat in the slip rising and falling with the tide. In the spring when the San Francisco Bay winds picked up, I started sailing lessons. That was thirty-two years ago.

I met Jennifer in the marina at Point Richmond while on a round-trip sail up through San Pablo Bay. I was single that day but had a couple of regular mates and their girlfriends with me. We were sailing east up through the inland channel for an overnight docking in Stockton. Somebody forgot a can of something so we stopped at the small harbor. While the giddy couples were frolicking down to the store, I pulled out the insides of a sticky winch onto the deck and began spraying it with an aerosol lubricant.

"You know that spray breaks down the ozone layer," I heard a woman's voice from behind me.

A steady twelve knot northeast breeze was blowing a few high cumulus clouds around while the bright sun took the chill off a San Francisco morning. Holding the chrome winch casing in my hand, I twisted my head to look over my shoulder and saw a Norwegian-looking pale blonde wearing a black and orange San Francisco Giants baseball cap. Her eyes trained on me like a hawk staring at its kill. But a bird of prey never filled out a bikini top the way this petite, fair-haired dock-buddy did.

There was a quiet confidence in her smile that I couldn't quite pinpoint. Her cheekbones were prominent with a slight blush of pink. Maybe she was flirting or maybe she told everybody about aerosol cans. But right then I had no crew in sight, oily fingers and a world of possibilities in a yellow swimsuit standing on the dock in front of me.

"They make it in spray cans and I'm just dumb enough to use it, I guess." I smiled.

My delivery was deadpan as I stared back into her laser eyes. She took a couple of steps toward the boat and scanned the machined parts that were spread out on the deck's surface.

"Oil won't help you anyway. From here it looks like the number two sprocket is worn and needs replacing. But you can't get one here. Probably have to order it at the boat works in Alameda," she said. "I'd throw that thing back together for now. It'll last through your little booze-cruise today."

I picked up the sprocket—she was right. "Aye, aye skipper. I'll get right on that," I said. "But cruising-the-booze requires a few more mates than I have. Can I count on you to join our merry crew and swab the decks for the afternoon?"

Okay, it was one of my worst pickup lines ever. When those words oozed through my lips, I figured this little rendezvous was going down in flames. She stood there unfazed, though. Her face showed no signs that I could read. It was like I didn't say it, like she was allowing me to discreetly remove my foot from my mouth so we could go forward. I glanced up to see a group of gulls flying overhead, screeching and circling back and forth over the empty masts that silently floated in row after row above sleeping boats.

"So, you come here often, sailor?" she asked.

Without a second of hesitation, I broke into a snicker, my arms relaxed and dropped to my sides. I was saved from the moniker of cheap pickup artist and brought back to the land of the clever sailor. That's a lot of work for a small blonde, I thought.

"So hey, what's your name?"

"Jennifer, and you?"

"Richard Dennison, Captain Richard," I said.

"I'd go out with you guys but I have a few chores today. Maybe next time," she replied.

"Where do you live?"

"I hang around the boat harbor in Alameda most weekends. Stop by," she said.

She turned and strolled off down the pier, her thin frame casting a short shadow in the mid-morning sun. I wanted to jump onto the dock and try to see what boat she was on, but I was afraid it would look too needy, or whatever, so I sat down in the cockpit and just stared blankly at the disassembled winch.

That's how it started with Jennifer. A long time passed before I actually hooked up with her, but as you'll see, it was worth the wait.

Living on the boat, I had very few responsibilities, not much to hold me down, and I liked it that way. Then all that changed when in late 1983, I got a call from John Chakkera. He was a colleague at Intermediate Micro who had joined the company a few months after I did. The windfall from our stock options didn't entice John to quit working and wallow in life's pleasures like I did. He stayed with the company and worked his way up in technical sales. We both were riding the wave from our stock grants as the price moved higher on the market. But John was more conventional than me with his steady girlfriend and a membership in the Decathlon Club. He bought a house in Cupertino and prided himself on his "Silicon Valley network" of friends and acquaintances. I too had an extensive network, but most of them didn't wear shoes. John had an idea for a new company involving processor testing and he needed a management team to get it started. He wanted to talk it over with me, so we set up a meeting at Il Fornaio on the ground floor of the Garden Court Hotel in Palo Alto.

The Garden Court should have been apartments, tucked into a corner niche on a crowded street in this little town that is the hub of Silicon Valley. But somebody had the gumption to build a three-story hotel with thirty-eight rooms that turned into the "deal place" for the worldwide electronics revolution. I hadn't been there in a year but the maître' d greeted my arrival with, "Mr. Dennison, Mr. Chakkera has arrived and is seated at your table. Please follow me."

"Richard, how is life treating you?" John said as the waiter pulled out a chair for me. He rose from the table, his hand extended from his trim torso and slightly wide shoulders. The aroma of heavy garlic permeated the frenetic atmosphere of the large dining room.

John and I had just been over the niceties of life on the phone, so I didn't see the need to answer him. Instead I unfolded my napkin and laid it on my lap. I looked up and said, "So, tell me about this startup, Johnny Boy." A waiter pushed through the swinging doors from the kitchen behind us, ushering into the room the soothing aroma of fresh-baked bread.

3

The Restaurant

Bill Price crossed San Antonio Road and turned right from El Camino Real into the parking lot of the venerable Chef Chu's restaurant. He had chosen a popular lunch spot six miles south of Palo Alto for this meeting. The food was renowned, with specialty dishes created in the kitchen by the chef himself, which could be found nowhere else in the world. Bill walked in the front door and turned left past the live lobster tank, and stopped in front of two carved wooden doors. He straightened his shoulders, took a deep breath and walked into the private dining room. A glass case covered the far wall with bottles of Chinese liquor floating on a glass shelf over bottle after bottle of private label wine. The room was often set for small parties of up to twenty people, but today there was only a small table with a setting for two placed in the middle of the room under a cut-glass chandelier. Bill closed the door and walked straight to one of the chairs, pulled it out and sat down. He cleared his throat, gently pulled the linen napkin down to his lap and looked up.

"How did they take it?" asked a svelte, tanned, seventyish-year-old woman with only a hint of age in her face.

"How do you think they took it? Jimmy squealed like a stuck pig. Maureen hurled insults at Jimmy while Alice retreated into some inner mystic layer of the ozone."

"I know that, I mean did they understand the game, you know, the hunt?"

"If you're asking if they jumped with glee about a treasure hunt for millions of dollars of inheritance," Bill asked, "not really. Look, Jennifer, when you and Richard set this fun little game up, those coins were worth a few million. Now the game is fifty times that amount. This is a big deal."

"I did help with the details, but you knew Richard. He had to have his mind working all the time on some project or he," she hesitated, "well, usually he drank too much and nobody liked that." She lifted her water glass, took a drink and continued, "And a few younger women too, nobody liked that either."

"Except Richard," Bill said.

4

Richard / Palo Alto

Bill Price settled into his chair, once again opened the diary to the bookmarked page and began to read.

"I need you on the team, Richard," John said to me. I sat straight up in my chair and didn't utter a word.

The waiter placed the signature Il Fornaio bread on the table in front of John Chakkera as he laid out the plans for a startup company, from describing the management team, to pitching venture capitalists for startup money.

"Building a sales force and distribution network will be a real key to success, and that's where you'll be critical," he said. "Finally, an initial public offering that will be the cash-out for us all, and bring the train into the station."

When his spiel was finished, I noticed he was leaning over the table, his head in front of his shoulders like so many cerebral types, leading the charge—full speed ahead. Then he pulled his head up over the center of his shoulders, shifted back in his chair, flashed a big toothy grin and said, "And that, Richard, my boy, is when I learn to sail and disappear to one of those tropical islands you're always dreaming about."

One of the waitresses flew by immersed in that I'm-twenty-five-gotta-get-it-done-Silicon-Valley-scoot that is common in these fast-paced, high profile restaurants. Her bouncy dark hair gave her a wholesome down-to-earth look, and I started thinking about clever lines I could use to open up a little bit of conversation. I was bored with hanging loose around the marinas. And...I'm tired of blondes, I thought.

"So," John took a long pause, "what do you think?"

"I think you've thought of everything. Of course, not much of it will go the way you've planned, but you already know that. The big thing is that I'm not sure I need a job right now. I mean, Christ, I live on a boat. All my shoes except one pair are flip-flops and those are saturated with salt water. It's not like I'm lazy, but..."

John lowered his voice as a couple of young wannabe tech moguls walked past our table. "It's not about being lazy. It's about creating the right opportunity. It's about getting the right focus for a specific time frame, and then," he paused, "cashing out. Read my lips, Richard, out, gone, vamoose. This is not a life sentence. It's the Last Waltz."

I was trying to follow what John was saying, but the brown-haired waitress passed by again. Her curvy figure complimented that natural beauty and, best of all, she gave me an inquisitive nod as she scurried by the table. I thought again about the new company. I liked John's spirit and drive and he had a good business plan. I could slide into this deal with no capital, except my time, and if it didn't work, I'd just go sailing.

"What role do you want me to take in the company and what's the financial arrangement for the initial team?" I asked.

"I'm asking the startup team to get the ball rolling, but take no salary till we get venture funding. There will be four of us and I'm selling each of you ten percent of the company for a penny a share. That leaves seventy percent for me to negotiate with the VCs," John replied.

"How much are you going to keep?" I asked.

"All I can, but I know anything over ten percent will be gravy for me," he said. "We might see some dilution along the way, but we just have to go for it and see how the chips fall."

John was talking about the practice the venture capitalists have of extracting more ownership of the company by creating more shares that they keep. This reduces the value of the existing shares. It's a common practice when there is a perceived distress around financing. It can happen when the initial product is slower getting to market than expected, and more money is needed to keep things rolling, or a competing product from another company suddenly surfaces, or any number of other reasons. John and I saw it happen with Intermediate Microchip. We weren't part of the management team then, but we watched the whole deal go down. The specialty chip for video enhancement was hotly anticipated and potential orders were extremely strong, but the manufacturing ran into a glitch which set the product launch back six months. Cash was running short and the banks were not lending to startups at the time. The company was over a barrel and the VCs stuck it to the management. They coughed up the money but made the management issue new preferred shares which diluted everybody's stake by twenty-five percent. That's the way the game works and you had to be prepared for it. When the company went public, they all got rich anyway.

John wanted me to set up a marketing and sales system that would be all polished up for the VC pitch. He didn't have an office yet so we would be working from home, which meant boat to me. We would meet periodically until the office was rented. He had the patented technology licensed from a geek professor at Stanford University who was going to be part of the initial team, which bothered me some because these profs didn't usually have any business sense. They weren't used to normal business compromises and trade-offs. But they were the ones with ideas, they were the ones producing technology innovations in their academic labs. So, entrepreneurs frequently had to endure the "nutty professors," so to speak.

Our waitress set a warm plate of veal piccata in front of John and served a bowl of the restaurant's renowned spaghetti Bolognese to me. The conversation slowed as we ate.

"Give me a few days to think it over, but I'm feeling good about the whole venture," I said.

Finally, we pushed our chairs back and stood up to leisurely walk out of the restaurant onto Cowper Street. As we left the table, I glanced at my jacket slung across the back of my chair. I turned and kept walking out the door. John and I exchanged goodbyes and I stood on the corner watching him pull his new Volvo coupe out into traffic, turn onto University Avenue and drive away. I pictured him in a new BMW 640 convertible with a high gloss metallic finish. Yeah, that would be just the ticket for John. My mind's eye then pictured a fifty-foot Oyster sloop with two luxury cabins, an electric furling mainsail, bow thrusters, and Virgin Gorda off the starboard bow. Oh yes, and I was at the helm with a twenty-knot wind blowing in my hair. Maybe John would be my ticket to that new boat in the islands.

I turned and walked back into the restaurant, past the front podium and straight to our former table to retrieve my jacket and hopefully run into a certain brown-haired waitress. I rounded the corner to see the table neatly reset and my jacket gone. When I felt a tap on my right shoulder, I stopped and slowly looked around. As I turned, I heard, "Looking for this?"

Gazing past the jacket, I saw my picture-perfect, blue-eyed darling, ready and willing.

Her name was Samantha, but they called her Sam. She came from Mississippi to go to Stanford and graduated the previous year. Living with some friends in Woodside, she was taking a breather from career ambitions for a while. I told her she looked like a sailor and I just happened to have a boat with a crew spot open for this Friday afternoon.

5

Zach

"Did Dad set a time limit for this treasure hunt?" Zach asked.

"No, not really a time frame, so to speak. It's set up to go till somebody finds it," Jennifer told her son.

"Let's say nobody finds it and something happens to you. Is all this possible wealth just lost?"

"Your dad envisioned this as a test of character, stamina and will," she said.

"Jesus Christ, Mom, I've got all the character I can stand, and talk about stamina, it evaporates every day that I get older," he said. "As for 'will,' will you just tell me where this treasure is and I'll split it up like normal families do."

Jennifer was sitting having a private conversation with her only son, and the most levelheaded and reliable child Richard produced. But she knew even level heads had to question this over-the-top scheme to make heirs to an estate follow clues, like the board game "Clue"—*the murder was committed by Colonel Mustard in the Library with the Wrench*. She could feel the strain it put on the whole bunch.

Jennifer never saw a need to marry Richard, but for thirty years they never parted. She settled in with a partner who had character and commitment, a soul mate. Before they met, he had flings, but all of these women tried to tame his spirit and domesticate the wild stallion in his soul.

Jennifer never wanted to take anything from Richard, and most of all she never had expectations. But once settled in, Richard stayed close to her. She knew some people tagged her as the free spirit type. She was, however, very conventional in her thinking. But unlike most other people, she didn't try to be somebody else, nor did she feel influenced by fads or fashion to act a certain way. Jennifer always felt like Jennifer. She always knew her mind.

"I don't know where it is," she said. "In fact, I don't know what it is. Maybe it's not worth it and you should just forget about the whole thing."

"All the time Dad coached me to manage his real estate properties," Zach said, "he never gave so much as a hint about this trick he was planning."

"He planned it long before that. I doubt he was thinking about it very much at that time," she said.

"God, he was strange."

"Let's just call him unique, shall we?"

6

Richard / Bruce

Bill Price slipped into his study around eleven in the evening, exhausted from nonstop meetings preparing a network hardware public stock offering. He took a deep breath and picked up the diary.

Deep in my bag I heard my cellular phone ring. I pulled the brick-size plastic device out and pushed the green button.

"Hi, this is Richard. Bruce, old boy, what is shakin' on the high seas?" I said. "Well, I just left a meeting with John Chakkera."

"How's he doing?" he said.

"Yeah, well he's plugging along fine, but he wants to ruin my peaceful, happy life by getting a startup going."

"He's overachieving," he said.

"Yeah, I agree, but he is dead set on doing it—claims we can all retire to various desert islands. What's that? No, he didn't say anything about buying an island, but now that you mention it, maybe we could find a small one to buy."

I had turned onto University Avenue and was walking down to Mac's Smoke Shop to snag a couple of hand-rolled stogies for the boat, when I got the call from Bruce. Bruce Bundy worked for me at Intermediate Microchip in sales. After the IPO, he disappeared for a while, which was normal for a single kid in his twenties. But, usually the lower-level employees, who didn't have that many stock options, showed up ready for a new job opportunity when the money ran out. Bruce did surface at my boat about a year ago talking about the Caribbean Islands and his sailing adventures. He made himself a cozy perch in the cockpit and after a few painkillers, let me in on his little secret.

His grandfather had invented an obscure technique integral to the manufacturing process for drug delivery systems through the skin. A trust was set up to give him the first of five installments of ten million dollars when he reached his twenty-eighth birthday. He had known that there was a trust, but nobody mentioned the amount for fear of ruining his motivation. Clearly, it didn't work. Through the rum I learned that Bruce took off to Antigua, a small island about midway down the Caribbean chain in what's called the Leeward Islands, to hang out and get drunk with a pal for a couple of months. He knocked around, mostly with twenty-something bikini-clad chicks for about two years, and learned to sail racing boats. A saucy brunette from New Zealand convinced him that he couldn't live without her and the wedding bells were about to ring from high above English Harbour at a place called Shirley Heights where British cannons once belched hot steel balls out over the cliffs to scare away French warships.

The view from Shirley Heights was legendary and as the rum loosened Bruce's tongue, he said, "Richard, you're not going to believe this, but you can almost see San Francisco from that hilltop." I knew then either it was really good rum or Bruce had way too much of it.

The day of his twenty-eighth birthday, his dad arrived on Antigua in a private jet and presented him with a bank statement showing his full first payment. The next day he bought the eighty-foot racing boat he had trained on, and set sail for Martinique. He didn't mention the brunette, and in fact, she never was talked about until about twenty years later on a midnight watch sailing to Tahiti, but that's another story.

Bruce was calling this time because his boat was moored in the British

Virgins and he was inviting me to crew with him on a leisurely jaunt around the islands. My sailing had been limited to San Francisco and a few trips to Catalina Island, out of Long Beach, so I was ready for an island trip.

"Okay, what's your timing, Captain Ahab?" I asked.

"Anytime is my timing. Just book a flight and boogie on down. I'm at a slip in Road Town. It's the big red boat on the end. You can't miss it," he said.

"What do you want me to bring?"

"A smile is all you need, boss," he said, and the deal was done.

7

Richard / Samantha

Several pages of the diary were dog-eared and water-stained. Bill Price straightened them out and continued reading.

Samantha came strutting down the dock at a brisk pace. I was standing on the bow up near the forestay with a hose in my hand washing off the boat. She wore a pair of navy-blue Capri pants, a red Stanford T-shirt and white Nike running shoes with red trim. Her brown hair glistened in the mid-morning low light, transforming it to reddish-brunette. Stopping abruptly in front of the boat, I could tell she was anxious about showing up to sail with somebody she'd just met and only talked to for a couple of minutes. A low marine layer of clouds grayed the morning sun and put a chill in the air. In spite of a few light morning gusts from the east, the wind was calm.

"Hi Richard, are we still going out for a sail?" she asked as she let her canvas gym bag slowly drop from her left hand to the dock.

"We'll be underway as planned, but it'll be about an hour till the crew gets here. Meanwhile, you're right on time for coffee, come on up," I said.

I walked across the deck and back to the beam to help Sam step onto the boat. After showing her around the cockpit, we went below where the French press was sitting on the counter in the galley. I poured the boiling water over the coffee and began to fit the plunger on top of the carafe when she jumped up and took it out of my hands. Looking up at me gently, her hand touched mine. Then she put the plunger on the counter, picked up a spoon and stirred the coffee and the water together.

"Connoisseurs say this is the best cup of coffee in the world," she paused and looked up with a coy smirk, "but you have to do it right."

She watched the clock for four minutes then unceremoniously shoved the plunger to the bottom of the carafe and poured the coffee into a warm mug. It tasted better than anything I ever made. But that lesson in coffee making was not the only thing I learned from Sam over the years.

My normal line with younger women was to ask about where they grew up and what their parents did. Maybe it flattered them, but anyway it worked because they all liked to talk about themselves. Sam had never been sailing and she was interested in the boat and rigging and how things worked, so the flattery part was over soon, and before I knew it we were at the navigation station looking at charts and as quickly, on deck talking about sails, sheets and binnacles.

My buddy Jack and his latest "Jill" showed up about eleven o'clock to see a clearing sky and a pithy breeze ruffling the flags. The diesel engine purred as I punched into forward gear and nosed her out of the slip. I had just moved my boat to Alameda and was getting used to motoring out through the long channel. It is wide and dredged deep to accommodate the huge ocean-going cargo ships unloading at the docks there. I motored under the Bay Bridge and turned her upwind to raise the sail. Jack took the halyard and pulled the mainsail up by hand till he got to the last foot, then wrapped it around the winch and finished the job. I turned the boat away from the wind and fell off in a five-knot breeze which hardly gave us enough power to sail at all. But, you take what you get when you're sailing, and that was typical for winter in the Bay.

A thin cotton-like tulle fog hovered around the base of Alcatraz Island, as we passed slowly by it, heading out under the Golden Gate Bridge. We sailed in front of Bonita Point for a couple of hours. The clouds broke and it felt like a summer day. With the current flowing out at two knots and the ebb flow soon to peak at five knots, I fired up the engine and pointed her for home base. Jack and "Jill" joined Sam and me for beer and deep-fried salmon and chips at the Hang Ten Fish House at the marina. As fast as Jack could order the pitchers, we were draining them. Sam, it seemed, was best friends with everybody by this time, and the beer in her glass was evaporating as fast as it was poured, like the rest of us.

"Does everybody in Mississippi drink beer like you?" I asked.

She stopped and slowly looked up, spreading a glance around the table. "Pretty much, captain," she said.

In the morning, the aroma of fresh-brewed coffee, the best on the planet, woke me up. Sam was standing in the galley wearing a long T-shirt dangling over bare feet. I shuffled gingerly through the door from the front cabin and sat on the bench seat in front of the table.

"You want to go to the Virgin Islands?" I asked.

"When?"

"Tomorrow."

8

Jimmy

Fresh flowers sat in a crystal-cut glass vase on the credenza behind the conference table. Jimmy was sitting next to Maureen and Alice at the table as Zach opened the door and quietly walked in. Jimmy thought Zach's baby-blue collared golf shirt under a navy blazer looked conventional but mostly boring. As he watched Zach sit down next to Alice, he rested his right hand on the conference table while his fingers stroked the horizontal grain of the Brazilian maple.

"Is Jennifer going to be here?" Jimmy blurted.

Jimmy wore a long-sleeve pink button-down shirt, a white linen blazer and a paisley scarf casually draped around his neck. He always dressed to make a statement, but he saw the smirk on Zach's face and didn't have to speculate what he thought. Maureen stared at Jimmy. It was January in Palo Alto, but it was sixty-eight degrees—great day for a scarf.

"She isn't a beneficiary of the trust, so she wasn't invited," Zach said. "She won't be any help with this," he said in a low, unconvincing voice.

"How can you expect us to believe that, Zach?" Maureen asked. "Your mother knew everything Dad did. If she didn't plan it with him, he certainly told her about it. Randy thinks she should be part of this whole stupid game."

"Oh yeah, that's just what we need, Randy to straighten everything out—keep us on track," Jimmy shouted.

Jimmy looked over as Alice was shifting in her seat and looking at Zach, who did not react except to lean back and settle into the soft, brown leather chair. Alice left her Birkenstocks at home and was wearing brown leather flats with soft soles. Her one-piece olive-green dress came to just below her knees and her hair was pulled back in a neat ponytail.

"Jimmy, I'm going to wring your skinny little neck if you start in on Randy," Maureen said.

Zach waited for the fighting to die down as Jimmy shrugged, rolled his eyes and turned away from Maureen.

"Dad set this up as some sort of test for us," Zach said. "He thought it would build character. But you all should know that we don't know exactly what we are looking for and we don't know how much it's worth."

"Build character? What kind of crap is that? Dad had a chance to build our character when he was sailing around the globe with that loser Bruce and a string of topless babes, but he couldn't find the time. Now he's dead and he's giving it a shot from the grave," Jimmy said. "No thanks, I'm not buying this line of bullshit."

Alice shifted again in her seat while Maureen let out a long, frustrated breath and flopped herself into the back of her chair. Zach lifted his plastic water bottle to take a drink but stopped short of his mouth, setting it back on the table in front of him.

"Topless babes?" Alice said with a mocking gesture toward Jimmy.

"You know what I mean," he said.

"No, nobody ever knows what you mean," Maureen chimed in.

Everyone fell silent as Bill Price walked into the conference room with a two-inch thick folder. He sat at the head of the table and placed the folder on the table directly in front of him. Jimmy twisted halfway around and was looking through the clear floor-to-ceiling glass window and into the lobby of the law firm when Bill began to speak.

"Your father was very successful and the fruits of his labor are going to be divided according to the provisions of the trust I have in front of me. Each of you is a limited partner in the real estate holdings, as you are aware. Zach, as general partner, runs the operations and is responsible for its growth and success. The general partner controls the business and makes all the decisions."

"So, being nice to Zach is a good idea?" Jimmy said sarcastically.

Bill Price looked down and flipped through a few pages of the trust document in front of him, but did not respond.

Then he continued, "The operations of the properties take precedent over cash distributions, but the trust recommends that growth of the business should occur after each of you, plus Jennifer and Samantha, receive twenty thousand dollars a month. Your father has provided a steady income for each of you. Richard anticipated that the property revenue would grow and Zach is charged with increasing the income to all of you as that occurs."

Alice's eyes lifted slightly. She glanced at Zach, but he didn't react. Maureen pursed her lips, looked at Zach and then looked away. Jimmy squirmed in his chair. A car horn sounded a long blast below on University Avenue, but nobody in the conference room noticed.

"Well, we know that 'cause we're already getting that money monthly," Maureen said. "What else is there? And let's get to this scavenger hunt we're hearing about."

"I have a check for each of you for two million dollars," Bill Price continued. "It's yours to do with as you please."

"Two million? Is that all?" Jimmy blurted.

Zach uncrossed his legs and set both feet on the ground, lifted his plastic water bottle, and took a long slow drink.

"Your father was a modern-day adventurer with a playful side and I guess what we can call a sense of humor," Bill Price said. No one said a thing and for a unique minute, nobody even moved. "Richard buried a treasure for you four children to find. There are clues to uncover and to follow and there are rules of the road, so to speak, that will help you find it. The starting point is in this document I have for you today."

Jimmy jumped out of his seat. As his knees straightened, they propelled the leather conference room chair backward on its castor wheels and it slammed against the glass wall.

"Can anyone hear me?" he said in a shrill, shouting voice. "I don't have time for this shit. Somebody straighten this out!" He jerked his head around and looked down his nose directly at Zach. "Do something, for God's sake."

9

Richard / Beef Island

A week passed before Bill Price was able to resume reading the diary. The stock market was hitting new highs and along with it, the IPO market for new stock issues was buzzing. His firm was swamped with legal filings. But today he was finally home for dinner with his family. He read a chapter of The Secret Garden *to his daughter and then settled in with the diary.*

I stepped onto the jet platform at the top of the stairway and looked out on the Beef Island airport. A small, private jet lowered its wheels and was making its final approach over Trellis Bay, where a small island sat in the middle dividing the bay into two halves. Another small, round island called Marina Cay lay just beyond that in light blue, shallow water, west of the larger Scrub Island. The air was thick and warm and held a salty-sea aroma. Samantha followed me down the steps to the concrete tarmac. Her long, tanned legs in white linen shorts led her way, as we walked directly through the small terminal to a parked taxi. Speeding down the left side of the road, the driver was jovial and gregarious (the steering wheel is on the American side but they drive on the British side). In the first few miles we learned that he had lived on the Island of Tortola all his life, followed the National Football League, and his favorite team was the Philadelphia Eagles. His oldest child was a son living in Bozeman, Montana and working as an engineer. Sam asked him how the son liked the winters and he said that he liked them just fine. Was he planning to migrate back down to the islands in the future, was Sam's next question. No, he likes it there. In my mind's eye, I could see Bozeman residents mounting studded snow tires to prepare for the winter onslaught, and I could see red noses and frozen ears as they trudged in from shoveling the snow off their driveways. I looked out the window as my mind jumped back to the island and the side of the road, and the makeshift homes and leaning fences barely containing a few goats within their confines. No snow and ice in this tropical paradise, I thought. Our driver sped us over the small bridge that connected Beef Island to Tortola, the capital of the British Virgin Islands.

Our driver flew by white multi-story buildings capped with red tile roofs that surrounded Road Harbour and pulled up in front of the Village Cay Hotel.

"Walk around the building and you'll see Village Cay Marina. Just look for your boat in the slips. Have a nice time," said our driver, waving goodbye and flashing his wide, signature smile.

Sam picked up her backpack and slung it over her right shoulder and said slightly under her breath, "How well do you know this guy, Bruce?"

"Some company events, we got together a few times for beers, and he worked for me for four years in Palo Alto," I said.

"So, he's reliable, right?"

"Listen, Bruce is the salt of the earth—a filthy rich salt, but everything will be fine," I said. "He's spent two years sailing these boats with the best teachers in the Caribbean. Besides, there are beach hotels all over the islands. If we get tired of being drunken sailors, we can just jump ship."

A small alleyway opened to a view of the boat slips in the marina. To our left was an open-air restaurant with tables spilling over to the dockside walkway. The tangy aroma of fried fish hovered in the midday air. Patrons were casually sipping drinks and talking without regard to much else.

"My god, these boats are so big!" Sam exclaimed.

I looked over at the slips to see at least fifty boats moored, and each one made my boat back in Alameda look like a toy. We walked out on one of the docks and gazed around for a red hull and hopefully Bruce standing on the deck. Our eyes filtered through giant masts that seemed to pierce the scattered cloud cover.

"Over there is a red one," I said in a quiet voice humbled by the seeming opulence of these boats.

"Bruce, hey Bruce," I shouted. "Anybody home?"

Sam and I stood there waiting for somebody to emerge who could tell us if we were in the right place or not. She started looking around nervously. I imagined she was thinking, *What am I doing here in a strange place with people I barely know?*

Just then a redheaded young woman with soft brown freckles spotting her cheeks poked her head out the cabin door. She turned toward me and said, "Are you Richard?"

Sam let out a sigh of obvious relief and I said, "That's me reporting for duty."

"Bruce said to keep an eye out for you; we didn't know when you were coming. He's off shopping or drinking beer or something. Anyway, he'll be back later. Bring your stuff on board and I'll show you your cabin."

Sam walked up the stairs from the white concrete pier and stepped onto the deck, following our host into the cockpit and then down into the salon. I stopped in the cockpit, tossed my soft bag of clothes onto a seat and stared out onto the boats fitting snuggly into the marina slips. The air, so unlike San Francisco, was balmy and thick. My nose twitched with the fragrance of afternoon humidity. People were walking slower and even looked calmer than back home. And with only a handful of big boats, San Francisco paled in comparison to this fiesta of massive, beautiful, and expensive yachts.

Across the small Road Harbour bay, rows of charter boats made neat, straight lines in the slips, waiting for the vacationing skippers from the frozen North to mount the pristine, all white sloops and sail off like the pirates of old on the scripted booze-cruise of the tightly positioned Virgin Islands. Lobsters and rum bars awaited at every port, and that's why they came.

Sam and the as yet unnamed redhead stayed down in the salon talking with some giggling thrown in. I was glad she was getting comfortable and feeling a little more secure with things. When we changed planes in Miami on the flight down, I picked up a schedule of returning flights in case Sam turned sour on the trip and needed to jump ship early. Having known her less than a week, I felt I needed an escape option for her, and for me. Don't get me wrong, Sam was a hot ticket and she had some great innate traits that I really liked. Her soft Southern accent relaxed me, and gave me the feeling of being back home—not just in the South, but at home safe and secure in my parents' house with a hot meal of pork chops and mashed potatoes served up. She had a nurturing way about her even at twenty-two years old. And in bed? Yeah, well all these girls in their twenties could make a roll-in-the-hay come alive. My former girlfriend, Rebecca, was a steam engine with some sort of "thing" to prove. She never quit, and practically wore me out every night, and those "nooners" were a work of art, but Sam. Sam was calm, steady and nurturing. As for this trip, she was either going to like this loose sailing atmosphere or not, and we'd know pretty quickly.

"Hey, boss," a soft salutation rolled over the bow with the gentle afternoon breeze.

"Captain Bruce, I thought you'd never get here," I replied.

"I stopped over at the Moorings charter base this morning and hired them to monitor our calls in case we have a breakdown. They can be out in thirty minutes with a repair boat if we need them," he said.

"That's a good safety net," I said.

"It's only good for the Virgins. We're on our own if we head to the down islands," he said. "How was the trip?"

"Smooth as a baby's bottom," I said.

Bruce heard the talking below and turned his head slightly in that direction.

"Did you bring Rebecca?" he asked.

"Samantha," I replied.

"Sweet, where did you get Samantha?" Bruce cocked his head slightly down and shot a glance up at me from the corner of his eye.

"Il Fornaio, she's a waitress," I said with a nonchalant shrug. I was dating around, but I didn't want to cheapen the relationship and Bruce was leaning toward being caddy and boyish.

"Is she a sailor?" he asked.

"She's been out once with me, but she is from Mississippi."

"How long have you known her?" he asked.

"Four days, and..."

Just then the women emerged from the top of the stairs.

Bruce turned, stood up and with a kind of nervous giggle said, "You must be Samantha? I've heard a lot about you."

"Bruce, it's a pleasure," Sam retorted in a nonchalant Southern style. Almost every native Southern gentleman is a character study in "strange," and Sam had no doubt encountered many sappy Southern gentlemen in her young twenty-two years, and knew how to handle the social niceties. Plus, Sam knew how to be laidback.

Sam looked at me and motioning to Bruce's redhead, said, "Richard, this is Amanda."

I said hi to Amanda as Bruce started the tour of his boat. It was an Oyster built in 1981 for a very rich Saudi oil tycoon's son who suddenly got a lot richer as oil prices spiked. He bought one twice the size and never even set foot on this one. A syndicate bought it to charter in the Caribbean, and Bruce scooped it up from them. Each of the four cabins had a full bathroom, or head as they call it on a boat. Bruce took me into the owner's cabin, which boasted a formal sitting room and a library. The king-size bed had satin throw pillows all over it in bright colors exuding extreme opulence.

"This is over-the-top formal for a sailboat, and for you…well what can I say," I posed.

"More formal than that crash pad I had on Old Middlefield Road in Mountain View, anyway," he replied. "You're right, though. It's not totally my style, but this cheap old bucket is all I could afford."

We both broke out laughing, while Bruce shuffled the few steps over to a cabinet and pulled out a bottle of Habitation Clement Rum, and poured two shots into small crystal tumblers.

"The best they make in Martinique," he said. "Welcome to the Caribbean."

10

Children

Randy slumped into his big leather La-Z-Boy recliner with a tall summer gin and tonic on the side table next to him. The calendar squarely in February didn't faze him in his choice of drinks. He set the bound document on his lap and stared at the cover.

"The Joys of Intrigue and the Rewards of Adventure," he read aloud. "What kind of sick lunatic would leave his children an estate like this," he shouted and slammed his clenched fist on the chair.

"Dear children," he read in a low voice, almost a whisper, forming each word with his lips as if reading to a crowd. "Each of you has been provided for with a steady, reliable income. Over and above these necessities and through the fortunes of investing and some luck, my technology money has grown to an amount that has created an opportunity to have some fun. If you want to indulge me or more appropriately indulge yourself in a little game, I have created a treasure hunt with a few shiny baubles that I uncovered in the deep-blue sea. If you feel this game is not worth your while or you have important endeavors to attend to, then I wholeheartedly encourage you to pursue those and leave this adventure to your siblings whose time is less valuable. By the way, if my father had set something like this up for me, I'd have spit in his proverbial eye." Randy stopped reading and quietly looked up and said to himself, "Spit in his eye, my god!"

****

"Well do you want to play your father's little game or just forget it?" Andrew asked as he stared at Alice and closed the spiral binder, laying it on the coffee table.

"I don't know. Daddy was such a goofball sometimes. You know he told me about this treasure hunt when I was a little girl, but I didn't think it was real," Alice replied.

"I know he did. You've told me about a hundred times in the last week," Andrew said.

"I know, but he said there was a magic island with special prizes for a little girl when she grows up," Alice said.

"Yeah, but all parents say that stuff, fairy princesses, buried treasure, lost boys, Christ, all that stuff," he said.

"Yes, but Daddy meant it," she answered.

"What do you think it might be worth?" Andrew asked.

"There is no telling with my dad. I know he had the idea thirty years ago and he may have hidden something then. I remember him being silly and a little giddy about it. But, maybe he added to whatever it was or it's just some toys or something. I don't know."

"Do you think Zach knows more than he's saying?" he asked.

"Maybe, but he's keeping whatever he knows to himself. You know full well that he treats us all like spoiled rich kids, sending the checks every month and making sure we know nothing else."

"Has Zach ever mentioned this magic island or anything like that before?" Andrew asked.

"Not that I can remember, but I've told you before Dad always had games going, so talk of this one wouldn't have stood out as special," she said.

"Okay, but back to the businesses that Zach runs, how much do you really want to know about all that anyway?" Andrew asked.

"Well…I really don't want to know anything about all that stuff," she said.
"Right."

Alice gazed out the window then turned to Andrew and said, "If it is a lot of money, we could set up the summer camp for the at-risk kids from down in the valley. You know that whole project that the meditation group has been talking about."

"How much do you think it would cost?" Andrew asked.

"I'm not sure," she said. "But people have been talking about a million dollars."

Andrew walked across the room and sat down.

"If we had two million, maybe we could run the camp year-round," she said. "Let's look into this treasure hunt."

****

"Where have you been?" Jimmy barked. "You keep me waiting constantly."

"I was running late getting my nails done. Take it easy, they always have room downstairs in the hotel restaurant," said Amber, who was Jimmy's sometimes girlfriend.

"We're not eating at the Fairmont. We're going down to North Beach and eating spaghetti," Jimmy replied sharply.

"Spaghetti? North Beach? Have you lost your mind? Next, you'll want to go to Big Al's strip club," she said.

"I'm thinking about Big Al's. You have a problem with that?" he asked with a foul-hand gesture.

"You have never wanted to be caught dead in that sleazy part of town. Come on, Jimmy, spaghetti?"

"Well if I'm going to be broke, I might as well learn how to mingle with the riff-raff," Jimmy said with a sigh of resignation.

"You're not broke. Come on, you can tell your little girl all about it at dinner… at the Fairmont."

****

"I read the whole document and I must say it's not a work of literary genius." Zach and Jennifer were sitting in his living room on Taaffe Road in Los Altos Hills. The picture window looked north toward San Francisco over a panorama of low, rolling coastal mountains. Neither son nor mother were enjoying this million-dollar view. Zach was rolling a cube of ice around in a tumbler of twelve-year-old Talisker scotch while a glass of Ridge Vineyards 2006 Cabernet sat in front of Jennifer, untouched.

"You've been to Tortola plenty of times with Dad," Jennifer said.

"Of course, and Bruce kept his boat at Village Cay. But, this is like a silly board game. I've got businesses to run and responsibilities. Honestly, I feel like ignoring this whole thing. I don't need any of this.... whatever Dad buried," Zach said.

Zach's words stagnated and hung in the dry California air like dust blowing off a grapevine. A few crows cackled as they flew by the open French doors, and a fifty-eight-degree winter breeze ruffled the side curtains. Jennifer picked up the wineglass and brought it to her mouth for a taste.

"They say Cabernet Sauvignon is the second most complex liquid on the planet," she said in a quiet, serene voice.

"I'll bite. What's the first?"

"Why blood, of course," she answered.

"Yeah, I'm going to pass up this little test of character. Let the leisure class go on a treasure hunt," Zach said.

11

Richard / George Dog

The diary was waiting for Bill Price and he hastily sat down and started to read.

"They all seem so close together," Samantha said.

"That's the great thing about the Virgin Islands," Bruce said from behind the wheel of his eighty-foot sailboat he named *Found Treasure*. "You can navigate by sight."

The wind blew a steady twelve knots from the northeast and the seas were pleasantly rolling in, at about a foot or so. The bow was pointed into a high mid-morning sun as we made our way up the south side of Tortola headed past Beef Island to visit the Dogs, five small islands that formed a cluster at the east entrance to the Sir Francis Drake Channel.

I was on the helm when we pushed by Beef Island on a course of twenty degrees magnetic. The wind died down to around eight knots as we slowly approached the northernmost island.

"Nose her up till we get the jib in and then fall off a bit and head for that rock," Bruce called to me from the bow just in front of the cockpit. "Right in front of George Dog, we'll drop anchor in about fifteen feet, a good sandy bottom."

Amanda, Bruce's redhead, was calmly watching the action and then looked at Sam. "George Dog is a nice place to snorkel, and it's not too crowded. You'll like it."

"I'm liking everything so far," Sam replied.

Attached to the single mooring ball in the wind-protected inlet at George Dog, a forty-foot yawl, sporting its two masts, was floating calmly. Bruce called back to Amanda to pull in the jib. She moved to the port side of the cockpit while instructing Sam to loosen the starboard jib sheet from the wench. She nonchalantly gazed up at the pulleys along the port side and then depressed the electric roller furling. The front sail rolled up tightly, and the main sail filled as I fell off the wind. The boat slowed to about four knots, and the waves shortened and became very small as we neared the shore. Bruce jumped back in the cockpit and directed me to start up the diesel. The engine turned over and purred like a kitten.

"Keep it at four knots as I roll up the main sail," Bruce told me.

Then I reversed the engine to bring us to a dead stop and from the bow, Bruce lowered the anchor. When it hit ground, he hand-motioned to slowly back up, and when seventy-five feet of chain was expended, I stopped the engine and we let her swing.

I saw Sam break into a big smile as she looked down at the crystal-clear water, then up to the broken clouds above and then back at Tortola.

"Remind you of Mississippi?" I asked while tilting my head slightly with a bit of a childish smirk.

"Just like Mississippi except for the ocean and the islands," she quipped.

She looked east at the jagged rock peak of George Dog and seemed to be surveying the cliffs as she pulled her T-shirt over her head. I couldn't take my eyes off the profile of this Southern beauty. The wind ruffled her shoulder-length auburn hair, and her bikini top barely covered her round breasts. She shook her head slightly to straighten her hair and then dropped her shorts to the floor, preparing for a swim. Did I mention I was staring, and could not take my eyes off her? If I have to be honest, I think I fell for Sam at that moment, and everything that came after was just a ritual dance. She was on the young side for me and a bit impetuous, but I'm told I was too.

She jumped up, stepped over the lifelines and dove into the water. I followed her in, stayed submerged, and swam straight toward her, then grabbed her knees and yanked her under the water. We tussled and came up together, face to face, her arms around my neck, both laughing. My arms surrounded her waist and I kissed her. Her soft, warm lips drove all other thoughts from my mind. Yeah, I didn't fully know it, but I was hooked on Samantha.

12

Treasure Hunt

The wheels touched down on the Beef Island tarmac. The door of the private Lear jet opened onto the upper platform of the stairway. Randy emerged, as the flight attendant secured the door, his eyes squinting into the early-afternoon sun. He took the first step down the stairs shouldering a small carry-on bag followed by Jimmy, Maureen, Alice, and Andrew. A pair of Oakley sunglasses wrapped around Jimmy's eyes. He looked down at the first step before moving his foot off the platform. His salmon-colored linen pants broke just over his Top-Siders which he wore over bare feet, the sleeves of a light blue shirt rolled up just below his elbows. Alice and Andrew looked like they just walked out of a camping store, hiking boots, khaki shorts and rumpled shirts. Maureen was tastefully dressed in a straight skirt and matching blouse.

After checking through customs, they boarded a waiting white Toyota van and took off for Road Town. The white stucco, red-roofed buildings greeted them on the right hillside as they got the first glimpse of Road Harbour. The van skirted the small bay and pulled up in front of the Village Cay Hotel. Randy jumped out of the front passenger seat and started giving orders to the driver. He pulled out a wad of ten and twenty-dollar bills, peeled off a few, and handed them to the driver.

Then looking out in space, no doubt to a distant galaxy, he said to the driver in a slightly muffled yell, "Take the bags to the lobby."

Randy was fulfilling his self-appointed role as the titan-of-organized-responsibility, in his Silicon Valley uniform of a blue button-down shirt, khaki Dockers, and Cordovan penny loafers. Jimmy stepped out of the van, looked at Maureen, and rolled his eyes. She stared directly at him with a look that could have drilled a hole in a steel girder. Jimmy offered no resistance, turned and walked straight for the hotel.

"Everybody, find a table and order lunch," Randy announced. "I'll see to the rooms and meet you there shortly." His dark brown head of hair pointed toward the lobby while his slightly stocky torso and stubby legs followed.

Ten minutes later Randy walked through the narrow pathway in back of the hotel and emerged at the Marina Restaurant. He stopped and gazed out at the boats gently bobbing in their slips. His eyes fixed briefly on a large red-hulled yacht at the end of the pier. Looking to his left he saw two tables pulled together near the corridor nearest the water with his group sitting, mostly staring out across the bay.

"Zach should have come with us," Maureen directed her comment to the whole table.

No one said a word.

"I guess he's not interested in Dad's treasure hunt?" Maureen continued.

"Yeah. He probably knows where it is or even what it is," Andrew added.

"Oh, you think?" Jimmy blurted. "Zach must know it isn't worth finding, or he'd be down here with us. He and Jennifer know everything about this and they're sending the family losers on a wild goose chase."

Alice jerked her head up, her lips dropping the straw into her glass of cola. Andrew sat up immediately in his chair with a fearful look on his face.

"You can leave my mother out of your psychotic musings, Mr. Jimmy

Smartass!" she exclaimed with an uncharacteristic fire in her eyes.

Nobody said a word or even moved. Jimmy's eyes glazed over but he kept looking straight at Alice, respectfully attentive.

"And my brother, Zach, goes to work every day to make sure you have enough money for sailboats and whores. If you are too cool or more likely too wimpy to handle this thing, why don't you sail on back to Martha's Vineyard and shut the hell up!"

There was silence at all the surrounding tables as Alice's bomb-blast dissipated into the muggy air of the marina. Finally, Alice stood up with tears running down her cheeks, and walked briskly out of the restaurant.

"Okay, this is a good start," Maureen said with a sarcastic tone.

After a long moment of silence, Randy started squirming in his chair. He peered over his shoulder and out over the boat slips.

Maureen looked at him and asked, "Is everything okay, dear?"

"Right! Five fools following a fool. Why, everything's terrific," Jimmy interrupted.

"Shut up, Jimmy," Maureen snapped. "Randy, what's the matter?"

"Look everybody. I have a career with responsibilities to clients, so I can't stay down here indefinitely arguing about trivial stuff. The first clue in the trust said something about Gorda. I think we need to try to get started, and I think we should be looking for something on the island of Virgin Gorda. Can we all agree on that?"

Alice, who had returned to the table showing no signs of wear, placed a folio on the table in front of her and pulled out a document. "The clue reads, 'Gordy's little brother has what you desire under two green hats. The clue for you is to see caves and graves.'" Alice read the clue again to a silenced table.

"It's on one of the islands around Virgin Gorda. I'm sure of it," Randy pronounced. "It'll be somewhere near The Baths on the western end of the island, because that's where the caves are."

"All those islands are just rocks. They aren't real islands," Maureen said.

Randy shot her a cold stare, as in "don't contradict me."

Alice looked up and watched the blank looks around the table, then said, "Those little islands are more like children instead of a brother. I think Dad would have been more specific, but The Baths play into it somehow. That's clear."

"Dad was incredibly precise but he used nuances that were not direct, but each word was pointed and meaningful. Sometimes I felt like I had to be really inside his head to follow along with his conversations," Jimmy said. "But the word 'Gordy' has to refer to Virgin Gorda. What else could it be?"

Randy sat back in his chair, his lips tightened into a slight smile, then finally said, "I'll arrange for a boat tomorrow and we can go out to The Baths and take a look."

13

The Baths

The motored catamaran pulled out of the harbor about ten the next morning. The usual two-foot seas every thirty seconds providing a relatively smooth ride had been replaced that morning with bigger waves, a choppier outing and queasy stomachs for this ragtag band of treasure hunters. When they arrived at the grouping of rocks known as The Baths, Randy instructed the skipper to drive around the bottom of the island to look for rocks protruding out of the water big enough to be construed as islands that should be explored. The first stop was Round Rock off the western tip of Gorda. It was more than a rock but not big enough to be a real island. Nobody had ever lived there, but there was a sand beach for occasional picnicking. Just in front of the beach a small sailboat had grounded and been abandoned. By its looks, it had endured several hurricane seasons. There was no mast and the hull listed about thirty degrees from what was left of a rock-battered keel. The skipper anchored the catamaran, loaded Randy, Jimmy, and Andrew into a rubber dinghy, and motored to the beach. They quickly disappeared into the brush and rocks near the shore. At about two o'clock the men arrived and climbed back on the catamaran. Jimmy headed straight for the ice chest, pulled out a bottle of gin, filled a cup, scooped some ice, and added a splash of tonic. He drank it in one long pull and sat down in the covered salon area of the boat.

Alice sat outside on a stern bench seat in the cockpit and looked over at Virgin Gorda. "Well, any luck?" Maureen asked while settled into a swivel seat on the deck.

"We looked for anything green, but found nothing," Randy said, his voice trailing off at the end. "The only spot where we had a view of The Baths was on that rock face. It was almost vertical, and I couldn't see any hiding place there or any way to climb it, either up or down, to even hide a clue."

"Want a drink?" Jimmy asked.

"Gin and tonic," Randy replied.

14

Virgin Gorda

Around seven in the morning Zach picked up the wireless phone from the bathroom wall holder on the third ring. "Hi Alice, how is it going down there?"

"We've been riding a catamaran around Virgin Gorda for three days looking for a hiding place with green on it and a view of the caves," Alice replied.

"Do you mean around The Baths?" Zach asked.

"Randy is sure the reference to 'caves' is certain to be The Baths, but no green has shown up, and nobody can figure out the 'caves and graves' reference." Alice paused and took an audible, deep breath, and then continued, "Well, you spent so much time in the islands with Dad, I thought maybe something might ring a bell for you."

Zach pulled a towel from the rack and brought it up to dry his face, then wrapped it around his waist. The mirror reflected a dark, hairy-chested man approaching middle age sporting a girth that was growing along with his years. He pulled his gaze away, and looked out the window at the live-oak limb that seemed to float horizontally just outside, partially obstructing the view of the rolling coastal hills, and finally said, "Sweetie, I'll think about it, but Dad never even mentioned this treasure of his. And I'm not really focusing on…well, anyway, I'll think about it."

"Thanks, Zach."

How long are you staying down there?" he asked.

"Randy is flying back tomorrow for some big deal he has going, and I don't know about Maureen. Everybody is bickering as usual. Andrew wants to spend a few days on Marina Cay before we head back, but that depends on if we can get our farmhand to feed the cat on his day off," she said. "Zach, can I ask you a question?" She paused. "Do you think this whole thing is worth pursuing? And, does Mom know what any of this is?"

"That's two questions, and I don't know the answer to either one."

15

Richard / Marina Cay

Bill Price hadn't heard from Richard's family in weeks, but he was becoming more intrigued with the diary, as he read deeper into Richard's life.

When Samantha and I climbed up the ladder onto the swim platform, Bruce was stuffing something in a backpack.

He looked up and said, "Very little sediment is stirred up on this side of the island so you can see all the way to the bottom. Gorgeous visibility, wouldn't you say? We're packing a lunch to toss in the dinghy. I'm going to take you guys to see the babbling brook gurgling out of this island."

Our small dinghy floated the thousand yards to a small sand outcropping where we all stepped out onto the soft, white beach. Like a short river running half the length of a football field, this creek cascades over a shallow, rock-strewn channel dumping into the sea. Bruce picked a large boulder protruding from the middle of the stream to use as a table to unpack lunch. After our quick meal, Bruce led us up a narrow, parched path to the top of the island. He pointed out The Baths at the south end of Virgin Gorda.

"Tomorrow we'll sail over there. You guys will love tramping through the caves."

"Are the caves those big boulders over there?" Samantha asked while pointing nearly due south.

"Yeah, that's them." Then Bruce turned around and looked the other way. "See that little island jutting out? That's Scrub Island. A little-known fact is there is a forgotten pirate cemetery there on that point. It's a scruffy, windswept place, but that's the only patch the British military could find to bury the ones they hung."

"That's uplifting news, Bruce. Maybe we should talk about scurvy or food poisoning," Amanda said with a slight chuckle.

Bruce continued to give us the first day of the grand tour of the British Virgins. We sailed around the tip of Tortola to a little round island called Sandy Cay. Dropping anchor, we swam over to this picture-perfect island dragging a few cans of island brew with us. I felt like I was in a postcard or maybe a beer commercial for the rest of the afternoon with Samantha and Amanda sunbathing topless. Later we raised the mainsail and drifted back around Tortola to hook on a mooring ball at the small island of Marina Cay. There was an old stone house that turned into a bar at night with an island folk singer blaring out sailing songs through a scratchy sound system.

We had dinner on the boat and joined the crowd for the songs and the rum. A young New Englander named Robb White built it in 1937 during his dreamy, escape-to-a-desert-island stage of post adolescence. It was a rectangular one-story with a basement for storage. The walls were made of formed concrete that he brought over by boat to the island. The current bar area was an add-on with a tin roof open to an ocean view to the south.

The crowd of cruisers was feeling no pain and rocking to the music when we arrived. Snagging a table in the back, we ordered Painkillers all around, a Caribbean favorite. After several of these rum delights, Samantha wanted to see the inside of the concrete house just back of the bar. Night had dropped a curtain on our scarlet-red sunset, and a string of tiny holiday lights barely lit our way in back of the bar. I felt a little giddy because I could see Sam was getting lightheaded and she could be very frisky in dark places.

We opened the door and walked in the room. A window to our right overlooked the southern sea, and to our left were simple wooden steps rising to a four-foot-high concrete platform. I flipped on the small flashlight from my pocket, and shined it around the room. A portrait of an English gentleman hung next to the window. On the platform was a small table, a chair, and a lamp. Back to the main floor, my small beam of light found a large wooden hatch on the floor. Sam walked over to it curiously and tugged a bit to no avail. Handing her the light, I pulled on the planks and finally moved the hatch enough to create a small opening. The flashlight revealed a cool damp basement with the concrete foundation as walls and natural rock along with sandy soil as a floor. I kicked the hatch back over the hole and followed Sam up the few steps to the upper level. Across from the table was what appeared to be a daybed with a tattered cloth cover draped over it. Sam put the small light in her teeth and slumped onto the daybed with a move reminiscent of holding a long-stem rose in her mouth, her right arm extended over her head mimicking a flamenco dancer. I sat down beside her. Taking the light from her mouth, she said, "Kiss me, boy."

I leaned over slowly and kissed her gently. She pulled me closer and snuggled into the foam bed.

"I don't know about this. It's kind of a public place," I whispered in her ear.

"Ho, ho, ho and a bottle of rum. Make me feel like a woman, sailor," she replied.

Now, I want you to know the full impact of the moment. I was young and out for adventure, feeling that I had to grasp for all I could get out of life before it passed me by. Bruce and I had been drinking beer since the late afternoon and as I recall Sam had downed a few herself along with the rum. The tropical air was warm and comfortable. Samantha was twenty-two years old, exercised regularly, her breasts pointed up to the sky, and her skin was as smooth to the touch as a man could ever want. To top it off, she was clever, witty, and cheerful. You can see my feeble attempt at caution was overwhelmed by the circumstances—oh yes, did I mention the rum?

"Is this the way they do it in Mississippi?" I asked.

"This is the way I do it in Mississippi," she said. "I guess they check with the preacher first in Tennessee?"

"Only if you're nailing the preacher's daughter."

We both laughed, then she reached down with her right hand and pulled her T-shirt from her waist up over her head. Back then, Samantha kissed each time like it was a gentle discovery, an exploration into the unknown. The soft, warm flesh of her two lips blended together, and learned their way as they went.

Time sped up and finally we lay quietly in the dark with only a glimmer of light from the bar seeping through the window at the far end of the room. Just then the door creaked open and we heard voices.

"You see, this guy named Robb-somebody built this bunker…thought he'd live in it in paradise forever. 'Course the stupid kid forgot that you need food and clothes even in paradise. He took off back home. I heard he never came back here again," said the intruder.

"Jack, I think we've had enough for tonight. Let's go back to the boat," a female voice said.

What's up here?" he asked. He started up the steps while Sam and I lay still as church mice. He rummaged around the table and chair area while she stood only about six feet from our not-so-clever love nest. Then she turned and stared directly at us. Her eyes pierced our veil of darkness, and I was sure we were caught. I was ready to spring to my feet, when she turned and said, "Come on, Jack, it's time to go."

She barreled down the steps dragging Jack by the elbow. They blasted through the door, leaving it wide open. Neither of us moved or said a word for a moment.

"This calls for a celebration," Samantha said and locked her legs around me, while gently placing her lips on mine. You see what I mean. I was helpless.

16

Gordy

Zach sat at his desk doodling on a legal pad. He had nearly filled the page with the phrases "Gordy's son," "green hats," and "caves and graves." He was wasting the morning at a time when he should have been preparing for an afternoon meeting with his real estate team. He glanced over at the spreadsheet of the properties the trust owned. The office buildings were the worst. Rents had spiked for a few years but tough negotiations brought them down to levels of a decade ago. Operating expenses had doubled in the past ten years and thousands of square feet of new office space made the competition for renters fierce.

His eyes diverted to the lease agreement for the huge light industrial building across the bay in Fremont that was leased to Western Micro Digital. The four hundred thousand square-foot building was a signature part of the family portfolio. Lease negotiations for another ten years had been going well until the bombshell hit. The company decided to move the semiconductor testing business to Hong Kong, and the chip manufacturing to Mexico. They would not be renewing the lease. Zach knew he could find a new tenant, but it would take time to re-lease, and the expense to upgrade the facility would be huge. With twenty percent of the company revenue vanishing, things were going to be tight. He doubted he could keep the sibling payments at the current levels, and some staff cuts were certain. He looked back at his doodles and suddenly grabbed the phone and dialed.

"Alice, call me back as soon as you can," Zach practically yelled into Alice's voice mail. He sat back in his chair and stared at the notepad. Just then the phone rang.

"Zach, what's wrong?" Alice said the moment he answered.

"Gordy was our dog when we were in elementary school," he blurted.

"Yeah, the yellow lab," she said.

"Gordy is not Virgin Gorda, it's our dog," he said. You're looking for the Dogs, the little rock islands due east of Tortola."

"What?" she uttered in a slow, confused voice.

"The clue is on one of the small Dog Islands. Great Dog is the big one and the small ones are West Dog, George Dog, and Seal Dog."

"Didn't dad love to snorkel off George Dog?" she asked.

"He took me there almost every time I was with him," Zach said. Where is everybody now?"

"They all left. Andrew and I are on Marina Cay till Thursday."

"You can see the Dogs from there. They're southeast toward Virgin Gorda. Hire a boat and comb those islands tomorrow," he said.

17

Richard / Bitter End

Bill Price wrapped both hands around a warm cup of chamomile tea and resumed reading the diary.

After a morning exploring the caves on Virgin Gorda, Bruce installed me as skipper for the day, to sail us to the east end of the island and into the beautiful bay of North Sound. I tacked through the channel between Gorda and Great Dog and then pointed her northeast to a way point that gave me a straight reach into the Sound. My chart calculations utilized my amateur understanding of the technique and landed us short of our entry point near Mosquito Island. Bruce shrewdly left me to my mistakes as a learning tool—the student had become the master, Obi-Wan. Another tack out to sea and back, put us in front of The Bitter End Yacht Club, the most exclusive resort in the BVI. Bruce manned the stern lines with Amanda on the bow, as I backed that eighty-foot behemoth into the slip.

"I called for dinner reservations at that little island in the channel called Saba Rock," Bruce announced. "An interesting guy named Burt bought it and turned it into a restaurant."

"Richard needs his own island," Sam said. "How much do islands cost?"

"No idea," Bruce said. "The rumor is Burt found a box of Spanish pieces of eight on some old wreck out around Anegada. He sold off a little at a time so he wouldn't attract attention."

Samantha cocked her head and asked, "What exactly are Spanish pieces of eight?"

"During the Colonial period the Spanish used a standard-sized coin that most of the Western world also adopted over time. It refers to silver coins, but sometimes the gold coins were carelessly called pieces of eight," Bruce said. "Over a few decades many of the ships loaded with treasure sailing from Mexico and Central America to Spain were blown into the rocky shores off the Florida coast and the shallow reefs around Anegada by freak storms and early-season hurricanes."

"Okay, back to dinner, do they have lobster at Saba Rock?" I asked.

"The biggest in the world. They're from Anegada," Bruce replied.

"Gold and lobster. Just what I want. When are we going to Anegada?" I asked.

"A couple of days. Don't worry, the gold and lobster will be there waiting," Bruce said.

The mooring field at the Bitter End was the temporary parking place for a variety of sailboats over the next few days. Mostly smaller charter rigs looking the same—white hull, white sails, metal gray rubber dinghy floating off the stern. Our boat, *Found Treasure,* got a string of admirers from serious skippers to giddy teenagers. Bruce hired a shore maintenance team to polish up the deck and scrub down the hull. He was treating this boat like he might not be able to afford another one, just in case one of the $10 million checks bounced. One afternoon the wind started blowing in the Sound and Bruce hoisted our sails and took our crew out for a training mission. He gave the helm to Amanda, who took control, giving Sam responsibility for the jib sheet as we whipped around the bay pretending to pick up overboard crew. *Found Treasure* sailed smoother than any boat I had crewed. She cut through the water with no regard for the little waves and swells that rocked the smaller boats that I was accustomed to. Turning was smooth but it took more time and more area. Amanda handed off the helm to me for some practice while Bruce sat in the cockpit with a distant look in his eyes and a smile on his face. Scattered clouds dotted the light blue sky throughout the afternoon, and when the wind fell back to only a few knots, Amanda steered us to the dock, backing in like a pro.

I jumped off the boat onto the dock and headed over to the provisioning store to grab a few things. When I got back it was quiet down below, so I flipped through a cruiser guidebook and a few maps before boredom propelled me out of the seat, and I slowly began to meander around the deck. When I got to the bow, I saw Amanda perched comfortably facing Leverick Bay, holding a paperback in one hand.

"They're napping," she said. "I guess it was a big day."

"Yeah, this is a terrific boat," I said, sitting on the bow to her left. "I've wanted to ask how you met Bruce. Was it down here in the islands?"

"Not really. We met four or five years ago on a ski trip in Lake Tahoe. We were both with different sets of friends and we met while hanging around."

"So, you met in the Plaza Bar at Squaw Valley?" I asked.

She laughed and then paused. "Yeah, that's the routine, but he was late getting down a run, and his friends went up the chairlift without him. I was skiing single that morning, and he jumped on a chairlift with me and we started talking."

"A big wild weekend after that, I presume?" I said.

"That was his idea, but I wasn't going along. After all, I'm a nice girl, can't you tell?" she said.

"Amanda, you strike me as a very nice girl, but I know Bruce and I have a good idea what the pickup scene is like at a ski resort."

"Well, he called me a couple of times and we went to a concert in San Francisco, but nothing came of it. Then he called out of the blue from Antigua and said he bought a big sailboat and wanted to teach me to sail. I asked if my mother could come along as a chaperone. He knew I was joking, but he got the idea that I wasn't looking for a hot sailing adventure."

"You were already a sailor, right?" I asked.

"Never sailed and never had any ambition for it. I grew up in Burlingame just south of San Francisco. Some friends sailed in San Francisco Bay but it never interested me."

"You handled that boat today like you knew what you were doing," I said.

"I watched, and learned a lot from Bruce. Before that, I was in technical sales for a software startup south of Market in the City. They were on the ropes and finally sold out to Oracle. Actually, I think they just gave it to Oracle. Anyway, taking some time off in the islands seemed like a good idea for a while. I flew down and put Bruce on notice to behave, and he did. We actually dated and became friends for a while."

"Did you hear about his pending marriage?" I asked.

"He told me all about it. He practically left her at the altar. Inheriting that huge fortune shook him up. Anyway, I like Bruce, but I don't think he is a long-term kind of guy."

I felt uneasy extracting intimate details from someone else's girlfriend. The conversation about "long-term" was one I didn't want to necessarily have with anybody right now, and since Sam was brand new, I wasn't feeling any of that vibe with her.

18

Caves and Graves

"We found a box, Zach," Alice's voice crackled through the cell phone.

"What's in it?" Zach asked.

"We found it at the top of George Dog in a little cave. Two gigantic boulders were on either side with a barely moveable rock in front of the hole," Alice continued.

"What about green hats?" Zach asked.

"The boulders had eerie green lichen growing all over them. That's how we found it, and we could see the caves on Virgin Gorda. Get this, last night Andrew was lurking around in the small dusty library at Marina Cay and found an old book with a reference to a pirate cemetery on Scrub Island. You can see Scrub Island and barely some remnants of the cemetery right from where we were standing," she said.

"How did Dad hide that box? And what was in it?" Zach's voice rang with anticipation.

"We started scratching around those boulders and found a rock that moved a bit. We slid it to the side and could see the edge of the box."

"What was in it?" Zach's voice raised an octave.

"We're not sure," she said. "Just something written inside on the bottom in red paint: Anegada Reef Ho...Raise the Bar Still Look for Green," she said slowly.

Silence filled the airwaves from the Caribbean all the way to Silicon

Valley. Zach tried to speak, but found no words and Alice patiently waited for her big brother and family patriarch to respond.

"Great, the next clue is whores on Anegada. Dad really lost it on this one," he finally said.

"Hold on, Andrew thinks it may have originally said 'hotel.' The paint looks worn off," Alice said.

"Anegada Reef Hotel! Dad hung out on that island a lot ever since Bruce introduced it to him in the 1980s. I think the first time he went there was with Samantha," Zach said.

"Maybe she knows something about this clue stuff?" Alice said.

"I can ask Maureen to call her," Zach replied.

"Maureen thinks she was conceived at Anegada on that first trip. At least that's what her mother told her," Alice said.

"How do you know these things?" Zach asked with an uncharacteristic whine in his voice.

"Girls talk, that's all. Maureen told me," Alice said. "Maureen doesn't see Samantha very often. She lives in Florida with her new family. I say new, she's been remarried for thirty years and is a grandmother several times over. Jimmy goes down to see his mother at Christmas, but otherwise she successfully put the Dennisons out of her life years ago."

"Dad may have engineered this scheme after Samantha was long gone," Zach said.

"Zach, we're flying back tomorrow. I'll bring the chest with me," Alice said.

"Okay."

19

Richard / Anegada

Bill Price dialed Zach's number to ask him how things were shaping up with the treasure hunt. His call was picked up by the answering machine. After leaving a message, he laid the handset down on the table and picked up the diary.

"I am not seeing an island, Bruce," Sam said from a cockpit seat.

"We don't want to miss it, 'cause the next island we run into is Rhode Island." Bruce's quip got a chuckle all around.

"We won't see it till we're almost there. It's only twenty-six feet high, built up by coral reefs over millions of years," Amanda said. "You're going to love the color of the water, Sam."

Our compass was reading almost due north, and steady seas at near four feet pounded in from the east under a cotton-like sky, keeping the boat rolling slightly. Bruce steered us to a compass point at the mouth of the entry channel. As we neared the island, Sam jumped up to the bow to watch the ocean bottom rise as the depth fell to seven feet. Bruce took the wheel and I joined Sam at the bow with the hook to snag the mooring ball. As soon as the mooring was set, Sam stripped to her bikini and slipped in the water from the rear swim platform. I watched the sun's reflection off the white sand floor ripple and flow over her, like a dreamy iridescent oil painting. Bruce popped a couple of beers to celebrate the clock striking one o'clock.

"Where is this famous lobster?" I asked.

Bruce pointed to the shore and grunted out something about lunch. When we got over to the dock, Amanda showed us a large trap full of live lobster floating beside the dock.

"Pick out your lunch, sailor," she said.

Our table on the beach was in the shade of an old growth tree, a survivor of the many hurricanes and pounding seas. This beach restaurant was the sandy foyer to the modest but quaint Anegada Reef Hotel. The lobster was barbequed over hot coals and smothered in butter. The conversation was light small talk and as we sat, I started thinking about the startup and John Chakkera. The dirty truth was seeping back into my consciousness that my treasure chest from stock options was running thin. I was going to have to think about making money. I looked at Bruce carelessly chatting with the girls. No ten-million-dollar check would be flying in on a private jet with my name on it. Chakkera had a plan and I needed to get started while I still had some money. He left a message that there were commitments from the technology and finance guys, and he needed my answer to get the ball rolling.

"Let's jump on a moped to the other side of the island and do some snorkeling in the surf," Bruce said.

"You guys take off, I've got a couple of calls to make back to the States," I said.

When John answered, I told him I was in, and we set a meeting at Stanford for a week and a half out. He'd been throwing some teasers around to a couple of VC groups and the response was good. It was set. I was back to work.

****

Palo Alto was buzzing and traffic was bumper to bumper on University Avenue. I was driving through town to the Stanford campus for a management meeting with our team at Professor Orion's office. A venture capital partner was sitting in to get a flavor of our strategy. Chakkera had the plan on paper tight as a drum. I listened to the technology presentation followed by the sales and marketing plan as it rolled off John's tongue. The vagaries, uncertainties, and pure fabrications were slipped into a masterful disguise of self-assured success. The VC guy was smiling and eating it up. Easy sell, I thought.

Three months later we moved into sparse offices on Charleston Avenue and started hiring a skeleton crew. Needless to say, most things didn't go like the plan. But the product was working beyond our expectation, and everybody was excited.

Sam spent more and more time on my boat in the Alameda Marina. She alternated waitressing shifts between lunch and dinner but made it out to the boat most nights. Summer arrived with the cool light breezes of the San Francisco Bay, but Sam and I rarely left the dock after work began. I could say the job was forcing me to stay late into the evening almost every night, but the truth is I was pumped up with adrenaline and excitement. Everybody on the team was too. Sure, we all could see the rainbow at the end of the tunnel in our mind's eye with dreams of Maseratis and big, new houses. But honestly the momentum of everyone working together, overcoming obstacles and solving problems was infectious. It snared everybody on the team.

I shortened the commute by moving the boat to a small marina in Redwood City just two exits north of Palo Alto. Sam bid a hearty farewell to her roommates and moved onto the boat. Yes, it was cramped and yes it was too small, but we were living like bohemians and loving it. I was keeping Silicon-Valley-startup hours. In other words, I went to the office late and stayed late. One morning my eyes opened to the smell of coffee. I looked out but didn't see Sam. With a cup of coffee in hand, I climbed the steps to the outdoor cockpit—still no Sam. I walked up front and saw her sitting on the bow and sat down beside her but neither of us spoke.

Finally, she broke the silence with that little bit of Southern humor in her voice and said, "Well Mr. Tennessee, do you want to be someone's dad?"

"Really?" I said.

"Really."

When Saturday rolled around we slipped the boat out of the dock and motored through the narrow channel out into the Bay, pointing her north toward San Francisco. The wind was light but bearing down on our bow so I kept the engine running until we passed under the San Mateo Bridge. Where the narrow channel widens, I raised the main sail and fell off to a starboard reach, and crisscrossed the channel until we rounded McCovey Cove in San Francisco. The afternoon wind was picking up through the slot. I kept Alcatraz Island off our port bow, darted through Mosquito Pass and motored into the marina in Sausalito. I took Sam down to the cabin and kept her busy straightening up from the voyage, and then watched while she climbed the steps to the outside, hearing a loud cheer. Bruce was leading the applause and Amanda planted a long, bear-like hug on Sam. I put on my tuxedo coat over my T-shirt, all matching perfectly with my yellow swimsuit, and emerged to another roar of giddy cheers. The minister made his way over to Sam as I slipped in beside her. When he asked, "Do you take this man to be your lawfully wedded husband?" Sam paused, looked over at me and said, "You dog!" After another roar from the crowd, she said, "I do."

20

Vivian

"There was nothing else on it, Zach," Alice said. "Andrew used a magnifying glass looking for scratches or words or any other clue, but found nothing."

"'Anegada Reef Hotel…Raise the Bar Still Look for Green.' Well Dad didn't make it easy, but I don't think he would have tried to make it impossible," Zach said. "Anegada is twenty-six miles wide but the hotel grounds are relatively small. We'll find this clue. I'm going to call Vivian at the hotel and get her help."

Zach swirled his desk chair around, punched a few keys on his computer and dialed the international area code and then the number for the Anegada Reef Hotel. After about ten rings a man answered. He said Vivian was in St. Thomas until tomorrow, so Zach left his number, and turned back around to Alice.

"Do the others know about the chest?" Zach asked.

"We wanted to talk to you first to see what the plan would be," Alice replied. "Randy is behaving but he's quick to come to conclusions and doesn't wait for all the evidence, so he's encouraging wild goose chases. Maureen would also like a quick conclusion and is following Randy down these rat holes."

"And Jimmy…?" Zach inquired.

"You have to ask? We need to take Jimmy to the nearest kennel and have him put to sleep! There is no other solution."

"Let's keep this a secret," Zach murmured.

The next morning Zach picked up the phone on the second ring. Coffee in hand, he brought the receiver to his ear.

"Hello Zach, it's Vivian," she said with a faint but distinctive British accent. "I'm glad you called. It's been a while since I've seen you here on the island. I heard about your dad and I wanted to give you my condolences."

"Thanks, Vivian. It wasn't a surprise 'cause he had been in hospice for a few months, but I guess it's always a bit of a shock when a parent dies," Zach replied.

"Richard probably ate more lobsters on my beach than anyone ever. Heck, one season except for a couple of trips to Road Town, I think he lived here on that forty-foot boat."

"Yeah, that was the year after Dad and Bruce sailed to Tahiti."

"He was in rough shape then. I remember," Vivian said.

"After Tahiti, he went back to California and drove to the house and it was empty. It turns out Samantha sold it and moved the kids back to Mississippi," he said.

"Believe me, I heard all about it for a month. Then when Jennifer arrived everything changed," she said.

"I was born at Stanford Hospital ten months later," Zach said.

"Your mom was the only one who could handle Richard. She let him be himself all the time. Samantha needed more of a hold, as in commitment, and she was young. But Jennifer was fine staying loose. How's she doing with your father's death?" Vivian asked.

"As usual she's stoic about it. It'll leave a hole in her life, but you know Jennifer. She's always on the move and getting into new projects," he said.

"Vivian, the reason I called is that Dad left a final teaser for us to solve. It's kind of a wild goose chase and I was wondering if you could shed any light on it for us."

"Big surprise, right? Not really. He loved to think of clever games to stump his friends. What have you got?" she asked.

"He called it a treasure hunt and left clues all over the islands, but I think it's mostly in the British Virgins. We don't know what this so-called treasure is. Did he ever talk about treasure to you?" Zach asked.

"Everybody talks treasure around here since the rumors that Bert Kilbride found part of the San Ignacio wreck, that Spanish ship loaded with gold and silver that was blown into the Anegada reef sometime in 1742. Everybody's looked for that wreck," she said.

"Do you think Dad or Bruce or both of them found a part of it?" Zach asked.

"Who knows, but a kind of strange thing happened one day. Their boat pulled in the harbor around three in the afternoon. They pulled up chairs at that first table next to the pier and ordered bottle after bottle of champagne. I strolled around to say hi and your dad motioned me over. He opened my hand and put a coin in it. He said he found it while kicking around on the beach and wanted me to have it. It was solid gold with Roman numerals and Spanish insignia stamped on both sides. I think I still have it," she said.

"I guess those coins wash up on the beach from time to time. Maybe they found a few of those, or some Spanish jewelry." Zach paused. "The next clue is on Anegada and I thought it might trigger something for you. It says, Anegada Reef Hotel…Raise the Bar Still Look for Green." Zach waited in silence as the international phone connection lightly crackled.

"That's a good one. Richard is displaying rare form even from the grave. I'll give it some thought and if I come up with an idea, I'll call you."

21

Traveler

Two weeks passed while Zach and his marketing team devised a plan to fill their vacant office space around the Valley. The Sunnyvale properties were filling up, but the older spaces in Menlo Park were lagging. Jennifer called and invited herself to Zach's house for dinner. She warned him not to be late, so he left the office at five, sharp. The temperature was a bit too cold and the sky too gray for a convertible ride home. He nosed the roadster out of Palo Alto and onto El Camino Real, a right on Page Mill Road, he flew under I-280 and geared down for the winding ride to the top of the ridge. Punching through the cloud cover to a sunny sky, he saw behind him a river of fog rolling in from the coast. The warm land was sucking the marine layer inland for its nightly cold, wet bath. When he pulled in his driveway, he saw his mother's car tucked in snuggly against the retaining wall next to the garage.

"Well you're not late, so I have a reward for you," Jennifer said when Zach walked through the front door.

Zach smelled a comforting aroma and guessed it was Jennifer's pot roast with potatoes and carrots. He hoped the strawberry Jell-O was not for dessert, but of course he would eat it if served to make Mom happy.

"Sit down and close your eyes and get ready," she said while Zach could hear glass clinking beside him. "Okay," she said. "Give me your hand." She put a small glass in his hand and instructed him to drink a sip. He tasted the light, smoky flavor, a hint of cocoa and the familiar bite of a smooth scotch whiskey.

"Nice, Mom. What is it?" he asked.

"It's Sullivan's Cove. But get this. It's made in Australia."

"You can't make Scotch in Australia. Isn't there a law against that?" he joked.

"Not yet," she replied. Zach sat back in his chair, his shoulders dropped slightly, and a faint smile came across his face. Jennifer didn't appear to notice, but walked to the oven and opened the door to peer in at the roast. With a stemmed glass of red wine in her hand, she came back to the table and sat across from Zach. She straightened her three-button, beige vest, aligning it with her off-white silk shirt as she settled onto the chair.

"How is the treasure hunt going?" she asked.

"Not much new. Everybody is quiet except Jimmy, of course. He's calling Bill Price's office constantly. I don't know what he's trying to get out of them. He's convinced there's a shortcut to this whole game and wants answers that nobody has. You think he has a money problem?"

"I want to talk to you about that. Samantha called me yesterday to talk about Jimmy. He flew down to Florida to ask her for money. Said it was just a loan, and he needed it really quickly. She knows he just got two million and can't figure out what he needs it for."

"Remember four or five years ago when Jimmy almost got his knees broken by that gangster in New Jersey? He wasn't gambling or buying property. He was helping a friend by guaranteeing a loan the friend got for some kind of inventory swap in the fashion business. It had ironclad collateral backed by a flood of orders for knockoff purses from China. The collateral disappeared when the friend slipped out of the country and vanished." Zach finished with a sigh.

"You mentioned it to me."

"It was only a hundred and fifty thousand. I coughed it up for him and made him pay me back with the year-end bonus from the company. I tried to scare him by telling him that was the last time I was bailing him out. By the way, how is Samantha doing?" Zach asked.

"She sounds okay. Jimmy told her about the treasure hunt."

"What was her reaction?"

Jennifer sat back in her chair and looked out through the picture window as the evening darkness was closing in, "She wasn't laughing, but she wasn't surprised. She talked about how when Richard walked into a room he filled it up, sort of sucked the air out of the room. Then she said something that struck me. She said, 'Richard understood the pleasure of being a Traveler in Life rather than a Tourist.'"

"What did you say to that?"

"Not a single thing. What's there to say? It's like she summed up his whole life in one sentence."

Zach followed Jennifer's gaze across the room to the picture window and out to the scant light remaining. "I guess he's still traveling. I wonder if we're just tourists?"

After dinner Zach updated his mom on the current status of the clues. She quietly listened while interjecting a few, short questions.

"We haven't told Maureen or Jimmy about the box with the Anegada clue yet. Alice and Andrew think we should not tell them, see if we can find the loot, whatever it is, and then split it up four ways. But I'm not sure I want to go down that path," Zach explained.

Jennifer said nothing. She knew the clue without being told, "Anegada Reef Hotel...Raise the Bar Still Look for Green." Knowing that finding that one on Anegada would take them to the Soggy Dollar Bar, she offered no help and no advice.

"This clue is somewhere at or around the Anegada Reef Hotel. I talked to Vivian and she's going to think about it," Zach offered. "I may ask Alice and Andrew to go down there and see what they can find."

"Do what you think is right," Jennifer said.

22

Jimmy

The intercom on Zach's desk hummed slightly as it always did just before a voice came through.

"Zach, your brother Jimmy is here to see you," his secretary said.

"Jimmy is here?" His voice raised a little, revealing his surprise.

Jimmy walked through the door and up to Zach's desk. Zach leaned back in his chair clasping his hands behind his head, and prepared for the unknown. Neither said a word for a few seconds. Then, out of character, Jimmy asked how things were going for Zach in a feeble attempt at small talk. Zach noticed that his usual flamboyant clothes were replaced with a classic-looking blue button-down shirt, gray Dockers and a navy-blue blazer...kind of like he belonged there.

At first Jimmy was asking subtle questions about the business and what he could expect in distributions this year. He asked if the payments could possibly go up, saying he thought Maureen and Alice could benefit from it. Then the pointed questions about the trust and the treasure hunt started. He showed Zach a memo that a high-powered New York lawyer wrote with techniques to break the trust and stop the treasure hunt.

"Jimmy, what if this works and we can break the trust? Where is the money?"

A deafening silence filled the room before Jimmy practically screamed, "Somebody has got to know where this pile of money is!"

"Following the clues is the only way I know to find it. And one more thing, Jim. What is it we're looking for? Is it money, a deed to raw land in North Dakota, a patent on the newest gadget, mineral rights to oil wells?" Zach paused. "Are you in money trouble again?"

"Of course not. That last time was a fluke," Jimmy replied. "Everything is just fine."

23

Andrew

The inter-island ferry pulled away from the dock at Village Cay in the center of Road Town. The ride to Anegada was about two hours. Andrew rested *The Cruising Guide to the Virgin Islands* on his knees. As the boat slowly sailed past the navigation buoys in Road Harbour, Andrew turned to the Anegada chapter. He had heard Alice talk about the island and the long history the family had there. She'd gone there as a child with Jennifer and Zach many times. Richard was there too, but was darting around with scuba and day-sails to the neighboring Jost Van Dyke and Virgin Gorda. Although the island was only eleven miles long, white sandy beaches covered the shoreline. Unlike the adjacent island's volcanic formations, rising high above the sea, Anegada is merely a low coral reef formed over millions of years. What is not visible from the surface is the ten miles of reef lying shallow in the water to the southeast. Coral reef heads close to the surface and tricky currents snagged many hapless sailors in giant wooden ships filled to the brim with newly minted gold and silver coins. Andrew read further that gold was impervious to the salt water, could be pulled out of the ocean after two hundred years, and have the same shiny luster as the day it was submerged. Silver, on the other hand, corroded into a black lump. Coins would fuse into piles of seeming rubble, making them hard to recognize underwater and even harder to bring to the surface.

Alice fidgeted with her smartphone. She punched the keys in an anxious attempt to reach their daughter, Bev, with a text. Bev was facing a big math test and was very stressed over it. Alice always wore Bev's stress on her sleeve, feeling every anxiety, and every adolescent trauma of her daughter. As the boat rounded the harbor and turned left into the Sir Francis Drake Channel on a due east heading, the cell phone signal went from bad to nothing. Alice opened her bag and tossed the phone in with little regard for where it landed.

The shallow reefs made navigating into the Anegada Harbor nearly impossible until enterprising hotel entrepreneurs dredged the bottom and placed marker buoys, creating a narrow but safe channel. The ferry slowly inched next to the end of the pier in front of the Anegada Reef Hotel. Andrew stepped onto the wooden dock and looked up at the azure-blue sky and then to the water. The shallow white sand reflected the bending light waves back up to the surface and left him almost speechless.

He turned to Alice as she appeared on the dock. "I've never seen a more beautiful color of water."

Alice gazed nonchalantly at the water and replied without astonishment, "Yep, welcome to Anegada."

Vivian greeted the couple as they approached the modest hotel office. The concrete block one-story buildings looked more like a motor inn on the drive to Sacramento, Andrew thought. They settled into their room for the three-night stay. Alice plopped her soft suitcase on the double bed to the right and stretched out on the adjacent bed. Advance dinner orders were required and Alice ordered grilled lobster for two without consulting Andrew.

"Okay, we're looking for a bar and something green. You know the grounds. Where should we start?" Andrew asked.

"I'm starting down at the dock and picking out two live lobster for tonight," Alice replied.

"What are you talking about? We have three days to find that next clue. Please…get focused! Work with me, Alice."

"Andrew, button it up! We'll find the clue. Why are you stressing out? We'll find the dadgum clue!"

"It's just this could be really big money. It could change our whole lives."

"What do you want to change? Christ, Andrew," she gasped.

Andrew paused and looked out the window to a gentle breeze blowing through the trees. "Yachts, airplanes, a villa on St. Barts. Small stuff like that. That's all."

24

Richard / Panama

Bill Price leafed through page after page of the diary that described the new startup. His law office handled the meltdown of the management team including the Stanford professor turned chief technical officer who couldn't grasp the concepts of timeline, product development and launch. He knew all the details of the new team that was put in place before the initial public offering. His law firm had taken part of their fee in stock options and when the stock opened at $15 and soared to $40 on the first day, he was ecstatic. But his fortunes took a bigger bump as the stock eclipsed $100 over the next two years. On the IPO, the only 10 percent holders were John Chakkera and Richard Dennison. They were each worth $40 million that day. It took Richard another year and a half to lose interest in the company. He negotiated a three month leave of absence.

In a steady fifteen-knot wind, Bruce's yacht cut through a calm sea between Papeete and Bora Bora in the Tahitian chain on the day the leave of absence ended. Richard was at the helm that day. He returned to the company, but only for a short time.

Price slipped a recycled envelope into the pages of the diary to mark the place where he'd started this evening.

Bruce called one morning during a tense marketing meeting when the battle was between the old guys, like me, and the young guys fresh out of business school. They had some good ideas but it was going to be too slow to implement and cost more than it was worth to sales growth. When the meeting ended, I dragged myself back to my corner cubicle and called Bruce back.

"I'm glad you called. Let's pull up anchor and set sail for somewhere warm," I said, exhaling with a sigh.

"You're a mind reader," he replied. "I've been planning your escape from tech purgatory. We're setting sail for Tahiti and your cabin is being provisioned with Talisker single-malt and oven-roasted cashews as we speak. You're first mate unless I'm too drunk and then you'll be skipper."

I sat back in my chair and neither one of us said a word. Finally, I broke the silence. "When are you hoisting the sails, skipper?"

"Five weeks, mate. I'll be through the Panama Canal in two weeks and then to Panama City preparing the boat for the trip to the South Pacific. I hear they grow limes the size of grapefruit down there. Gin and tonics here we come."

The next morning, I strolled into John Chakkera's office around nine. I told him that Neil Butcher, on my marketing team, was ready for more responsibility. He could handle the team and he understood the vision of our company. John had been working with Neil closely for almost two years, so he readily agreed. Then I told him that it was time for me to get some space from work because I was feeling burned out. This wasn't a surprise to him. Everybody in Silicon Valley was in one stage or the other of burnout mode. Before I could say another word, John piped up and suggested I take a three-month leave of absence.

"Three months, though! Your place is still here with this company. Neil can handle the program while you're gone, but I'm going to need you back a few months before the July board meeting. Is that cool with you? How does it sound?"

"Where do I sign?" I quipped.

I arrived in San Salvador from Los Angeles about two in the afternoon. The layover was six hours waiting for the flight to Panama. Bruce was through the Canal and in a boat slip at La Playita Marina in Panama City. It took him eleven hours to transit from the Gulf of Mexico to the Pacific Ocean, stopping in Gatun Lake overnight. Eighty-five feet above sea level, the lake was created to reduce the amount of excavation needed for the canal. A series of locks on both sides of the lake raise boats to lake level and then lower them down again to sea level. It was first opened in 1914 following the United States completing the original, unfinished French project.

Sailors all over the world talk about the passage around Cape Horn on the southern tip of South America. Some go through Drake Passage and others through the Strait of Magellan, but I never heard anybody say they'd do it again. The sea churns in all directions and the wind gusts are equally chaotic. Yet before the canal, that was the only way to get goods and people to the West Coast and the burgeoning markets of Los Angeles, and San Francisco among others.

I slipped my travel book into my red backpack as my flip phone rang. It was Samantha. I'd only been gone overnight, but she wanted to give me an update on the live-in nanny she hired to help with Maureen and Jimmy while I was away. I planned a month of sailing and then I'd jump on an Air France flight to California. She was cool with the trip, although she was a little suspicious of Bruce. We all partied and sailed in the old days, but Bruce never settled down and she took him for one of those who never would. I never agreed with her out loud, but I knew she was right. Hey, it was a guy's trip, I told her. Sam was generally happy with everything in those days, but a little fidgety. We bought a five-acre plot with an old but huge house in Portola Valley. It had stables for six horses and a riding ring, and she was shopping for her second horse. Her first was a sorrel quarter horse and now she wanted a white jumper. She loved the open space of our property, so I put the house in her name for a Christmas present.

25

Blake

The Island Air 6:14 arrival from Puerto Rico taxied to the terminal. The twin engines sputtered to a halt as the outside stairway was rolled up snug against the forward door. Jimmy was the first passenger through the door followed by Jack Stenson, the bodyguard, and Blake Sorrentino, the consultant. They walked through the terminal to the car waiting at the curb. Speeding to the Village Cay Hotel in Rhode Town, Jimmy assumed an air of leadership, but came across more like an arrogant brat. "We'll start with this, Gordy's little brother has what you desire under two green hats. The clue for you is to see caves and graves." Jimmy paused and thought about the first clue from the trust. Blake put his right hand to his chin, his thumb and forefinger gently massaging the skin. There was no chance, he thought, that he would solve that clue in this muggy backwater part of the world. The forensic consultant from New York City wearing shiny, new Topsiders, khaki cotton slacks and a white linen shirt, knew how to consult. Jimmy was paying him $2000 a day so he rubbed his chin and began his mission of "digging into the facts."

The intercom buzzed on Zach's desk and the secretary's voice announced, "Maureen is on the line." He gracefully reached for his reading glasses with his right hand but then meticulously laid them back on the desk. Picking up the receiver, he greeted Maureen and then she started.

"Zach, Jimmy will kill me if he finds out I'm calling you." Zach sat back in his chair. He thought about growing up in this family. His mother kept things on track, calm, mostly lighthearted and fun. Maureen and Jimmy arrived every summer from Mississippi for a month's visit to become part of the family for a time. Their mother, Samantha, loaded them on the plane and Richard picked them up at the San Francisco airport. In the beginning it was all fun. The water park in San Jose was about all it took to keep four kids occupied. Later Dad bought a modest mountain cottage in the Lake Tahoe neighborhood of Tahoe Donner. Two community pools, and a private beach on Donner Lake filled the bill for summer fun. Zach and Jimmy went to a two-week camp with rock climbing and mountain hiking while the girls went to horseback-riding camp. As an older brother, Jimmy held the upper hand because he could do everything Zach wanted to learn to do, and Jimmy kind of mentored him. It wasn't till the summer before his senior year that Jimmy's arrival turned sour as Zach watched Jimmy tell some lies to Jennifer, like the boys were going to the store on the corner for candy bars but got cigarettes instead. Zach started to wonder if his half-brother was sincere and totally trustworthy.

"Let me hear it," Zach replied to Maureen.

"Jimmy called me from JFK Airport yesterday and it slipped out that he was boarding a plane to Tortola with some guy he hired to find this treasure thing we're all looking for."

"Did he say what he was going to do down there?"

"Just that he has the right guy to crack this puzzle."

"Okay, I'm glad you told me. I guess we'll see what he comes up with," Zach replied.

Zach didn't give Jimmy much hope of getting anywhere with his search, but he was sure that on the off chance that he did, the rest of them wouldn't hear about it.

He hung the phone up and dialed Alice's cell phone. She picked up on the fourth ring.

"Any progress?" Zach asked.

Alice looked out over the sailboats hanging on mooring balls bobbing up and down in Anegada Harbor. The salty sea put a flavor in the air, an island aroma, that was hard for her to describe. She took a deep breath, exhaled and spoke into the phone, "Nothing new. Andrew is running around trying to solve the mystery, but I'm chilling out in a chair on the beach in front of the Ritz Carlton."

Zach knew she was referring to the Anegada Reef Hotel that resembled more of a motor lodge than a Ritz. He chuckled to himself, knowing that not many motor lodges had a view of the Caribbean Sea on one of the most pristine harbors anywhere. For a moment in his mind's eye, Zach saw himself with Jimmy slipping heavy gloves around each hand and fighting a live lobster, finally extracting it from the submerged cage. He felt the exhilaration of success from those many years ago, for a brief second, and then returned his attention to Alice.

"I need to let you know that Jimmy arrived on Tortola yesterday. He brought some detective to snoop around. I don't know his plan or where he's going, but you should be on the lookout," Zach said.

"Does he know about the Anegada clue?" she asked.

"Not yet, but we probably should tell him, don't you think?"

"Not really. Jimmy is a spoiler and a distraction. I'd be happy if he disappeared," she replied.

"I don't think that's going to happen."

Zach told Alice about Jimmy's visit and trip to Florida to ask Samantha for a loan. Alice pleaded with him not to tell Jimmy about the clue, not just yet anyway. He relented and said he wouldn't say anything for the moment.

They ended the call, as Alice jumped up from the white plastic beach chair and headed toward the hotel grounds to find Andrew. Her leisure time was over. She needed to stay one step ahead of Jimmy.

26

Richard / Equator

Bill Price resumed reading.

We motored out of the harbor in Panama City around four PM. The weather was calm and the wind steady around twenty knots. Nosing into the wind, Bruce hoisted the main sail and then the jib. We fell off into the wind watching the sails fill with a breeze from the west by southwest. The sun was low in the sky, but we still had a few hours of daylight. Once I took the helm, steering the boat for the first shift, I could feel the stresses of work, traffic, and even family begin to slowly drain out through my feet into the deep, blue Pacific Ocean. I thought about the days bobbing up and down in that slip in Oakland before I knew how to sail. The calm freedom I felt and, I have to admit, a certain edge I held on to about my future and how it would turn out. The success of the company solved a lot of that anxiety, but what was next and who was next, were the thoughts that crept into my mind.

We hired a weather router from New Zealand, Derek, to help guide us into good sailing weather and away from storms and rough seas. The satellite connection was spotty at times but did provide a periodic download of a grid file to pinpoint wind locations and alter course. Derek sent messages through the satellite which at times were lifesavers.

On the fifth day we were flying wing-on-wing in low wind, blowing from behind. The main sail was out on starboard, and on the front, we pulled out the spinnaker and let her fly on port. The spinnaker's big parachute-like nylon filled with what little wind was blowing from time to time. A yellow vertical stripe decorated our front sail, and ran from the top to the middle, accompanied by orange stripes on either side. Horizontal bands of red, orange, and yellow covered the lower area, all paintings on a backdrop of the blue Pacific sky. That day we crossed the equator heading toward the Galapagos Islands. Sighting San Cristobal, the governing island in the group, we entered the harbor with sails flying into the bay almost to the marina before we engaged the engine to pull us into dock.

The Spanish discovered the islands, and names were given to the individual islands here-and-there by buccaneers, naming British royalty and noblemen as well as fellow pirates. After Ecuador took over the island chain, they gave them all Spanish names. Sailors use both mostly interchangeably. Cristobal is also known as Chatham, for a British earl. The volcanos here are always blowing smoke and lava, and some islands have disappeared under the sea. We were hoping this one would stay afloat for a few days. After securing the boat, Bruce gave the order to head to the bar for a celebration on the equator. It was a small bar with tables sparsely occupying the floor areas.

"Okay boys, listen up," Bruce said in his skipper voice. "We're going to tackle this map-dot tomorrow and see if Darwin knew what he was talking about. Right now, it's bottoms up in the Southern Hemisphere."

"North, south what real difference does it make," a voice came from behind us. "You're standing in the north, but see that hill over there? That's the beginning of the southern half of the world. There's no bar over there, gentlemen, so I recommend you anchor-down right where you are."

I turned around to see a sandy-blonde, five-foot-five frame in navy blue shorts, white linen shirt, and flip-flops. Bruce answered her shout-out,

"We're teetering on reality all the time anyway, why not teeter on the Equator?"

Okay, Bruce was caught off guard, but that was weak, especially for a notorious bachelor on the prowl. I could hear the seagulls screeching as they flew by the open wall of French doors in that island watering hole. There was one patron sitting at a table near the bar. He looked like he was a sailor who pulled into harbor to get his boat repaired and was patiently waiting for engine parts for the past twenty years. He alternately stared at his beer and out the open doors, but I guessed he was really listening to every word from this new cast of characters that the southern breeze delivered to his doorstep.

I looked back over to this fearless, brash blonde. Something was familiar about her, but I couldn't pinpoint it. I switched to a rum punch as daylight slipped away, listening to Bruce and the girl banter mostly about sailing stories.

Bill Price closed the diary, quietly closed the door to his study, and headed to bed.

27

Damn You Richard

When Alice found Andrew, he was walking between two of the cabins behind the hotel office. She stood in the shade of a tree and watched him pace along a path only to reverse and march back the other way. After a minute, she walked up behind him and said, "What on earth are you doing?"

"I've drawn out a grid and I'm covering every square inch of this whole place. We know it's here, and I'm going to find it," he explained.

Alice looked at Andrew and then walked out on the "grid" without a word. As Andrew continued his work, she retreated to the shade, and leaned against what appeared to be an old stone well. After a few minutes, she leaned over the crumbling stone and peered down into the well, where all she saw was pitch-black. She stared into the nothingness mostly thinking about Andrew and his newfound passion for riches. As she pulled back from the dark hole, her eyes began to refocus in the light. Attached to the outside of the well were wood beams capped by a weather-beaten wooden arch, with a slight green tint on the facing. She took two steps back to get a better look and saw that the whole wooden structure was once covered with weathered green paint. Stepping further back to the well, she looked again down the black hole. Still nothing.

"Andrew, get a flashlight, a big one, and get over here," she shouted.

The flashlight found the circular walls of old stone. "Point it straight down and see if you get a reflection off any water," she demanded.

Nothing but black. Andrew straightened his back and looked at Alice with puppy-dog eyes. She touched him on the shoulder and took the flashlight in her left hand. About four feet down, the light revealed a bar wedged into the stone. The bar traversed the center of the well and was also wedged into the other side. Alice leaned into the well for a better look at it, but only saw a simple, pitted iron bar. Her hopes collapsed as she straightened up into the light.

Over lunch they sat quietly, neither one speaking of the clues or the treasure. Lobster sandwich on white toast and an island beer seemed to be the only topics worth discussing. A soft Caribbean breeze blew the warm, salty air through the trees above them. Andrew eased his chair back and rose from the table. Alice offered a slight nod as acknowledgement. He left and walked inland toward their room. Strolling by the old well, he slowed down and then stopped, facing the structure. He repeated the clue to himself, "Anegada Reef Hotel…Raise the Bar Still Look for Green." His first thought was, *Richard Dennison, what a crazy old fool. What on god's green earth was he thinking about…. a treasure hunt, stupid, crazy clues?* He walked up to the stone rim and shined the flashlight down into the black hole. Then on a whim, he leaned into the blackness and extended his long torso, reached out and touched the iron bar. As he did, he felt a link of chain and gave it a tug. He repositioned himself with his left hand holding on to the top of the wall, and began pulling up the chain. He was able to pull his body upright and each length of the chain followed him up and out of the well. Finally standing with both feet on the ground, he saw a flat metal object dangling on the end. Pulling it into the light, he made out the word "dollar." He grabbed a water-bucket and brush, and began to scrub the surface. Holding the metal plate in both hands, he extended his arms to be able to see the whole thing. He read the words slowly, saying each word out loud, "The dollar you save without the dock you crave where sweet Brenda is waiting." He read it again, and one more time. Then he said out loud, "Damn you, Richard Dennison."

****

Zach put his glass of bourbon on the redwood side table. From his deck he looked out all the way to the Bay Bridge through an afternoon blue sky speckled with white, wispy clouds. He dialed Maureen and when she answered jumped right into it: "I called to tell you Alice and Andrew found a clue on George Dog island. Yes, that little one across from Gorda where The Baths are. Well it's some kind of riddle, but we think the next clue is on Anegada. Alice and Andrew are there looking around now. Yes, I talked to Vivian, but she couldn't think of anything helpful. I'll let you know if they find anything. Oh, and one more thing, I haven't told Jimmy about this yet. I'm hoping they don't run into each other down there. Yeah, I'll let him know later."

28

Richard / Jennifer

Bill Price hadn't heard from Zach in a month, but surprisingly he hadn't heard from Jimmy or the others in a few weeks. His firm handled the real estate business for the trust, but another partner coordinated that area. Nevertheless he had planned to make time for the diary that night. He'd never heard the full story of the Tahiti trip. After the kids were asleep, he slipped into his study.

Bruce told her about his trip from St. Martin to St. Croix when the ocean swells were rolling his forty-foot sailboat in a "death trap" for an entire night under a pitch-black sky. At the bottom of each swell, the walls totally surrounded him, making the boat vulnerable to colliding with steamships that he couldn't see. At the top of the swell, it was all about steering and keeping the nose at a quarter angle to the wave. Hitting the wave straight on would probably swamp them, and letting the wave hit on the beam would likely roll it over, turning them upside down. It was a good story, but then again it should be, he'd told it a thousand times, sometimes to blondes, sometimes brunettes.

With the boat in the harbor, we could finally get some normal rest, as in sleep eight hours, have coffee on a flat table, and see dry land. I eased out of my cabin the next morning halfway expecting to see this sandy-haired, precocious sailor-girl stumble out of Bruce's cabin in one of his T-shirts. I was putting my money on the shirt that read, "Sail fast, Live slow." I poured the dark, rich coffee grounds that we provisioned in Panama into the filter then drenched it with steaming water. The morning aroma filled the salon, and with a full cup, I ascended the steps to the blue sky and open cockpit. A little groggy from last night's celebration, I settled into a swivel chair and rested my feet on the bench seat in front of me. A few high clouds floated over the island, and I thought about how nice it was to be relaxing. I knew the next leg of the trip would be a grueling passage, but our next destination, the Marquesas, would be a treat. They're a newer formation, and the volcanic peaks are higher than the Galapagos. It'd be a couple of weeks in open ocean, but you never can tell what the wind might give you, or how long it might take.

I looked over my left shoulder, which I think was northwest, to see a tall peak on what I thought was Santa Cruz island, poke through the bottom of a passing cloud. Most of the people in this island group live there, and the Darwin Center is there busily breeding tortoises.

I turned to see Bruce take the last step up to the deck from below. He unceremoniously plopped into a seat and took a long gulp of his coffee. The distant squawk of seagulls was the only sound breaking the silence in our floating sanctuary.

"Think we can make it over to Santa Cruz island before we head south?" I finally asked.

"Maybe, if you want to. There's plenty of cool stuff here to see, though," Bruce replied without seeming to pay much attention to the topic. "The biggest freshwater lake in these islands is up in those mountains. They named it Laguna El Junco. It might be worth a look."

"Where'd a flat-foot country boy like you pick up all these data points?" I poked.

"Well, Cleveland is not exactly 'flat-foot country boy' territory. And hey Mister 'Data Points,' you're not in Silicon Valley anymore. You can talk regular English."

Bruce snickered as he spoke, and I managed a slight chuckle. I felt my shoulders drop slightly and another round of tension fade away. This was going to be a great month's vacation, I thought.

"We've got to go see the booby birds," Bruce chirped while I looked in his direction, my head slightly tilting. "Yeah man, these birds are like a poultry market for sailors. They land on your boat ready for slaughter. Grill 'em up. I hear they're really tasty,"

I let that pronouncement just lie there, not having any idea how to respond.

"Booby is from a Spanish slang term, bobo, meaning stupid," he said.

"You mean booby trap?" I said.

Bruce brought his right hand to his earlobe, gently rubbing it in silence, then said, "Maybe so. I haven't thought about it."

"Let's ask your little blonde girlfriend downstairs. I think she knows most everything about sailing," I said.

"You mean Jennifer? She's not on our boat, mate. Took herself home last night. It's a mystery how she could resist me, but I guess strange things happen." I nodded without a word. He continued, "She's in that little pale blue hotel for a few weeks. Said she is taking some time away and wants to soak up the Darwin vibe. Pretty cool gal, but kind of different."

Over the next week we hiked the mountains, watched giant tortoises maneuver around and even made it to the mountain peaks on Santa Cruz. It took three days of on-and-off wrangling to get clearance documents to leave the Galapagos and prepare for the three-thousand-mile trek to our next port. The morning before we set sail, I jumped off the boat for an early stroll around town. A small pebble slipped into my shoe, so I plopped myself on a bench to clear it out. When I looked up, I saw the blonde from the bar a few nights ago. She strolled up nonchalantly and sat on the end of the bench. She wore white bike shorts and a pale pink tank top. Her loose flip-flops revealed that she was on a casual stroll.

"You look vaguely familiar. Do you think we've met before?" she asked.

Okay, I said to myself. *I've used that line a thousand times to start a conversation with total strangers, most of whom didn't look half as good as this gal.* I fought the urge I was feeling to be self-conscious and nervous and for once just sat there with half a smile and counted to five. Counting *three, four, five, okay, here I go.*

"How about marrying me this afternoon?" I said in a slow, measured pace.

"I'm not sure I have the right shoes," she volleyed back.

We sat staring at each other, eyes locked like lasers, both fighting smiles. Two tourists walked by speaking what seemed like Spanish. One was waving his arms in front of him as he pontificated on some grand event. The other staring out at the bay as they passed by without a glance our way.

Finally, she overcame the silence and said, "Where do you sail when you're not chasing the rainbow?"

Sailor, rich widow, just divorced, I had no idea who she was, where she came from, or why she was on this map dot in the South Pacific.

"I cut my teeth in San Francisco Bay. Some say it's the best place to learn having to sail with currents, tides, flat wind and all-out gale-force winds." She sat listening as I continued, "Even on warm, calm days in the Bay, I always have storm gear packed and ready to go. The wind can howl under the Golden Gate Bridge at forty knots at a moment's notice."

"Where do you sail from in the Bay?" she asked.

"I was in the Oakland Harbor to start, but moved the boat across the Bay to Redwood City. It's a bit of a trip to get to the good water in San Francisco, but living on the boat was easier for work from there."

"Are you in Silicon Valley?" she asked.

"Yep, on dry land now. Stables, two horses, five acres. All that stuff," I replied.

She kept the questions coming for a few minutes until I coughed up a few questions for her.

"Are you a sailor or just famous for something that I never heard of?" I asked. She smiled and diverted her glance slightly. I looked down the street in the direction of our boat and thought I saw Bruce walking down the docks to the marina office. I hoped he wouldn't see us and head this way. The sun was rising and I could feel the air starting to warm up. A bank of clouds rolled in from the southwest, dark gray with bright white edges and sun peeking through fat holes in the cotton-like overcast.

"I sail. My dad took me with him on the water since I was six. Mom was not adventurous or athletic, so I got the nod to be Dad's first mate. He had a few buddies that sailed every now and then."

"What kind of boat did he have?" I asked.

"He started with a twenty-four-foot Swan and later moved up to a thirty-two-foot Island Packet. We liked that one 'cause it was heavier and held the heading better in high wind...and big water. Every couple of months we'd spend the night on it in our slip. Mom would come down and we'd kind of tailgate in the marina. In warm weather there'd be a small crowd of boaters there. Kids could run around so it was fun." She paused and I could tell her mind was picturing that scene from her childhood.

"Sounds like you were in the East, somewhere in New England?" I said.

"No, I gunk holed off the coast of Maine one summer, just exploring the islands and lakes. It was a great two-week trip."

I'd read about gunkhole trips with a lot of shallow water sailing into inlets made private because nobody else wanted to risk it. Those boats had retractable center boards that drafted four feet but could be pulled up as you entered shallow coves.

"My husband sailed some as a kid in that area. So, we gave it a try," she said with a slight, dry gesture from her wrist.

"Married, then?" I said.

"I should say, former husband."

The next hour flew by without noticing the time. She was married to an introverted, unemployed engineer who one day decided to look for a job. He got hired at a small, fledgling startup called NetTrip. They had software that helped people navigate web pages on the internet. It was a far-flung idea because not many people really used the internet and when they did it was a painful experience, because it was so slow. Everything took forever. Phone companies offered dialup connections unless you were close enough to a telephone pole special box to get what was called an ISDN connection. But the connection would mostly go in and out. So, this job was more of a trial run to see how he could handle a work week. The company didn't pay a competitive salary, but they gave everybody big stock options. Big deal, they thought. The options are worthless unless the company is successful, and we know how that goes. She went on to tell me the marriage didn't work out and I decided not to pry for now.

"What's your trip like from here?" she asked.

"Heading out tomorrow for the Marquesas. It'll be a trudge of a couple of weeks but all part of the fun," I said. "What's your plan?"

"No plan really. Just out to find the beautiful places and the beautiful people."

"You could meet us down island if you want; I think we're planning to hang there for a while. The mountains are higher there and I think there are some good hikes."

We both slowly stood up. I looked down at my feet for a second and then back at her. There was no rushing or shuffling by either of us to split the scene. She looked back at me with a gentle glance and said, "That might be fun."

I reached down and took her hand in more like a handshake than the other kind of gesture. She grasped my hand softly and we looked at each other for a split second, before turning to walk away. She took a step then turned and said, "Watch out for those sticky winches."

Something triggered in my mind, but I couldn't quite picture what "sticky winches" was all about. Passing a combo T-shirt and coffee shop, I stopped to stare out at the sailboats. I was feeling that high you get when you just met somebody that you really connected with on a personal level but, you know, it was more than that. Samantha, the kids, two horses, and a job all waited for me back in California. More money than I ever thought possible and the world was my oyster. I'd probably never see Jennifer again anyway. And, Mr. Casanova, as in me, didn't get her phone number, her email or her last name. I wasn't trying; I guess that's a good thing.

29

Glock

Jimmy settled into the front seat of the thirty-foot rented charter boat for the trip to Anegada along with his two companions. Jack had a friend on St. Thomas who he explained was in "the business," a term neither Jimmy nor Blake understood except that he acquired a 9mm Glock handgun, and wore it inside his waistband. Jimmy was nonchalant about the gun, but was satisfied with the professionalism it implied. Blake brought his laptop along not knowing what for, but it proved he was a consultant, and Jimmy gave an approving nod when Blake stepped onto the boat with it under his arm. The thirteen-mile ride to the island shook up this oddball crew. Ocean swells rolled in from the southeast about every nine seconds. The captain started out using the autopilot, but reverted to manual control as they rounded Jost Van Dyke and headed north in open ocean.

The Virgin Islands is the most popular tourist sailing destination in the world. Every port is geared up to make sailors welcome. Each morning these would-be pirates of old, alias middle-class weekend warriors, sailed away from the most beautiful place they'd ever seen only to arrive a few hours later, after never losing sight of land, in the most beautiful place they'd ever seen. The popularity had a great deal to do with the protected wind and water that the island chain provided. This merry band of clue-seekers were getting a sharp dose of what nature has to offer, and they weren't enamored with the experience. After thirty minutes, Jack rushed to the side, held on tightly to the gunnels and lurched from the waist. Pulling his upper torso back upright, he tasted the salt water dripping down his forehead from waves lapping over the sides, soaked from head to shoulders. Blake looked at him with a slight bit of compassion, but stayed glued to his seat. Jimmy didn't veer from his straight-ahead stare, looking for the flat island ahead that he knew so well.

The waves began to ease and the wind dropped as they approached the narrow passage to the only port on the island. Jimmy hopped up to the bow and looked down as the ocean floor rose and the shallow white sand transformed clear water to turquoise. Richard always required a child to stand at the bow to make sure they stayed within the slim channel, so Jimmy did it out of habit. The captain navigated using the buoy markers and paid no attention to Jimmy.

Alice turned to Andrew and yelled, "Get the binoculars, and I mean quick."

Andrew hated it when she'd hurl orders at him. But he gave up fighting it a long time ago. He would have been a broken man by now, if he'd ever feigned a backbone. Alice ripped the binoculars out of his hands and darting under a tree, trained them on a motorboat rounding the channel and heading for a mooring ball. There, holding on to the bowsprit, was her half-brother Jimmy. She was sure of it, white linen slacks and pale blue shirt, slightly bent forward. Jimmy all right.

"Go tell Vivian that we don't want him to know about us. Ask her if he has a reservation for tonight. Jesus! I have to call Zach."

It was six in the morning when Zach picked up his cell phone in California. He was stirring but not fully awake.

"The Jimster is making a grand entrance on Anegada. He's chartered a water taxi to bring him here," she blurted.

Alice was sitting on the new clue and had not told Zach about it yet, thinking she and Andrew might try to make some sense of it before revealing their find. She knew Zach was her ally, and he would play the new information the right way, but just the same she wanted to stay one step ahead of the process. She knew Zach had regular conversations with Jennifer, much more often than she, herself, talked to their mother. If she were honest, she'd admit that the obvious closeness of those two annoyed her, because as hard as she tried with her mother, that brand of intimacy never materialized for her. Although Zach believed that Jennifer knew nothing about the treasure hunt, Alice had paid attention to her parents' relationship; how they interacted and worked together on most things. Yeah, Dad could be spacy and distant, but on the big things…well, that was different. Their mother was clever, outgoing, and outspoken, but when it came to their dad, she had a measured response. When Alice watched them, she could see her mom almost fall into a groove behind Dad when he suddenly transformed from being quiet and removed to talking about ideas and strategies for anything from stocking the kitchen at the mountain house to buying a multimillion-dollar property. As a little girl paying attention to what Dad was saying, she felt like his thoughts came out in fully formed ways, and Mom absorbed all the concepts with a kind of reverence and respect. Not all those ideas were made into something concrete, but she could see that some of them were stepping-stones to new, sometimes bigger and better things. She took those traits of reverence and respect as Mom and Dad's love language. Alice saw this closeness in a way she was sure Zach, and also Jimmy and Maureen never did.

Before Zach could organize his thoughts about Jimmy's arrival, in a quiet, measured voice Alice said, "We found the next clue, but we haven't figured it out yet."

"So it isn't easy to decipher. Why am I not shocked?" Zach said.

"No, I didn't think it would be obvious, but why so obscure?" she said.

"Email it to me and I'll see what I can come up with," Zach replied.

Just before lunch that day, Zach read over the clue. A second and third time but he couldn't focus on it, or even think about what it might mean.

"The dollar you save without the dock you crave where sweet Brenda is waiting."

He clicked on "forward" and typed in Vivian's email address.

"Hi Vivian, I know this is a weird one, but take a look at this and see if anything comes to mind," he wrote. "It's the next clue, and I can't make heads or tails of it. Thanks, Zach."

30

Richard / Skipjack

Bill Price impatiently opened the diary and began to read.

The calendar lost its meaning after days in open ocean. Sometimes we had full sails and other days the wind slacked and left us meandering and languid. We counted the miles in a seemingly endless trek across the South Pacific. One morning Bruce was up on the bow and called to me to come up front. The sun was high closing in on midday, the visibility was good, and the waves were rolling at one to two feet in the direction of the wind. When I reached the bow, he was pointing at the water ahead of us. I immediately saw a strange line of whitecaps formed at a distance. A few minutes later we splashed into this mini-cauldron at about fifteen knots and could see a strong ocean current smashing into the waves, creating the whitecaps. I was watching the water's action when Bruce uttered, "Washing Machine Effect." I looked up and he repeated it, then said, "I've heard about this…never saw it before."

We estimated the current's flow at around three or four knots. Bruce walked below to the navigation station, picked up the satellite phone and punched in Derek's number in New Zealand. Derek explained that this was common in this part of the ocean. He did a quick scan of the wind conditions and weather forecast in the surrounding area. After some back and forth discussion, he recommended a course change. On our present course, we would hit twenty-five knot winds, gusting to forty knots in about two hours. This new current was accelerating our arrival time into the bad weather where Derek estimated sea swells at five to eight feet. We fell off our current course knowing that the weather pattern was wide, moving in our direction, and dangerous. Derek told us that it would be chasing us even on our new course, so get all the speed we could.

After a few hours the wind picked up and we were moving at a quick fifteen knots, running southeast away from the storm, but also away from our destination in the Marquesas. If we could outrun the storm, we'd resume our proper course and not lose too much time. As the sun dropped below the horizon, no stars peaked through the solid cloud cover to light our way, and no moon shone through to rescue us from the pitch-black night. We could feel the frequency of the gusts quicken; at times it felt like they were tearing through the sails. Bruce had us reef the main sail by flipping the switch on the roller furling, decreasing the sail area by half. The spinnaker was flying in front so we pulled it down and ran up a reefed jib, giving us wind power but limiting the effect of the gusts.

The current was still pushing on the port bow, rendering us uncertain about our forward progress. Simply put, we weren't sure whether or not we were outrunning the storm. Our crewmates ascended from below wearing full storm gear, so I took the hint and headed below for mine. After slipping them on, I put Bruce's gear under my arm and fought my way through the rolling and bouncing up to the open air of the cockpit. Bruce was finishing his shift and when I took over I resumed steering up and down ten-foot troughs. Waves were breaking over the side of the boat from the beam, in the middle. As the bow dug into the churning sea, gallons of water rushed through the deck and into the cockpit drenching every inch, including me. I hunkered down low, and the waves broke over my head, collapsing on me. While straightening up, a rogue wave hit us broadside on the beam. The surprise force tossed me to the side, and I slammed to the edge, bouncing back, but off balance, while the boat lurched left. I felt the top of my body bend and start over the side, then grabbed the rail with my right hand and fended off the gunnel of the boat with my left. With both hands on the rail, I pulled myself back into the cockpit, exhausted. Lying on the deck, I shifted to one elbow before getting up, and wiping the salt water from my eyes. I was stunned and scared but the wind and waves were still pounding; I still had a job to do, so gathering myself, I sat behind the helm and put both hands on the wheel. Every move of my left wrist shot a biting pain up my arm—sprained or broken, I wasn't sure—but I dropped my left hand to my lap and made do with one hand. With the helm securely on autopilot, I thought about slipping downstairs to get dry clothes and wrap the wrist to keep it from moving, but never got the nerve to leave the deck. I shivered through the end of my watch even as the sea started to calm and the gusts relented into longer intervals. While the night sky hovered over us, a few stars began to twinkle through broken clouds. When I was relieved, I took my turn in the sack and in gently rolling seas, I slept like a baby until I smelled the warm aroma of fresh coffee.

For the next few days, I thought about my life in Silicon Valley. Work was fun and exciting, but how much money do you need? Challenges were good, but it's all about making money, and I wondered if too much money could be boring. Chakkera was not slowing up and it hadn't occurred to me to ask him about that island he was going to buy. He was evolving into that guy who is "more…more…more…. win…win…win." The adrenaline rush.

Samantha was sliding into a conventional routine. A lot of that was because of the kids, school, and other parents she was meeting, all of which she pretty much handled on her own. It was a dance I called the "middle-class boogie woogie," or the "bourgeois scoot." I know that's weird, but what can I say? I was in the kind of "what's life all about" mood, and it was hitting me right between the eyes.

Bill Price looked at the clock as the hands rounded the midnight hour. This was his signal to close things down and head to bed. But he looked down at the next paragraph, and was drawn back into the middle of the south Pacific Ocean.

Slack winds were making our progress slow and we filled the days fishing to bolster our provisions. We threw out two lines at a time and although we'd pull up anything we caught, skipjack tuna was mostly the catch. There's a huge population in these warm waters, growing up to three feet and weighing usually around twenty pounds, although a seventy-five-pound catch is not unheard of. Bruce was bragging about this feast we were having nightly to Derek on a satellite call, and in between the chuckling, Derek told us to be careful because sharks and marlin gobble up skipjack. A little silky shark would be a good catch, but you want to watch out for the big ones. Catch a skipjack and then a honking-big-ole shark catches you, he joked. Later, when the sea floor rose and our depth was under thirty feet, we hauled 'em in, like they say, "shooting fish in a barrel."

On days when the wind was brisk, we sailed along at fifteen knots and struggled pulling in twenty-pound skipjacks against that speed. If a big fish chomped down on our catch, he'd snap the line or we had to be ready to cut it. Our calculations showed we were doing about 200 nautical miles a day, with average speed around eight knots.

At the halfway point to the Marquesas, with a nine-knot wind, I hooked a feisty skipjack. He was giving me a fight and as he got closer, the gray-blue stripe across his middle flashed in the morning sunlight. I felt the line slack as he rose through the water, and broke the surface in a straight vertical jump. As if on cue, a huge dark blue fin pierced the surface preceded by a razor-sharp spear and in one choreographed motion swallowed the skipjack whole. For a split second, I simply marveled at this surprise attack. Then my left hand reached for the knife to cut the line and liberate me from this monster I was clutching. Just as I found the knife, I heard Bruce yell, "Bring him in. Come on, sailor, bring him in!"

The knife missed the shelf and dropped to the deck as I let it slip away from my hand. I put both hands on the rod and looked up at Bruce grinning ear-to-ear. I knew what he was thinking: *Game on.* For the next half hour I fought my "nemesis of the sea." Bruce sat behind me and said simply, "Eighty or ninety pounds... what a feast!" I offered the rod to Bruce and begged him to spell me, but no way that was happening. This was all mine.

By the time we pulled him into the boat, the marlin and I were both exhausted, but fighters like that don't give up easily, so we had to stay clear of the lethal spear of a nose, and the sharp edges of the dorsal fin. Bruce shoved his foot just barely below the fish's head, slowing his frantic lunges on the deck, and a hammer did the rest.

On the fourteenth day out, the wind abruptly changed direction, coming out of the southeast right on our nose. You can't sail directly into the wind, so we had to find a new heading. Derek's recommendation was to head due south, putting the wind at about two o'clock on our bow, filling the main sail nicely, and although Bruce had us ready the spinnaker to replace the jib on the front, the higher winds postponed that decision. Derek gave us a waypoint on the compass that marked where to turn east. He told us to stay on the southern heading even past that point if we still had the wind; explaining if the wind shifted a little south, we'd be in the same situation as now. The further south we got, the easier to catch the easterly straight to the Marquesas.

As evening fell, the wind died down to six knots with quiet seas, and we decided to set the dinner table outside in the cockpit. It might come as a shock, but we grilled marlin steaks with frozen corn-on-the-cob, and green salad. The monster fish was actually a species of marlin called a longbill spearfish. We weighed him in at ninety pounds and a bit over seven feet.

As we sat down to dinner, I felt calmer, a lot of anxiety was lifting, and I wasn't giving much thought to business or the kids or the horses or the house or even Samantha. Out of sight, out of mind maybe, but this trip and bouncing around in the middle of the ocean completely changed the perspective for me, as it did for all of us for that matter. Were all those things a dream, or a long-lost past life? Was it real? I'd tell you this trip was a dream come true, but I can't remember dreaming an excursion like this; never knew it existed. I merely jumped on a boat with Bruce, because Bruce is my friend, and I wanted to get some air in my life, a little space to rest up.

I did have dreams when I was younger. Tennessee dreams, like going to Atlanta, or bigger yet going to New York City, or even bigger, going to London and Paris. There are more lakes in Tennessee than any other state, and I had dreams of bigger and faster ski boats. Like everyone I knew, I dreamed of prettier women, more beer, and prettier women. I liked horses and the smell of an old barn and thought for sure I'd have a gentleman's hundred-acre farm... tractor, porch swing, pretty wife who likes my jokes, two sons and a daughter. I never dreamed about the South Pacific... except when I saw Elvis in the movie, of course.

We needed wine for this special dinner, and luckily in Panama I smuggled onto the boat a bit of contraband from my frequent wine tasting weekends in Napa Valley, where the summers were warm and dry with never a hint of rain. We'd get a sitter for Jimmy and Maureen, and would rent bikes on Route 29. Sam never got tired of the same wineries where the staff viewed us as regulars. The wine business felt more rural and off-the-beaten-path than it is today. The early struggle of wineries to be taken seriously in the marketplace was difficult, and credibility was measured against Rothchild and others from the century's old vineyards in France and Italy. The crowds hadn't found the place yet. The first tasting room we ever visited was Charles Krug and to this day, it's my first-choice wine. Krug had more big-red Cabernet Sauvignons than anybody on the 29-strip. Each year I tasted them, and bought a case of the ones I thought would age best. My policy was to store them for at least ten years before a test drive; finding that for most of them right at twelve years was the sweet spot. I brought two bottles of the estate cab on the boat, that were right in the pocket. Bruce took the honors of uncorking the first one; a perfect complement to spearfish.

Around ten thirty that night the wind picked up, clocking in at twenty-five knots, and it took all four of us to crank the jib in to half-reefed. The sea swells rose for a rocky, rolling ride, peppering us with salt spray. Later, heavy rain battered us till just before daybreak. As the sun rose, the wind died down and we saw nothing more than ten to twelve knots for the next five days.

Finally, we hit the waypoint target and turned due east, straight to the islands. From twenty miles out, the rocky spires of these volcanic ocean dots made a sharp outline on a pocked, cotton sky. We picked out Hiva-Oa, one of the big ones, for our first stop. Unlike most of the islands near the equator, we would not be protected from the pounding of the ocean by coral reefs fringing this island. There were a few sheltered anchorages to pick from, and Bruce chose Ta'a Oa bay resting in the crater of a collapsed ancient volcano. Its walls rise more than three thousand feet and a newly built seawall afforded good protection from sea surges. Dry land never looked so good.

31

Drowned Island

Jimmy stepped onto the concrete block patio leading to the double doors of the office at the Anegada Reef Hotel. A single step led into the small, dark room that served as the front desk. The blocks had missing chunks randomly dispersed and several of the whole blocks were broken into two or more pieces laying in place. Jimmy entered the familiar room. Looking to the right, he saw the stack of horseshoes, croquet mallets, and ping-pong paddles that had brought him in many times as a kid looking for summer activities. No one was manning the desk, so he wandered through the back door and called out. He heard a screen door open and slam shut, then a tall fellow walked in the room. Jimmy asked for Vivian but was told she'd be back in a couple of hours, so he retraced his steps out the front door and found his team standing near the beach. He dispatched Blake next door to Potter's Bar and sent Jack down the beach to Neptune's Treasure. Blake had formulated a list of things to ask about, and other points for the team to look for, like suspicious people, eyes not steady on you when you spoke to them… all guarded and worth noting. Jimmy stayed on the hotel grounds looking for suspicious activity, himself. Blake had scheduled three hours of discovery here, then it was off to Virgin Gorda for the evening and more "broadband reconnaissance," Blake's newly coined consultant phrase.

From her hotel room, Alice watched Jimmy leave the courtyard and walk down to the beach and then she quickly darted to the office, through the back door to order dinner brought to their room, where she and Andrew barricaded themselves. She had not heard from Vivian and was not taking any chances at getting found out by Jimmy. Alice was having grilled lobster and Andrew wanted fresh swordfish… and a bottle of white wine.

Vivian looked out her office window in the hotel gift shop. It was a separate building behind the hotel's beach bar. On first look, you might think this hotel was a grouping of random buildings that were expanded and used as needed instead of a single-purpose hotel. And that's just what it was. As business grew and more boats were making their way to the island, the hotel expanded organically. The bar and courtyard were a mishmash of random patches of grass and sand. Nobody paid much attention to maintenance, or raked it or groomed it in anyway. It was simply the beach on Anegada with the nickname, *The Drowned Island*.

She saw Jimmy walk through the courtyard and after a while, return back to the beach. Knowing he had no plans to stay the night, she just sat tight and waited. Staring at her open email page, she read the clue again: "The dollar you save without the dock you crave where sweet Brenda is waiting." All at once her fingers hit the keyboard and she began typing,

"Zach, the clue, *without the dock you crave*. There's no dock on White Bay at Jost Van Dyke. Maybe that is a place to look?' She hit the send key and leaned back in her chair. Then she sprung forward and again began to type: "Zach, *the dollar you save*… The Soggy Dollar Bar is on White Bay. Your dad used to go over there just to drink beer for the day. He loved that bar. I think you should head to Jost." She hit send.

Zach punched in the phone number for his travel agent. "Hi, Marci. See if you can book two tickets to Tortola tomorrow. Any time but maybe not too early. It's Jennifer and me going. No. No return right now; we'll need to wait and see."

Zach waited on hold for a couple of minutes until Marci came back with the reservations.

"I'll send a courier with the tickets this afternoon," she said.

Zach hung up and phoned Jennifer. He told her they were booked on a flight tomorrow.

"Zach, I can't go to the islands tomorrow. I've got stuff to do, and besides I'm not involved with this treasure hunt. You kids have to do this."

The call shook Jennifer's nerves from a pleasant morning, into a near panic attack. She knew she couldn't go down there and act nonchalant, naive, and disinterested. Somebody would catch on, probably Alice, she thought.

"Thanks for asking, dear, but I'm staying right here in California," she sheepishly uttered.

The next morning Zach ascended from the Town Car in front of the American Airlines baggage kiosk, planted both feet on the curb and did a 360 look around before he leaned over to the car door and offered a hand to Jennifer as she arose onto the sidewalk. She was in mid-sentence as she looked up at Zach, "—and I'm staying at the Village Cay Hotel, not traipsing around the islands on a wild goose chase. Zach, are you listening to me?"

"Yes, Mother, I'm listening, and you have a reservation at the hotel…in your favorite room overlooking the harbor and the big boats," he replied.

Zach stood up from the table when Jennifer arrived at the marina restaurant for dinner. They had arrived at Beef Island Airport in Tortola at six that evening, and after checking in the hotel began winding down the evening.

"How is your room, Mom?" Zach asked. He was hoping his surprise appearance at his mother's house that morning to convince her to take the trip would be forgotten now that they were here.

"Everything is fine, as usual. I miss seeing Louise at the front desk. She apparently retired last fall, but is still on the island. Maybe I can find her and try to catch up in the next few days while you're on your mission," she said.

"What I remember is, she was around fifteen when we first started coming here. Never been off the island except for St. Thomas, which is only a twenty minutes' ferry ride," Zach replied.

"She was always so nice, would babysit all of you guys. Richard treated her exceedingly well, lavishing her with tips and gifts. He could really lay that Southern charm on when he was in the mood," she said. "Once he hauled her on that forty-foot sloop with us and we did a five-day loop around the islands starting at Jost Van Dyke."

Zach remembered chasing her around the boat and playing hide and seek, but couldn't picture which trip it was. He sat quietly while Jennifer recounted story after story in these islands, beautiful sunsets, lazy days snorkeling and swimming, but also sea swells and rolling water, rains and squalls that were challenging.

He was watching his mother to see if she picked up on his distracted mood, but she gave no sign of it. He too was worried about accidently running into Jimmy, and what he would say, and how much trouble that might be for everyone. But, mostly he was thinking about Jost Van Dyke and the clue. The last ones to make any headway would have been Alice and Andrew, he'd thought, but they were moving things along, even though this clue was stifling. Although he had a far-flung suspicion that Bill Price knew more than he was admitting about this search, he was convinced that Jennifer was in the same situation as they were. Hearing her reminisce moved him to bring her in on the latest findings.

"Alice has found two clues, one on George Dog and the other on Anegada," he admitted. "The way Dad wrote these clues is so obscure, it's going to be really hard to track all this down."

She sat intently, allowing him to roll out the story.

"You read the first clue in the trust, 'Gordy's little brother has what you desire under two green hats. The clue for you is to see caves and graves.' The second one on George Dog was painted on the inside of a buried chest. It said, 'Anegada Reef Hotel…Raise the Bar Still Look for Green.' I can't figure what Dad was thinking with these kinds of clues. Did he smoke much weed back then?"

"How did you find it?" she asked.

"Alice and I figured out that the Gorda reference was our dog, Gordy, and get this, Andrew found a reference to an old pirate cemetery on Scrub Island while he was knocking around on Marina Cay. You can see the caves on Virgin Gorda and the cemetery on Scrub from George Dog. After that Alice and Andrew just stumbled on the chest," he told her.

Jennifer knew she should say something, but her tongue was tied in knots. Her mind raced with the thought of "knocking around" Marina Cay. If they "knocked around" too hard they could ruin this fun little excursion. Richard insisted on making the whole thing challenging, and when she wrote the clues, she fell into his spell of being clever, hoping not to be perplexing. Now she was not so sure she succeeded.

Zach told her about finding the third clue and how Vivian figured out the Soggy Dollar Bar, but it was a guess at this point. He was meeting Alice and Andrew there tomorrow and asked her to come along.

"No, I'll stick around here and enjoy the Road Town atmosphere," she said. "You can give me a report tonight."

32

Richard / Marquesas

After a robust Saturday morning golf game at Palo Alto Hills Country Club, Bill Price pulled in to his driveway and entered an astonishingly quiet house. Not even the dog was in sight to break the silence. He guessed the whole group was on a shopping trip. He'd just walked eighteen holes at the hilliest golf course in the entire Bay Area. But the early morning brisk air, fresh dewdrops, and views of San Francisco Bay were always a rush and made up for the rough walk. He grabbed a cold club soda, and wandered back to his study, and picked up the diary.

We had traveled 3,000 miles from Panama and I'll never forget the experience, but not sure I want to do it again. Yes, I was scared to death, happy as a pig in.... you-know-what, and about every other feeling you could get. The old life, yes old life, I can't believe I'm saying it, didn't feel important to me and most days didn't even feel real. Floating in a cloud of thin Jell-O, deprived of sensory sensations, just me and my thoughts would probably be an overstatement, or a gross indulgence.... Or maybe not.

I was bursting out of my bubble-of-a-life... growing up in the South, Silicon Valley rat race, and now the largest tiki sculptures in all of French Polynesia. I knew so many people who had fine, stable, and successful lives just staying home... in the town they grew up in. Look at it, everybody knows you, your brothers and sisters, your parents and maybe your grandparents. You spend no energy opening up new social circles. If you have a problem, plenty of people rush in to help. If you get divorced, somebody steps in that you've known all your life, and she knows all about you already. Easy is the key word here. Well, the key word right now, right here in the middle of the ocean is adventure. Giving up all the "easy" for adventure. It has its high points, but you pay with the low.

We pulled into one of the few slips in the marina, about two in the afternoon. The boat needed some fixes including a ripped jib. This front sail was only a few months old and could easily be sewn up as good as new. The traveler winch was sticking and needed repair or replacing. Bruce was starting a search of the island group to find the right part. He was on his own, and declined my help with these jobs, so I started thinking of hiking around to the tiki sculptures.

Carving deified ancestors with wood and stone sculptures was common throughout the Polynesian islands, but here on Hiva Oa the human-like figures reached their pinnacle in size. Tiki was the name for the first man in Polynesian lore. He created a companion to ward off his loneliness and when the urge finally struck, children came along and that's how the world was populated. The whole thing sounded familiar to me!

I took a small bottle of water and started my trip to see this first man for myself. The most abundant grouping of stone statues is on the northeast coast near the village of Puama'u, but travel to that area was only by boat as the roads were rugged or nonexistent, so for now I was satisfied with our side of the island. I walked for about an hour among lush green, on dirt trails. A tall canopy of indigenous trees stretched high above a twenty-foot cover of low-lying trees, accented with broad-leafed native greenery for my walk. Stacked stones in a kind of wall began to crop up along the road until I entered a small clearing. An earthen terrace was ringed by two rows of three and four-foot-high stones, and in the center was Mr. Tiki himself. This twenty-foot stone figure was partially covered with green moss and lichen, while a bright-white fungus, like dusted powder, highlighted the surface in a random, earthy pattern. Iron deposits in the stone leached out to the surface along his torso and left thigh, adding a terracotta patina to the composition. Companions surrounded the central figure, some seated, others standing, no doubt protecting and keeping company. I sat in the silence of this clearing on a rock with an orange crusty coating.

Wondering if I had entered sacred ground, I thought for a minute about the whole idea of "sacred ground." What is sacred about it? What about "Holy City"? What makes it holy? These are special places to a culture for spiritual or most likely political reasons. It's subjective and has literally nothing to do with me or the present time, nor does it display any innate specialness. But right now, for me in the presence of these ancient carvings, I felt for a minute this was my special place. When I look back, it was more about being out of my normal loop in life, eliminating the noise that clattered through my mind, and the sound of responsibility and civilization ringing in my ears. Some people call this an epiphany… a flash of perspective in an otherwise surface existence. I had a vague feeling that nothing would ever be the same for me after this. I couldn't have known how right I was.

Arriving back at the marina, I smelled fresh coffee, but it wasn't a Starbuck's fragrance, deeper and richer than that. I followed my nose into a café just in time to see the plunger of a French press descend on the thick island coffee grounds. With a hot cup in hand, I picked a small table outside and started to sit when, from a side view, I recognized something about the woman at the next table. It was something familiar, maybe an air or a vibe; I couldn't tell. Just then she rolled her head to look over her shoulder and there was Jennifer, in the flesh.

I stood transfixed. The air around me seemed to grow thin, small breaths were facile and easy; the sunlight peeking through the outdoor canopy suddenly was brighter and colors on the patio were vivid. I know, only a lovesick weirdo would write this gibberish, but honestly, I can't think of another way to describe it. You might think one of us would reach out a hand, or say something clever. But, nothing happened, nothing at all for what seemed like a million years. Finally in silence, I took two steps to the empty chair at her table, placed my cup down and pulled the chair out to sit.

Jennifer began speaking, "Well you probably think I've stalked you by following you here. Okay, so I'm not calling it stalking because I am on a quest to see the South Pacific islands, and the Marquesas is hardly a group to be missed. And come on, Paul Gauguin made his most mature and popular work here, paintings that influenced Picasso and a whole raft of others. So…. I did make a guess of when you guys might arrive, and you did invite me to meet you."

"Yes, I invited you, but honestly I don't even know your last name and if I'm not mistaken, that kind of invitation literally never works." I paused to assess my words to get a feel for if what I'd said made any sense. I wasn't quite sure which way it went, but a wave of calm came over me when I realized I didn't much care how I sounded. I was on a map dot in the middle of the ocean, with a woman I didn't really know who wanted to get to know me, and it felt like my whole life was open and up for grabs, and it was eighty degrees with a cool wind from the south weaving adventure straight into my being. "Tell me your life story… all of it… every stitch and seam, every high and low."

She leaned back in her chair and I got a sensation that she owned the place, not the café, or the tables and chairs, or the wall and roof, but the air inside the building… it was a natural confidence and a knowing that I could sense but not really explain.

She carefully brought her coffee cup to her lips, and as she placed it back on the table, she said, "First of all, we met several years ago on the dock at Point Richmond. You were a beginning sailor and had the insides of a winch spread out all over the place. No way it was going back together, but I didn't want to tell you that at the time."

"So, that was you." I paused. "You're right, I bought a new one. But, how did you know I was a beginner?"

"It was all over you, looking awkward, unsure… and nobody can fix a winch. It's like a Swiss watch… you have to get a new one."

Okay, she nailed me on that. What else is coming? I wondered. I took a sip of my lukewarm coffee and tried to remember right now, I had no agenda, nothing to prove, nothing to accomplish, nowhere to be today. Relax and let things roll out.

She continued, "I was married at the time, but things were starting to splinter. NetTrip was getting a real big buzz around the Valley and the IPO was on the docket in the early summer. My husband made the transition from lazy no-ambition, to obsessed greed. I'll be straight with you, I didn't mind a little greed and I was already opening up to a lavish lifestyle coming my way in the near future. But over the next year, he found more and more reasons to stay in the Valley near work than he did to drive home to Oakland. I thought we'd move over there or even rent a house, but he never got around to it. Of course, I found out later the reason was a brunette named Lisa. She worked on his engineering team and I guess they shared the passion and fury of getting rich quick in Silicon Valley. At the time, a big hit IPO was the exception, not the rule. Half of everybody was from Ohio or Michigan living on a hope and a prayer until they could go home rich. Most didn't, but NetTrip was an exception, with the papers publishing daily the number of new millionaires that the company produced."

I remembered that story unfolding, but my little company was on the sidelines then and anyway, I never thought I'd get rich and move back home. I was day-by-day and wasn't worrying about it.

"I got half the stock and didn't sell much of it for a couple of years, unlike my ex and the brunette. The best run of the stock was after the IPO, so that's where the big money was made. It went up 600 percent" she said.

"What did you do after that?" I asked.

"I bought a Beneteau forty-five-foot sailboat and sailed around San Francisco some. Then joined a club and went with some flotillas to Greece and Croatia as well as a romp around Tahiti. I never got the urge to do this trip you're on, the long grueling overnights didn't appeal to me," she said.

"Never tempted to remarry?" I asked.

"The whole married thing lost its luster for me. Maybe that'll change, but can't really say. I did hang out with one of the sailing crew on the Croatia trip and that lasted a while after we got home. Problem was, home for me was Oakland and for him was wherever he laid his head."

You might guess that Jennifer and I ambulated to a beach bar for drinks as the afternoon progressed and to a fresh-catch dinner later. She slowly rolled out more of her story, including growing up in the East Bay of the San Francisco area. She pried out an overview of my time in the Bay Area. But I kept the early years in Tennessee for later. She was staying in a small hotel at the marina, so I walked her in that direction, both of us moderately drunk, which at certain times in my life opened up a plethora of possibilities. I walked her to the lobby door, with neither of us saying a word; I stopped, nodded slightly, turned and walked away, so noncommittal, I didn't know what had come over me. It just seemed like the right thing to do.

33

The Boss

Blake pulled a cashmere, olive green sweater from his suitcase, slipped it over his blue, button-down dress shirt, and stepped out of his ground floor room in the morning light at the Bitter End Yacht Club. He and Jimmy, accompanied by Jack, arrived at Virgin Gorda's most exclusive resort after dark last night. The clocks were one hour ahead of Boston time, and as he pulled out his phone, he saw an email from Lester Carducci that read, "Where are you? The boss is getting worried, REAL worried."

Blake had the newest model Apple phone that had email and text messaging, but he couldn't get calls or text down here and none of these island scrubs could tell him why. He was tense about it with good reason. "The Boss" was demanding and paying him a lot of money, double what Jimmy was paying, to verify whether or not Jimmy was for real with this treasure thing. Even though he'd just paid a million, Jimmy still owed a couple more to the Boss. Blake knew these were rough guys and didn't love working with them, but falling into it from a friend's referral was making him a ton of money. He usually worked for bare-bones operations or low-budget individuals. He suspected that Jack was on the Boss's payroll too, but couldn't be sure. Lester told him to follow Jimmy and be ready to do whatever he was told.

He walked into the hotel lobby through cut-glass double doors to look for a pay phone to give Lester a quick call back. He found it next to a six-foot-high iron ship's anchor textured in a flaky, green patina indicative of a two-hundred-year stint on the salty-ocean floor. The phone was exposed and offered no privacy, in addition to having three hotel guests waiting in line for it. Blake walked over to a corner of the lobby, sat in an antique, mahogany chair, and returned Lester's email.

"No money, no gold, no silver yet. There may be some truth to his story, 'cause he knows his way around the islands, and knows people here. My phone won't receive or place calls. I'm working on it." Blake hit send.

****

Jennifer skipped breakfast with Zach, but knew he was catching the eight AM ferry from Village Cay Marina to Jost. At eight thirty she strolled through the narrow walkway between buildings to the traffic circle and got in the back seat of a private island cab. They headed east toward Beef Island. Just before the airport, the cab pulled into the Trellis Bay Market where Jennifer planned to look through the store for the half hour till the ferry arrived. She and Richard had used the store to provision the boat for trips around the islands over the years, and she was excited to look around and reminisce.

Forty minutes later Jennifer stepped onto the dock at Marina Cay, walked to the "T" and turned left on the wooden landing toward the island. She had called the operations manager, a sweet girl and island native named Sherry, telling her she was arriving, and when she walked into the office, only a few steps from the pier, was greeted warmly. Sherry was employed by the small local company that leased the whole operation, which includes a hotel, a restaurant and gift/clothing store, and the infamous Hilltop Bar at the Robb White House. Sherry knew Jennifer was associated with the owner of the island, but had no idea that a shell company called the White Clan Trading Company owned the island and Jennifer was the only stockholder.

During the big economic downturn in 1989, Richard overheard someone talking about the island being for sale by owners who needed to raise cash. He made a few calls and a price was floated. He let it sit for two weeks without a response and then offered half the asking price. Three weeks later, while on a sailboat, a courier motored up and delivered a package of documents. It was an executed sales agreement to sell the island at Richard's price. He and Bruce brainstormed a name that would mask ownership as much as possible, and even though Jennifer never liked the whole idea, when Richard got sick, he transferred the reins to her.

After a quick chat with Sherry, Jennifer walked out of the office, took a right turn, and then a left onto the trail toward the cabins on the south side of the island. She reached the first cabin and stepped onto the deck; walking to the front, she stopped to gaze at the tip of Tortola; then to the southern end of Virgin Gorda before shifting her eyes to the closer Dog Islands. She thought about how she loaded that old beat-up chest with the clue on it into the dingy, and how she and Richard carried it over the gurgling stream and up to a spot on the island where both the caves on Virgin Gorda and old cemetery could be seen. When Richard first got the idea for a treasure hunt, she never thought he would follow through on a scheme this big. Nevertheless they planned the whole thing out, researched the locations of the clues, even did dry runs of the whole process, all just for fun, she thought. Making up games and adventures, escapades, creating unique languages and even accents, was the glue that held them together. Richard called it the super glue of the "R and Jen show." All the children, all the friends, and even Samantha knew it. These two were joined at the hip. Still Jennifer never, ever thought this fantasy treasure hunt would be played out.

On the trail overlooking the water, she rounded the island and headed up to the small peak that was home to the Robb White House. There was a makeshift stage rimmed by island grass, a wooden stool, microphone stands, and sitting alone was a small silent kick drum. She pulled a chair away from one of the tables and sat for a moment quietly in her thoughts. A short bluster of wind was her only distraction. So many times, she was here, with new, unique, interesting people from all walks of life from all over the world. It was such a rich life, such a gift, such a plethora of memories.

Walking around in back of the bar and into the "residence" space of the house, she recalled the story of the young Naval Academy graduate, Robb White, who met a young girl named Rodie, vacationing in the islands with her mother. Rodie fell for Robb as well as for his adolescent fantasy of escaping the world to live on a desert island. In 1937 the newlyweds began building their concrete house with two-foot-thick walls incorporating a chilly underground basement for food storage. World War II pulled them back home after which, neither ever returned to the island.

Jennifer stopped at the open door to the one-room main living area, her loose-fitting linen shirt starting to cling to her in the muggy air. Slowly scanning the room, she saw an old portrait of what looked like an English nobleman, a chair, a table, and a dusty old daybed on the second level toward the back of the room. She circled by the portrait and with a meandering, nonchalant stroll stopped near the east facing window. Taking a deep breath, she reached for a three-inch square of white brick that was neatly wedged into the concrete wall. She gave it a back-and-forth jiggle, but the brick wouldn't move. After taking a shoe off and rapping it a few times, she located a screwdriver behind the bar and pried the brick loose enough to wiggle it slightly. Eventually she got enough out to grasp it with two fingers and slide it out from the wall. Holding the white brick in one hand, she gazed out the window onto the trail that brought her up to the house, a little overgrown and unkept, the small brown line of dirt cut through a glut of random greenery.

Then without hesitation her fingers reached into the small dark space and clenched a little round object. Her fingertips patiently scoured the surface of both sides like it was a Braille map leading to a mysterious destination. She probed the room with her peripheral vision and then looked back over her left shoulder to the open door. Convinced no one was there, she extracted the object and in the window's light, looked down on a glittering gold coin.

The edges were rounded but irregular due to the handmade process of minting in the early eighteenth century. These were called "Cob" coins, an abbreviation of the Spanish phrase, "made from the end of a bar." Hammered and hand stamped, one side was struck with the phrase, "By the Grace of God-King of the Spains and the Indies," while the reverse side showed the coat of arms of Phillip II and the date, 1705 in Roman numerals.

Jennifer rolled the coin over and over in her hand as her mind raced with memories of the past forty years… never letting her mind hold on to any memory, time or place, event, or person. When she turned to walk out, her eye caught a glimpse of the wooden lid covering the large square hole leading to the basement. She noted that it looked in order, but didn't linger there, instead darted out of the room and down the path, past the office and onto the boat dock. Minutes later she stepped onto the ferry and settled in a seat for the short ride to Trellis Bay. She thought about Richard prying that brick out of the wall, reaching in the box of gold and silver coins, and pulling out that coin. With a silly smirk and a chuckle, he shoved the coin in the gap and crammed the brick back in place. She asked him why he was doing that. He was silent for half a moment, and then said simply, "Just because." Her right hand reached into her jacket pocket, took hold of the Spanish Cob, and held it tight like it was a baby squirming to be released.

Zach walked through the outdoor corridor leading to the open-air dining and bar area of the Village Cay Marina. Jennifer watched him walk to her table and sit down across from her. He seemed preoccupied and Jennifer looked out over the naked masts of 150-foot sloops swaying in the breeze lit by a low, western, setting sun. Across the bay she could see the Moorings Marina populated with smaller charter boats for rent. As far back as she knew, the BVI was the most popular charter destination in the world. The protected waters of the Sir Francis Drake channel, and the accommodating attitude surrounding the tourist business were huge draws.

She reached for her wineglass and took a sip, waiting for Zach to start.

"When I got there Andrew was combing the grounds of the Soggy Dollar. He kicked every inch of sand in the table area. You know, the roped-off place where the tables are. It was early and nobody was paying attention to him, so nobody asked questions. I asked him what he was on the lookout for and he blurted, 'anything I can find,'" Zach said.

"So looking for everything, he's liable to find nothing," Jennifer said.

"Right. When I left he was on a jag about finding a pier with a boat named *Brenda* tied to it. Mom, again the crazy clue is, 'the dollar you save without the dock you crave where sweet Brenda is waiting.' I don't get it. This one may stop us cold. There's no dock at White Bay. There are those new mooring balls, but no dock," Zach moaned.

Jennifer remembered Richard thinking up this clue. She told him it was too hard and that they shouldn't rely on people who come and go. But he thought it added to the adventure, and she let it go.

"They're staying in a cabin over there, so I told them I'd be back in the morning. How was your day around Road Town?" he asked.

"Relaxing, uneventful," she replied as her fingers caressed the coin in her pocket.

34

Richard / Pep-in-my-Step

Bill Price opened the diary to his last stopping place and continued to read.

I showed up at the hotel around nine AM and called Jennifer in her room. I was feeling a bit of fear and uncertainty as well as elation and adventure. There were really good things about these feelings and some really bad things too. Years of laser focus on work in my geographic bubble in the Valley, making money, kids, all of it was losing urgency. It's like a month on the water with days of relaxing punctuated by hours of fear and terror in the storms, and time, lots of time, all eroding the mountain, and silt of the past was cascading off my skin into the blue ocean.

Last night Jennifer had mentioned a hike up to the peak of the crater, but we hadn't made any plans. She wasn't surprised to see me, although I get the feeling she wasn't expecting me. After coffee and a small breakfast, we started the walk through the old village with flowers and fruit trees, and shops, and then coconut palms and then into a small rainforest created by clouds dumping water after smashing into the sharp peak of the crater. This year was wet and the forest was lush. We weren't alone in this hamlet, but there were no crowds pushing us around. The first creek was easy to cross, and Jennifer found a path jumping rock to rock to the other side. The humidity picked up in the dense growth and the trail was muddy and slippery until after an hour, when we came to the first lookout. The crater rises more than three thousand feet above the sea, and from our lookout we got a magnificent view of this natural phenomenon. The boats looked like toys and the rippled sea surface appeared smooth and calm.

As we looked out in silence Jennifer's eyes moved over toward me and said, "I never had kids. The time never was right and the man never was right, and…." Her voice trailed off.

"Did you want them?" I asked.

"I don't know." She paused. "I never not wanted them. I guess I thought I'd know when it was right. Time is ticking, though," she continued. "Tell me about your kids."

"Okay." I paused for a bit too long while I thought about what I wanted to say. This conversation was busting me out of the South-Seas-fantasy I was basking in: savoring the moment, relishing the experience, living in the present, shirking responsibility, dancing on the head of a pin, pixie dust in my eyes…. You get the idea. "Jimmy came along on his own time and Sam and I got married because of him. Maureen was expected, but honestly, I was working and hyper-focused on the company. Don't get me wrong. I was there for her birth, and took a few days off when we brought her home. But after that, it was Sam and the nanny who took over."

"Tell me about Samantha," she asked.

For the next hour I told her about Sam; how we met, her family in Mississippi, and why she picked Stanford instead of one of the Southern schools where her friends went. Jennifer had never been to the South, never had catfish and hushpuppies, never said "y'all" and never sweltered in the blaze of a Southern sun. Sam's family was large and cohesive, which she thought was mostly because of her mother and her innate ability to read people and know what they need. After watching the whole family dynamic for a while, I told Sam that a big part of the glue that held it all together was her mother's innate ability to kick all their collective butts at the first sign of insurrection. She thought about it for a while and had to agree. All in all, it made Sam a little compulsive.

"Are you in love with her?" Jennifer asked out of the blue. Well I thought it was out of the blue or green or out of the ether, but looking back it was probably a question that was on the mark and needed asking. I was on a great adventure, but Jennifer was rebuilding her life and navigating the best way she knew how. She was asking because she wanted to know where she stood and how to deal with this dating we were doing. For the record, I didn't feel like we were dating. We were respectful friends that just happened to be on a faraway island in the middle of the ocean spending all our time together. What was I thinking? I told her what any respectful husband would say: "I think so."

I knew I had a renewed pep-in-my-step. I was beginning to face the fact that this innocent adventure was more of an intrigue, a quest, and more and more like a mission. Trouble was brewing, but my life in California was so many miles away, so distant in head space. Did I just write "head space"? I was sweeping it all under the table, but I could tell Jennifer was not sweeping anything. She was putting it on the table.

We both let the conversation sit in silence as a midday breeze showered us in a warm bath of tropical air. After we reached the peak, the three-thousand-foot descent was a welcome relief. That night Jennifer accepted my invitation to have cocktails on the boat. Bruce was making his special version of BVI Painkillers, a rum concoction with fruit juice, and a twist of about everything he could find... all a trade secret of Bruce's. The crew guys were on hand telling the marlin story and others from our month on the water. Jennifer had some good stories of sailing the San Francisco Bay. She told about the time her dad donated a sailing trip around the San Francisco Bay to a charity auction.

"I was eighteen and Dad and I could sail his boat by ourselves. He was the skipper and I was always first mate. Our passenger, Doug, had black hair combed neatly across the top of his head, and fashionably long on the sides. Blue deck shoes, Bermuda shorts, and a collard golf shirt rounded out Doug's yuppie look. His wife, Pat, was neatly put together with short, stylish hair, a short casual skirt and a V-neck short-sleeve shirt, cut tastefully high so as not reveal any of the goods. As they stepped onto the boat she appeared a bit annoyed. We soon found out why. In the first few minutes I noticed that Doug seemed a little too happy for that early in the morning. It turned out Doug was celebrating some big business deal and polished off a pitcher of Bloody Marys before he left home.

"We sailed out through the Alameda channel, past Treasure Island and straight for the Golden Gate Bridge. The wind was steady from the northwest at about ten knots and we fixed a close reach, heading for the center of the span. Outside the gate near Point Bonita, the sea was calmer than inside so our passengers were enjoying a leisurely weekend cruise. Doug held his own still celebrating with a constant beer in his hand. I was at the helm when Dad suggested we come about and head back in. We sailed through Raccoon Straits to the mouth of Richardson Bay, letting Doug et al get a look at Sausalito from the water. To Californians it looks like a European coastal village, something reminiscent of the Greek island of Santorini. We were on a port tack when a gust from the middle of the gate came roaring from behind, almost blowing the boat over. I yelled out with all my might to ease the main sail, but before Dad could react, the boat tipped, taking the mast almost parallel with the water. Dad flipped the locking cleat open and let the boom swing wide. The boat responded immediately, and the mast retracted to almost straight up. Doug and the other passengers were thrown to the floor of the cockpit but started to pick themselves up as the boat leveled.

"Dad looked up at me and could tell that I was in control of the wheel.

From the front of the cockpit, he shouted to me to fall off and head for the Bay Bridge. I was hoping we could run down, through the wind tunnel blowing under the Golden Gate, known as 'the slot' before it turned to gale force. I pointed the bow south and we scooted by Angel Island into the slot. I yelled to the passengers to get their wind jackets on. Doug's wife looked up and shouted that they didn't bring them.

"'But you were told to,' I replied.

"'Doug said we didn't need them,' she sheepishly muttered.

"Doug was shaky and pale. He looked up at me with a worried cat-got-your-tongue grin. I pointed over the side. He nodded, rolled onto his stomach and leaned over the side. In an instant half those Bloody Marys were gone and floating in choppy, waist-high rolling seas. The beer was next, I thought."

"Unbelievable," Bruce interrupted. "You really can't make this stuff up."

"Yeah, but wait till you hear the rest," Jennifer continued. "The gusts rolled in at forty knots and everyone had to hold on with all they could muster to stay in the boat, except Doug who couldn't even sit up, much less hold on. I was afraid he might fall over the side where he would only last a few minutes in that frigid water, and it was questionable if we could even locate him in this churning cauldron, if he went out. Fog was rolling through the slot like a river of gloom over four-foot swells. We could have tied him to a bunk down in the cabin, but he would have been blowing his cookies all over the ceiling, making a royal mess. That was not an option. So in between gusts, Dad grabbed Doug around the waist and hauled him up to the front of the mast. With a spare rope tucked under his arm, he shoved Doug's back against the mast and quickly coiled the rope around it and Doug. He tied it off with a clove hitch while Doug appeared close to unconsciousness. As the boat lurched left, I ducked as

Doug started up-chucking the remaining beer onto the deck. His collared shirt was soaking wet with salt water, but at least he wasn't going to drown.

"The slot is an amazingly narrow wind tunnel, and as soon as we rounded the San Francisco Peninsula, the hills deflected the sharp wind gusts and the water laid flat under a lazy afternoon sun.

"Doug dropped to the deck like a wet rat when the ropes came off. Dad helped him to his feet with neither enthusiasm nor obligation. This guy gave pencil-pushers a bad name—an idiot who probably wore patent-leather shoes to a clam bake. Pat unloaded their soggy belongings like a yeoman—just working, getting the job done. She piled it all on the dock making no eye contact, and then presented herself at the bottom of the stairs waiting for Doug to be handed down. By this time, the swirling smoke from Dad's victory cigar wrapped gently around both Doug and me, as we stood waiting in the cockpit. When Pat reached for his arm, she looked up and gave me a wistful glance, and that was it. We never heard from them again, and we never did another charity auction," Jennifer said.

My stomach was throbbing from laughing so hard, and the others were rolling around on the benches. We gulped down our second drink and walked into the village for dinner. Afterward, the boys splintered off to local bars as Jennifer and I took a slow stroll toward her hotel. The fruit trees and coconut palms of this morning receded into the night shadows along our way. We'd had a long day together, and the drinks were hitting us both. I was feeling comfortable and calm, but also anxious, my mind buzzing with a myriad of possibilities for Jennifer and me. When we reached the hotel, I went blank; I took her hand, gave it a soft squeeze, turned and walked away.

35

Brenda

Jimmy woke in a cold sweat. A puddle of water on his pillow dripped onto the bottom sheet as he lurched and rolled over in bed. He knew better than anybody that he needed two million and he needed it quick. It was a legitimate deal, and how could he have known what would go wrong? The oil was in the ground all over the northern US, and the pipeline was approved by all the states it would run through, and the Feds passed off on it. This was a slam-dunk money maker, so he took a big stake in it. The payoff here would make him independent of Zach and the trust, and his whiny siblings, making their money just a little bonus, and he wouldn't have had to worry about this ridiculous treasure hunt that his wacko father set up. He rolled over on his right side, jerking the top sheet, pulling it around him. A glint of light peeked through the curtain telling Jimmy that it was finally morning, but he made no effort to get out of bed. *Our dad was always playing a game, even if nobody else was,* he thought. *He considered people just players in his contests… and now I'm screwed.*

He mortgaged his Manhattan apartment and sold the condo on the Cape, used all his cash and committed one million to the project. Monitoring the permitting and construction plans for the pipeline, he watched the budget and had his accountant review and advise him about the financial side of the whole deal. This was a dream deal. A key to success of the project pivoted on the banks lending money to build the four-hundred-mile pipeline, bringing oil and gas to the population centers in the East and Midwest. Eventually the pipeline would bring fuel to shipping centers in New Orleans and other ports on the Gulf Coast with potential to export worldwide.

"Help me out! This was a gold mine," Jimmy shouted at the top of his lungs. His voice quivered as the last words left his mouth and slammed against the empty walls.

Banks need collateral for a project like this, so as part of the agreement, investors signed a note that they guarantee the bank loans. No way that would be happening, he was assured by the developers. In all the deals they'd done over twenty years, never has the possibility even been entertained of using that collateral. This was just a formality that the banks have to go through for the regulators. You know these regulators are there just to make things hard for honest people, they said.

Jimmy submitted a financial statement that pledged a net worth of ten million dollars, even though he had tapped all his assets to get the first million. His share of the real estate in the trust was surely worth more than a measly ten million, so he thought what the heck, it's never going to get used anyway. Jimmy looked up as he heard a slight knock on the door.

"Are you awake?" A tepid voice called out.

Jimmy turned and looked at the hotel room door, when again the voice repeated his call.

"I'm awake. What's going on?" he replied. "I'll see you at breakfast in half an hour." He paused. "I'm in the shower."

Jimmy swung his feet onto the floor and sat upright, focusing on the growing sliver of light peering through the curtain. He was dizzy and disoriented, just like the day the banker called to tell him he had thirty days to deliver the three million collateral. Jimmy screamed, "bullshit," into the phone, "that never happens."

"Mr. Dennison, I assure you it is happening," he replied. "Three state legislatures rescinded the permits on environmental grounds. They don't have any hard facts. It's just politics. When can we expect your bank wire?"

Property had been bought as well as millions spent on equipment with long-term leases that carried obligations. None of it was going away and the timeline to solve this dilemma was unknown. Jimmy called his lawyer, who quietly told him that uncertainty was a nasty concept for bankers, and "unknown" was uncertainty on steroids. The loans had been called, and Jimmy was up a creek. Bankruptcy was steaming his way like a freight train, but his lawyer hinted that submitting falsified financials to a federally chartered bank was a felony. He begged his lawyer to find somebody to lend him the money. You see his dad just died and he was going to inherit more than enough to cover the debt, he explained. Two days later a guy named Vinny called and said they checked out his story with the inheritance and all that. "Your dad was pretty rich," Vinny told him. The interest rate was two percent a month, but after three months it was two and a half a month. "It's all due in six months," he told Jimmy. "No exceptions." In three days, a wire hit Jimmy's account which he sent to the bank. The next disaster was the estate meeting in Bill Price's office, and this insane treasure hunt. The interest on the loan was nearing a quarter of a million dollars, and cold sweats were a way of life for Jimmy.

He skipped the shower, walked out of his room onto the stone pathway, and through the lobby, where he saw Blake and Jack sitting in the restaurant next to a wall of windows. He gazed out over North Sound to the ancient volcanic peaks protecting this oval-shaped bay from the open ocean. He saw the small anchorage of Leverick Bay, where he first took diving lessons from a guy named Bert Kilbride. In his spare time, Bert looked for gold and silver and became an expert on the wreckage sites around the BVI.

Like every other morning, the bright sun was punching through scattered cumulus clouds on a deep blue-sky background. The morning temp was around seventy degrees on the way to the low eighties. Jimmy declined the breakfast buffet and ordered scrambled eggs and wheat toast.

"Okay, let's find this treasure today," Jimmy barked, jumping out of the frightened shell of the man that woke up in his body this morning. Jimmy was in charge now. Blake could tell that, but wondered just exactly what he was in charge of, treasure or hot air? The owners of the resort lived in Boston and Jimmy knew them well enough to get invitations to Boston parties. He also had phone numbers and had called to announce his arrival on Virgin Gorda. Just as the eggs were served the manager came over to introduce himself and inform Jimmy that the owners were in Europe, but sent instructions to comp his room during his stay at the hotel. Rooms were $400 to $900 per night, but Jimmy shrugged it off. Blake made a mental note; yes, this guy knows the right people. He must know how to find that treasure.

Andrew was scouring the area in back of Ivan's Stress Free Bar, when Zach and Alice walked up behind him. Their quiet entrance on the soft sand startled him and he jerked his torso up from a bent position to standing upright.

"Nothing to report," he blurted. "But we'll find this bugger," he said with the self-assurance befitting a man who found the first two clues.

Alice and Zach left the master clue-finder to his own devices as he moved to the sand in front of Ivan's. They walked down the beach past the Soggy Dollar and to the White Bay Sandcastle Hotel, where they stopped to sit on the sand and talk.

"I haven't heard from or about Jimmy lately, and honestly that kind of scares me," Alice said as her eyes lifted to look out across the water, the short distance to the northern shore of Tortola and Cane Garden Bay. The light wind occasionally flipped a sporadic wave to a tepid whitecap, but otherwise the channel was lying flat.

"I'm on pins-and-needles with Jimmy too. Something is going on there, that I can't make sense of," he replied. "But besides that, I have to confess, this clue may trip us up in Dad's treasure hunt. We're sitting here on a white sand beach, in a place we have been to a million times, looking for a needle in a haystack, and we don't even know what we're looking for."

"Do you think there is anything worth finding to keep up this rummaging through the islands?" she asked.

A couple of minutes passed while neither said a word. Zach wasn't even thinking about the whole thing. His team had an apartment building to sell and they had a reluctant buyer with a contract, closing next week. The building had been in the portfolio for years, but never really fit. They bought it cheap, but out of their geographic footprint. It had become a priority for Zach, and he wanted it sold.

"I don't doubt that Dad hid something precious, but how valuable it is, is anybody's guess," he said.

"Does Mom know something that she's not telling us? 'Cause I think she's holding back."

"I don't know. You sat through two years of psychic training in Berkeley. She's telling me she knows nothing. But when you think about it, she and Dad did everything together. I have no inkling; I guess it's your call on this one. Come on, let's get a fish taco at the Soggy Dollar," he said. "We'll put it on Jimmy's tab," he snickered and Alice smiled.

The legs of their white plastic table were anchored in three inches of sand. Zach pressed back in his chair and wiggled the back chair-legs down a little deeper so he was leaning back a bit, while kicking off his shoes to nuzzle his toes into the warm sand.

The waitress walked up with a smile, white cutoff shorts, and a halter top, with less cloth than skin, leaving very little to the imagination. Before Alice could speak, Zach ordered two Painkillers. They both knew this drink originated here, and spread like rum in a hot bath to every bar in the world. She came back with the drinks and put them on the table. Zach tried to keep his eyes away from the halter top, but wasn't succeeding. They both knew what everybody knows, that the girls wear those to get guys to look, and ogle, and hit on them… the big game. She was succeeding with Zach.

Alice took a sip, looked up and asked, "I don't know if you're a boater, but any chance you've seen a boat named *Brenda* around here?"

The waitress stopped dead in her tracks, pulled a chair up to the table, and with a mammoth grin said, "I've never seen a boat named *Brenda*, and I'd remember that, because my name is Brenda."

Alice was speechless. Her left hand dropped to the table with a thud; her mouth gaped open. "You are kidding me!" She was saying it more to herself than to Brenda, who placed both elbows on the table, cupping her hands as a cradle for her chin. She looked ecstatically happy and intrigued by these strangers and the happenstance of them seemingly falling out of the sky, into this beach bar.

"Brenda, do you have any idea what is going on here, because we don't." The words stumbled on her tongue, out of her mouth, and into the air.

Brenda wistfully cocked her head, maintaining her fixed smile, stood up from the table and said, "I have something for you. I'll be right back."

A few minutes later she appeared with a small plexiglass box. It was faint red, and opaque with an oversize clasp made of burnished brass.

Holding the clasp down was a wax seal with some sort of imprint embossed on it. She handed it to Alice, who accepted it with both hands, turned it slightly from side to side, careful not to shake or damage it. She regarded it like a sacred object delivered from the grave... Dad was reaching out, she thought. Zach sat mostly not reacting. He'd seen Alice cross over into the ethereal plain many times, and seen her coast back into reality without a glitch... well, mostly no glitches.

Zach cleared his throat. "Thank you, Brenda. Is there anything else you can tell us? Is there anything we should do to move on with the box?"

"No, sir. That was my job, to give you the box. I can get you some lunch if you'd like."

Zach gobbled up two fish tacos before Alice finished her first one. The box sat on the table between them, both looking at it like it was a hallowed, special gift on Christmas morning... untouchable. They left the restaurant and walked down the beach to Alice's room to regroup and talk this over. Neither one showed any inclination to open the box right away... hallowed, untouchable.

Brenda walked to the back of the restaurant, rifled through her backpack till she found her phone. In the search bar she punched in "Brenda." Clicking on the highlighted number, she let it ring until a voice answered. She simply said, "delivered," pulled the phone from her ear and punched the button to end the call. She walked out front and over to the bartender to check in with him.

"Hey Saundra, why was that couple calling you Brenda?" he asked.

"It's a long story," she said. "I'll tell you later."

36

Richard / Simply Fell in Love

Bill Price continued reading the diary.

"Hey Richard. Old buddy, we've got room on the boat. Let's invite Jennifer to sail to Tahiti with us. After all, she's a better sailor than any of us, tells great stories, and is terrific eye candy for us scurvy sailors," Bruce said. "I know you'll like the idea; how about it?"

I sat back in my swivel chair, staring at the navigation controls off to my left. Bruce had just bounded up the stairs from the salon. He sat across from me on a teak bench seat watching steam roll off his hot cup of coffee in a bathing suit, no shirt. The wind was pumping around us at about fifteen knots, and I could smell rain on the way, probably later that morning. Bruce had that giddy "why-not, what-have-we-got-to-lose" tone in his voice, so I sat, and didn't say a word. But to be honest, Bruce lived by the rule of "what-have-we-got-to-lose." I'm not implying he was frivolous. He was a cautious sailor and was becoming wiser on the water with each experience. While I was building the company, he was logging hours and days on the water. I learned a lot by just watching him sail. But life was a breeze for Bruce, a playful game, and people were an amusement, players in the game.

"An interesting idea, but we don't have room for her; all the cabins are occupied," I replied.

"No, it's going to be cool. The boys are going to rotate into the crew bunks. They'll take turns between the cabin and the bunks. Really, they're cool with it," he said.

"That's asking a lot of them, and besides Jennifer has other plans, and she can't stay away that long," I said.

I readjusted my position in the chair to alleviate the twisting feeling in my gut. All the possibilities of a two-week trip with Jennifer on a luxury eighty-foot sailboat flashed in front of my eyes. A full range of excitement and elation matched up against terror, trepidation, and potential disaster. The look in her eyes and the feelings in my gut couldn't be disguised. I hadn't been able to stay away from her on this island, I thought, but I couldn't let it go any further. This game for Bruce, would end up being a calamity for me. I let the words sit for a few seconds, and then thought, what's there to worry about, she won't agree to it anyway.

"Well, I'm a no vote," I said. "I don't think it's the right vibe."

A quizzical look came across his face, before breaking into an all-knowing smirk. He knew exactly what was going through my mind and the tension this whole proposition was creating.

As often happens, the skipper of the rig gets his way. After a day thinking it over, Jennifer signed on for the cruise to Tahiti. I switched cabins to be at the other end of the boat from her, needing to take some control of this pending catastrophe. Bruce assigned Jennifer the first watch right out of the harbor, from noon to six in the evening. At first, I found ropes to coil and anchor chain to clean up on the bow, staying as far away as I could from the helm and our new crew member. For two days, I rode a gentle southeastern breeze along with the others and let Jennifer get used to the boat and crew. A series of squalls began toying with us for the next two days, bursts of frenzied energy that passed as quickly as they came. The afternoon of the third day out, Bruce gave the order to trim the main sail and the jib to three-quarters. "If you know you need to trim, it's too late," he yelled, meaning anticipate the adjustment, because it's a lot harder to achieve when you're getting blown all over the deck. We had ridden through the squalls with both sails up, bearing down on the wind, but this one did not blow past us, but built wind speed along with occasional water-walls, the size of a house; whole areas of our seascape were masked from view, too much water. Before we could manage to pull both sails in, we rolled starboard, both mylar sails scooping up turbulent seawater like gigantic ladles. Mother ocean completely filled our cockpit with fizzling, cold salt water three times. The hatch door was mostly closed, insulating most of the living quarters below from the soaking.

An hour into my graveyard watch, a wave slammed us broadside. My left hand was laying on the wheel and as the impact hit, my fingers tried to wrap around the metal spokes but were shoved away by the stinging water-nozzle-ocean. I was flopped against the swiveling, attached deck chair like a wet noodle. The chair was rotating wildly when my chest smashed into the chairback and I dropped to the deck. This four-day gale took us off course and no closer to our destination and as you can tell, shook us up noticeably.

Getting a few hours' sleep at any one time was the most that any of us could hope for. We tried to prepare food when the wind dropped below thirty knots, which we came to anticipate in the early hours of morning. My discussions with Jennifer were restricted to grunts and grumbles, and acknowledgement through a look or a nod that we might survive this blender-ride we were on. If the old saying is right that you get stronger from what doesn't kill you, we were all on the road to body-building nirvana.

The first day after the wind and seas calmed down, we had a steady easterly that put us back on course and closer to our schedule. Then the sea went flat and we had to rev up the twin diesel engines to bring us to an eight-knot traveling speed.

I pulled a windbreaker over my head onto my shoulders, and in bare feet ascended the stairs, past the helm where Bruce was on watch for his shift. With the auto pilot engaged, he was laid prone on the bench seat and didn't notice me slipping past him on the way to the bow. The sporadic, gentle, warm wind rustled my hair as I sat near the forward hatch. It was barely first light, but I was accustomed to being awake at odd times, and my watch started in about half an hour. What a quiet paradise lay in front of me; the light barely breaking through the gray night to wake up the world on all sides. If the feelings of terror and panic still buffeting my memory weren't enough to remind me, my bruised ribs wouldn't let me forget the pummeling we took on these high seas.

Each one of us learned to be alone in a group, on a small boat for weeks at a time with the ocean for a coach in the fine art of patience, and time as our scorekeeper. Sitting on the bow, with the sound of the wind in my ears, I relished being alone, but then I sensed something, a feeling, a presence, a sensation. Turning my head, I saw Jennifer sitting beside me looking out, lost in her own daydream. She glanced at me, nodding without a word.

"How are you feeling?" she finally asked in almost a whisper.

"I doubt they're broken. They'd hurt a lot worse," I replied. Nothing came to mind, so I sat and looked out. Father time was keeping a slow grinding scorecard with nothing but blue sky on our calendar.

"You've drawn a moat around you so far this trip. I didn't see any alligators, but the water looks pretty deep. Are you feeling okay?" she asked.

"Yep. I'm doing okay."

After a minute, she grabbed my right hand and stood, pulling me up with her; our hands lifted up over our heads, turned, pirouette-bound on a fiberglass deck at eight knots, two hundred miles from Tahiti. She spun away a quarter turn, then full around and back to me, face-to-face, eyes locking. And that's when I fell in love with Jennifer. I didn't say anything, touch her, look at her, think anything about her, think anything about me, think anything about anyone in the universe. I simply fell in love with Jennifer.

37

Cold Empty Sheets

Jennifer always rented a local mobile phone in the islands. Cell coverage for the major carriers was spotty and she and Richard liked to slip their boat into any out-of-the-way cove they could find and anchor there for as long as they felt like it, and they liked to be in communication for emergencies when possible. Today Jennifer stayed in Road Town, had breakfast, walked the few blocks to Main Street to browse around the shops. She grabbed a late lunch at the waterside restaurant and bar and watched the yachts and dinghies coming and going into the marina. About three her phone rang. She dug into her pocket, looked at the display and saw no caller ID. She punched the answer button.

"Hi Jennifer, this is Liz in Bill Price's office. He asked me to call and tell you the package has been delivered and five-thousand-dollar wires have been sent to the original Brenda and to Saundra," she said.

"That was fast work. These kids are turning out to be quite clever. By the way, where does Brenda live now?" Jennifer asked.

"I'm told she's back home in Ohio, somewhere near Cleveland," Liz said.

"Okay thanks, Liz. On to the next clue. Say hi to everybody. I'll probably wander back into town sometime next week." Jennifer ended the call, not even trying to stop the grin progressively growing on her face and leading to a slight chuckle. *There are still some mysteries for them to solve, but they're getting closer,* she thought. She was glad that Zach was taking a part in the hunt. Over the last decade, he pulled away from the family, and who could blame him. He was a businessman focusing on real live things with real live people. Although Maureen had a conventional middle-class lifestyle, Alice was continuing her march into the ethereal, mapped out in her subconscious as a teenage dreamer, and Jennifer couldn't be sure Zach ever got over Jimmy's fall to the "dark side." It was hard to read Zach around Jimmy unless you were his mother. Zach was embarrassed by him, she thought, even more than everybody else. After his wife, Debra died, Zach lost interest in social gatherings except for a round of golf occasionally. He weaved into Bill Price's Saturday game and sometimes during the week. A couple of divorcees at the club took an interest, but Zach never followed through. Jennifer wanted him to get out and do more things, and she harped on him some, but nothing changed.

His foot slowly worked under the covers to the other side of the bed. He felt the cold empty sheets even through the fog of sleep, as he turned to lie flat on his back. Suddenly his eyes flew open as he tumbled back from deep slumber, back into the night, into this bed, in a bay, on an island, in the Caribbean Sea.

Zach exhaled and felt a familiar haze surround his head, flow through his ears and rest somewhere between his eyes. His roving foot found no solace, no rest, no peace, no companion. He rolled over on his stomach begging for escape, but it would not arrive, just as it never arrived. He pictured Debra in the bed when his foot would find her foot or sometimes calf, but always a furnace of warmth on his perpetually cold extremities. He felt this weight, this tulle mist blowing in from another dimension, would most likely debilitate any movement, any plans, or anything else, relegating him to lie in bed and suffer. He lay still for a moment, then commanded his legs to move to the side of the bed, but they stayed still, unmoving, in defiance. He lifted his head and let his consciousness push through a miniscule chink in the mist surrounding him, and again commanded his legs; they finally obeyed. He sat up, and then felt himself lifting upright and taking the few steps to a water glass on the counter. Sitting in the desk chair, he took a long drink; it would go away, he knew, like it finally did every morning.

Jimmy hired a boat and driver for the day and all three of the "investigators" headed west out of North Sound to the tip of Virgin Gorda and the popular tourist spot called the Caves. Not only was it a favorite of his dad's, "caves" were mentioned in the clues. His plan was to scour the dark reaches and crevices to look for green hats and any sign of graves.

"Okay, look for writing on the cave walls, look for green and any reference to a grave or graves," Jimmy instructed the boys.

They looked puzzled and confused, and when Blake asked, "Okay, we need to get this straight," his voice bore down with more than a hint of frustration. "Read us the actual clue, boss."

"The clue reads, Gordy's little brother has what you desire under two green hats. The clue for you is to see caves and graves," Jimmy read from his small notebook.

"I'm not saying I'm the sharpest tool in the shed, but I think we have a better chance of finding a needle in a haystack," Jack said.

Jimmy stood there dumbfounded, at a complete loss for words. He loathed the negative, can't-do attitude, but at the same time he knew this whole exercise was hapless and random. Blake was silent while looking down at the sand below his feet. Jimmy regained his fortitude.

"You're right. We're looking for that needle, but when we find it the other parts of this puzzle will fall into place like dominos. Look, I know how my dad thought; I can follow his meaning. Just find that first bit and we'll cruise right to that treasure. Jack, you go to the far end where the caves open to the beach. Take a good look then work your way back. Blake, come with me and we'll fan out. Remember, look for something out of the ordinary, maybe even a little bit contrived. Let's regroup right here in two hours. If we come up empty-handed, we'll head over to the Dog Islands. I want to comb Great Dog and then move to George Dog." Jimmy paused, took a deep breath and said, "We'll find this thing."

Jack stood silently. He knew even better than Blake or Jimmy that they'd better find it and quick. His boss was a master at cutting his losses and moving on. He's seen it happen too many times. One day, poof! No more Jimmy.

38

Richard / Doctor Coins

Bill Price was becoming obsessed with the diary. It wasn't as if he knew nothing about what went on, he just had never observed the events from this perspective. He was a young associate in the firm when the IPO made Richard a wealthy man, and subsequently divorced. It happened more times than not that the sudden big money turned people upside down or right side up, depending on who you talked to. Divorces were common in the Valley, but seeing this story unfold from the inside was turning his head.

My watch ended about nine in the evening. I went down into the salon, opened two beers, walked over to Jennifer's cabin and rapped gently on the open door. She looked up from her book with a slight smile, so I stepped in and sat next to her on the queen-size bed. I asked what she was reading, she said the book was set in sixteenth-century France and the king was putting pressure on the church, thinking they had acquired too much influence and he wanted it back. I paid little attention to the story, my eyes trained on her. We sipped beer and after a while she inched closer and laid her head on my shoulder. It wasn't suggestive or aggressive, just comfortable. Small talk trailed off and the next thing I knew, I awoke sometime in the middle of the night to see Jennifer still lying next to me. I found out later that Bruce had come to her cabin to rouse Jennifer for her watch, saw us lying on the bed, turned off the light and took her turn on the helm himself. I felt like calling somebody and saying I didn't mean for this to happen, and I'll make up for it, or we can fix it, or something... just to get some resolution, but there was no phone booth in sight, no Western Union, no video conferencing in the middle of a big blue ocean.

I had called Samantha before we left the Marquesas to tell her that our itinerary had been too aggressive, and we were likely to need to add a couple of weeks to get to Tahiti, and then try to get on a flight back. She was okay with it but not great. She seemed agitated and short. I assumed it was being alone with the kids and not enough adult time. In addition, her new horse had an ankle problem and she was irritated. The big storm probably set us back a few more days, so I felt the ice was getting thin with Sam. I was fighting the feeling that I was starting a whole new life, parallel, but somehow in a different dimension. Knowing it all still existed, the people, the house, the business. There was certainty that back there my life was waiting for me, but ambiguity crept in when I looked out over the open ocean devoid of a tree, a mountain, or any trace of a landmark, no signal buoy pointing the right way to go. I blew it off, assured that time would resolve it all, and then looked over at Jennifer... and felt my eyes melting in the vision. *Come on, Mr. Time, I'm over my head, work your magic.*

When neither of us were at the helm, we gravitated to my cabin a few days after that night, and then later she stayed with me all the time.

One evening Bruce, Jennifer, and I were hanging around the salon talking over the upcoming approach to Moorea, our first island in the Tahiti group, when Bruce pulled out two coins. The edges of both were irregular with the silver one slightly bigger than a quarter, and the gold coin just smaller than the silver dollar coin we'd see occasionally around town. Bruce handed the silver coin to Jennifer.

"This is a piece of eight," he said. "The Spanish minted these coins in Mexico and Central America for centuries."

"I've heard about pieces of eight," Jennifer said. "How did they get that name?"

"No other country had reliable coinage back then and much of the Western world adopted these coins as stable currency. The precise weight of each coin was exact, at least for those days, and the silver was measured in what they called a 'real,' while gold weighed out in escudos, kind of like ounces and pounds. They minted them in denominations of half, one, two, four, and eight reals. Anyway, the gold coins were called doubloons from the word 'double' because they weighed two escudos. One coin was double the value of the one below," Bruce explained.

"Hey Jen, Bruce has a PhD in pieces of eight," I joked.

"I can see that," she snickered. "They call those Spanish pieces of eight, don't they?"

"Yep, they sure do," he replied.

"I want to look at the gold one," Jennifer said.

Bruce held her wrist and placed the doubloon in her open hand, closed her fingers around the glistening coin, and said, "Be careful with this, it has the curse of Captain Hook on it, and anybody who lets it slip into the dark ocean is doomed to…"

"Okay sailor, I got the picture; I'm not going to drop it," Jennifer said as I tried to hold back a snicker, but failed, and then we all laughed out loud.

Jennifer grabbed my beer can, poured some into her glass, took a sip and put it back on the table while Bruce paused from the coin lecture to grab another beer from the fridge.

"This has a cross on it, and lions, and what looks like little castles. What's up with that?" she asked.

"Go on 'Doctor Coins,' give her all the answers," I jabbed.

Bruce cleared his throat and looked at me with one eye raised and an "I'll get you back, later" look.

"That was their symbol of affiliation with the church and signified Spain was the most powerful Catholic nation in the world. There was some sort of cross on all the coins made during hundreds of years."

"What's this side about?" Jennifer asked as she turned the coin over.

"That's the coat of arms and it's supposed to show all the countries that the king of Spain controlled. The coins changed when the countries changed or when the king changed... you know, died or was murdered. Now look at this one." Bruce slid a gold coin across the table to me with a big grin beginning to form. "Anything look familiar?"

Jennifer leaned over and we both took a hard look at it, turning it over and back again.

"Well there's no coat of arms on this side," I said.

"And no cross on the other side," Jennifer chimed in. "What gives, oh infamous doctor of coins?"

"I found this one diving off the coast of Key West, in only twenty feet of water. Instead of a cross, it has two pillars with a kind of a crown between them. But look at those pillars, and tell me what you see," Bruce said.

"Looks like ribbons winding around them," I said.

"And something's written on them," Jennifer said.

"One ribbon has Utraque on it, and the other says Unum." Bruce paused and then said, "I looked all this up after I found the coins, so I'm not that big of a genius, okay?"

"Okay then. Thanks, Mister Humble," I replied.

"Anyway, it means 'both worlds are one,' and it celebrated the old and the new worlds Spain had conquered in the past two hundred years. Anything else you see in those pillars?"

Bruce stood up and walked to the navigation station, opened the desk, and came back with a tablet and a pencil. We were watching him but couldn't figure out what was next with our captain. He lifted his beer can, took a slow, meticulous sip, replaced it on the table and proceeded to draw a large dollar sign. He looked up without a word, or a hint of what he was doing.

"Look at the straight pillar on the coin, intersecting the curves of the ribbons. Does it remind you of anything?" he asked.

I could feel a smile forming on my mouth, and Bruce smiled too.

"Right. It's thought that the dollar sign came from this doubloon design."

"Wow!" Jennifer exclaimed.

"Now flip it over," Bruce said. "This one was made in Guatemala in the early 1800s."

"Looks like George Washington," I said.

"Yeah well, they started putting the bust of the reigning king on it, replacing the coat of arms. It was called a 'Bust Dollar,' and it looks a lot like our dollar."

"You mean ours looks a lot like the Spanish coin," Jennifer said.

"You got it," Bruce replied.

We all handled the coins and I noticed Jennifer was rubbing her thumb slowly over both surfaces of the first doubloon we saw, like she was memorizing the contours of the surface.

"I don't get the piece of eight thing, totally," Jennifer acknowledged.

"Two pieces of eight equaled one escudo; a doubloon was two escudos, so it was equivalent to four pieces of eight; and a four-escudo gold coin was the same as eight pieces of eight," he said.

"Now I know I'm drunk," Jennifer said.

We all laughed at that, and the discussion moved back to our remaining itinerary and the landing on Moorea. The wind had picked up, so we'd been under sail for about a day. I liked when the sails came up and the engine turned off, and we got to lose the diesel exhaust always surrounding the boat.

Moorea is surrounded by coral reefs and passage into the inner circle is tricky in daylight and not navigable in the dark, so our timing had to get us to the island with plenty of daylight left. Bruce hailed Derek in New Zealand on the radio to get his take on weather and wind conditions for this last leg of the trip. We had a good tack on a northeast breeze heading south by southwest, but the wind was picking up and our speed was reaching about twelve knots. Derek was afraid we'd get to the waypoint for our turn west too soon, and arrive in Moorea at night, so he recommended slowing down to eight knots. We reefed both sails, taking our wind power down to around two-thirds of full. It was still tricky, because you can't predict the wind. Derek was running interference for us and he thought this would work.

39

Silly Clues

Alice and Andrew woke up at the Village Cay Hotel after taking the last ferry from Jost Van Dyke yesterday. The box was sitting on the table unopened. Andrew insisted on waiting overnight and opening it when everybody was fresh. Alice didn't object and Zach felt emotionally exhausted, and after thinking about it agreed. When Alice's cell phone rang, Andrew was walking by the table where it was lying, and picked it up.

"Okay. We're up, come on over," Andrew said. "That was Zach. Said he'll be over in fifteen minutes," he announced to Alice.

Andrew opened the room door, looked both ways down the dark hallway, his eyes settling on a framed photo of a sailboat winch that was on the wall directly opposite the door; a closeup revealing details and texture of the shiny chrome gear essential on all modern sailboats. He stared at it for a moment, then looked down, and kicked a shoe in front of the door, preventing it from closing.

Zach walked into the room a few minutes later, sat down in front of the box, and said, "We haven't told Jimmy and Maureen about these clues and where things stand."

"Well, do we have to?" Andrew asked. "I didn't see anything in the trust that said we have to share what we find. I'm seeing this as every man for himself."

"Does Mom say we have to collaborate and share?" Alice asked.

"Mom is not saying anything about all this. Not even a hint," Zach said.

"We think Jennifer knows not only something, but a lot about this," Andrew said.

Zach paused. He wasn't thinking they were wrong. He simply didn't know what to say.

Then after a moment of silence, he said, "Listen, how about if we decide here and now that whatever we find, we split four ways. We honestly don't know if there is anything of value there and if it's even worth our time."

"Oh great, you think Jimmy will happily share four ways if he finds it?" Andrew exclaimed. "The answer is no, he won't. And Randy is iffy at best."

"Maureen can handle Randy," Alice chimed in.

"I know Jimmy is a loose cannon. I am well aware of that," Zach said. "If we go under the assumption that there'll be a split, then we won't feel like we have to tell them about the search, and most of all we can keep Jimmy out of our way."

"I don't know; it doesn't sit right with me," Andrew said. "We've solved three really hard, obtuse clues and we're about to tackle another one. I just don't know."

"Zach, if we don't share, will you feel like you need to tell them everything?" Alice asked.

"I'm not feeling right about the secrecy," he replied.

Zach lifted his head, looked through the window, and his eyes fixed on the marina and the empty masts bobbing in the wind, while Alice stood up and took the few steps to the kitchenette to pour more tea in her standard-motel-issue white mug.

"How about we open the box after lunch. That'll give us time to slow down and think about it," Alice said.

When Zach left, the box still sat on the small round table, unopened. Alice plopped herself up on the bed and dialed Jennifer.

"Hi Mom. Let's have breakfast and catch up a little. Well, we've been busy over on Jost, and before that on Anegada. Back in Road Town now. I'll tell you all about it. See you in twenty minutes," Alice said.

Jennifer walked to the restaurant and just as she turned to enter the open-air venue, she looked out at the Village Cay Marina where Bruce moored his boat on and off for years. She looked at the big boats parked in the long slips at the end of the pier, picturing the boat Richard bought and owned for a few years. It looked stately with its dark blue hull and bright-white sails. She remembered sleepy mornings, and lazy afternoons here in this marina, and she missed the carefree life, but mostly she missed the friendships and more than that she missed Richard. Being here was hard on her, but at the same time delighted her. She could see both feelings clearly, understood them, and cherished it all.

She walked up to Alice's table, pulled out the chair next to her, and leaned over for a peck on the cheek.

"Well dear, tell me all about this adventure you're on, and how is my favorite, Anegada Island?" she asked.

Alice was cautious at first and only talked about the small things on the island; like the weather was beautiful, and the lobster was as good as ever, even if it was a little tough from over-grilling. She mentioned the treasure hunt nonchalantly, not showing much interest in it one way or the other. Jennifer nodded, agreed, and generally made nice, like ladies do over breakfast. Alice was looking for an opening, a wedge, a way into tips or important nuances for their search, while Jennifer watched this little exercise with a quiet, non-discernable interest. Finally, Alice broke ranks a little and put on her little-girl-I could-use-some-help-Mommy face and sighed.

"These silly clues are so hard, and we don't know what we're looking for, and if we just had some help, and Andrew is getting snappy, and I'm afraid the whole thing is going to damage our marriage."

It was a mouthful and she surprised herself with the marriage bit, but it felt like part of the flow at the time. She sat back and watched to see how the "little girl" thing was playing with her mom. A bit of the victim-look still dangled on her face when Jennifer looked up at her, but make no mistake, Alice was finely tuned and ready to pluck out whatever nuggets Jennifer let slip, and process it into the hunt calculations. She was sure there were useable tidbits, if not the whole story lurking in the ether surrounding her mom, sitting next to her.

"Your dad and I were very close, and I want you to know that I heard about this treasure hunt over the years and even talked about it with Bruce and Dad, but I didn't ever take it seriously, and frankly didn't think it was worth keeping up with. I just didn't feel this scheme would ever see the light of day; or ever make it from the drawing board to reality," she said.

"What 'drawing board' are you talking about."

Jennifer took a deep breath as she felt a slight breeze blowing off the water onto the pier. She thought about what to say next and more importantly, how to say it. What if they find it, and there is a glitch, trouble, fighting, or worse? What if they never find it? What's she going to do with a hundred million in gold and silver? Which ones will take that much money and promptly and totally ruin their life? Well, Jimmy for sure. Randy, probably. Not sure if she trusted Andrew to be able to maintain. What if she were to reset the clues, or remove all but around a million and let them find it, and be done with it? She took another long, deep breath.

"Not a literal drawing board, just a figure of speech. Those guys were always thinking up games, tricks, adventures, and things like treasure hunts. Who knew this one would be played out?" she said.

"It doesn't feel like play to us, Mom. It's disruptive, and what if the stress of it breaks up Andrew and me?" Alice replied.

Jennifer's thoughts kind of crackled like breaking bones in a sack. She knew Andrew hadn't worked a day since he left college, and he knew where the paycheck came from. He wasn't going anywhere, and good ole Mom knew it, but she was amused at Alice's dramatic stab at coercion.

"What if there's a lot of money at the end of this game.? What would you do with it? Have you thought about that? I mean more than you can spend?"

Alice seemed to puff up a little, but managed to answer, "Mom, I can't see how that question could possibly need answering until we find it and know what's there."

Jennifer quickly worried that she may have implied that she knew something about the treasure hunt, and Alice might pick up on it, so she buttoned up and resolved to listen rather than talk. Alice's mind seemed to abruptly stop when she replayed the phrase, "more than you can spend." It was clear her mom knew what was at the end of this trek; and it was big. She got her clue and decided to let this conversation end…she wanted to run it by Andrew. *I'm not letting Jimmy get his hands on this,* she thought. *Zach maybe, Maureen, questionable, but never Jimmy.*

40

Another Box Checked

"Let's load up and head to the Dog Islands. We have four hours of daylight, and we're making progress. At least we eliminated the caves… another box checked," Jimmy chortled. As the boat approached Great Dog, the driver began slowing down, and pointing the bow toward the one beach that could be landed on, when Jimmy yelled out over the engine noise, "Slow down, we're going to the big one, there on the right."

The driver turned to his left to see Jimmy sitting in the swivel chair next to him, and thought, *What a smug little twerp.* He caught Jack's glance that acknowledged his feeling with a slight wink.

Jimmy gave orders to "comb the island," and yes, "look for small caves and any sign of a grave… maybe an animal buried, you know stuff like that. Now get going and bring me some clues," Jimmy concluded.

Blake found a grown-over trail that led over the high point of this oversized rock and down to the northern end almost to the water. He sat on a flat rock and stared out at a coastline across the water due west, as planes floated in and out of the Beef Island Airport in an even, orderly minuet. The expectation that this gig would be a big moneymaker was unraveling. The words "short-lived" came to mind. He started thinking about other potential clients he should line up… he'd be back a lot sooner than he hoped… Monsieur Jimmy was hopeless, with no chance of finding anything of value. He hoped Jimmy had a backup plan… he was going to need it.

In the absence of meaningful clues, and daylight fading, Jimmy ordered the driver back to Trellis Bay on Beef Island, ending the day's search. Approaching the bay, Blake noticed a small, round island on his right circled by sailboats bobbing up and down on mooring balls.

"Is that an island or one of the dog rocks? I'm seeing buildings. Is that a pier?" Blake threw the questions out rhetorically, not to anyone, not expecting an answer.

The driver began to form a response when Jimmy cut him off and blurted, "It's a stupid little island with a lame bar on the top and an even lamer story behind it. I've heard the quaint little story of that island so many times I want to vomit. Dad gushed with it all the time. What love he had for that island, I'll never understand. If I owned it, I'd sink it."

Jimmy led the band of treasure hunters to the roundabout to catch a taxi to Road Town and the Village Cay Marina Hotel for the night. As the car pulled up, Jimmy balked just before getting in and told them he'd catch up later. As the others sped off, Jimmy turned back toward the pier. A small dingy had just pulled up and Jimmy flashed a fifty, and in half question, and half demand, he said, "Run me over to Marina Cay."

He stepped onto the pier and took his time meandering to the island. Looking over to the rows of docks, his mind's eye could see he and Zach running down toward the water with Maureen and Alice chasing after them, wanting to be part of the fun all those years ago. He stopped, took a deep breath, and in a brisk gait walked onto the island, strolled past the office, and up to the Robb White House. The folk music venue was empty as he walked past the mic stands and tables, started to stop and sit, but kept walking around the outside, through the side door and into the house. Cool, damp air greeted him, the familiar "old guy" portrait was hanging in the usual spot, and random furniture seemed glued to the floor, just as he had last seen it. Over by the window his eye caught a small white brick sticking out of the wall that looked a little out of place. Then he saw the square wooden lid covering the basement. One board came loose as he tried to slide the cover to the side, so he stepped around to the other side, held the loose board and easily moved the lid, exposing the hole to the dark basement. The dim light from the room revealed the old stepladder; the same one from all those years ago.

He reached into a small niche between beams just inside the opening and his fingers found the cylinder of a small flashlight. Amazed that it was still there, he flicked the switch and a dim, but adequate beam of light illuminated the earthen floor below. When his right foot touched the ground, he hopped off the last step of the ladder, and watched as the thin ray of the flashlight showed him a fort, a situation room, a puppet theater, a trading floor, and a speakeasy… all the fantasy rooms from a boisterous childhood. He could see Jennifer leaning into the room from above and could hear her saying, from all those years past, "You're in a refrigerator, don't stay down there too long." A few boards left over from props Jimmy didn't recognize lay on the floor as he ascended the ladder into the relative warmth above. He allowed his mind to ramble back to those days, feeling the safety of being taken care of and knowing that Dad would be in charge of problems. Who had problems? None of the kids did. Dad had it handled.

The anxiety he felt back then crept into his thoughts as well, moving like a wave of summer fog, first twisting his stomach and then becoming a chilling shiver all over. They were private feelings back then and he could see them all flashing in front of his eyes, welling up from some dark, cloistered recesses of his thirty-eight-year-old mind. He kicked the lid over the gap and hustled out of the room and down to the pier, blowing off all thoughts of Marina Cay, the postage-size, creepy island.

At the hotel, Jimmy checked in and went straight to his room. He pulled a half-full bottle of Kentucky bourbon from his bag, poured a glass-full over ice, then dialed room service.

Zach looked at the box, unopened but ready to reveal the next "exciting clue." He was getting bored with the drama and anxiety of personalities, and meaningless machinations on places and things he cared nothing about. And could he trust anybody, anymore? Mom might know more than she's saying, Alice and Andrew were turning into different people, especially Andrew, devious and greedy. And as usual, Jimmy could act out at any time, and get very scary, and he couldn't be trusted to not come off the rails; Zach was just glad they hadn't run into him so far.

Zach eyed the box and wondered whether or not they opened it already; no trust. But the wax seal looked intact. He ran his fingers over the raised surface, looking down at the red wax. Even in the dim light, he could make out the image of a coat of arms in the center, a rectangle with rounded corners on the bottom. He jumped up and reached for the window curtains, flung open both sides, exposing the room to the morning light. Sitting back down, he picked up the box, held it up and let the full windowlight illuminate the faint seal, and then, he could barely make out the word "Philip" around the outside edge, even though the letters were reversed. Turning the box slightly askew, he read "1607." He sat back in the chair, letting all this sink in.

"In 1607 Philip the Third was king," Andrew volunteered in a low voice.

Alice responded with a reassuring nod. Both she and Andrew were sitting across the table from Zach, but weren't looking at the box or the seal, both focused entirely on Zach.

"And you knew this arcane bit of trivia just offhand?" Zach asked.

Alice turned slightly to look at Andrew, who returned her glance without a word.

"We looked it up on the internet last night," Alice said. "It looks to be a stamp made from a gold doubloon probably minted in Mexico. We think this coin would be worth either four or eight pieces of eight, it's hard to tell from the pressing. It was a currency system like nickels, dimes, and quarters."

"We took a picture of it, and we are thinking it might work to scrape the seal off with a knife to preserve it," Andrew said.

When Andrew slipped the blade under the seal and slowly pushed down, the brittle wax crumbled into a pile of small, red pieces on the table. He looked up at two nonplussed faces, with a mere shrug from Zach. Clearing the pile away from the box, Andrew stood up and with a wave of his hand offered Zach the seat facing the box. Zach sat and lifted the clasp, meticulously opening the lid. Laying on the bottom was a small, velvet, maroon-colored pouch. In one concerted movement, Zach reached for the pouch, laid it on the table, and opened it. He pulled out a rolled piece of parchment and a coin. The coin was rounded with irregular edges, slightly bigger than a quarter, silver looking with some sort of black tarnish or patina in the crevices.

"I think it's a piece of eight," Andrew said.

Zach looked up with a "wow, you're all over this" expression on his face. He put the coin on the table, loosened the string that was tied around the paper, and unrolled it. Alice and Andrew leaned over his shoulder, and they all read the calligraphic script at the same time.

"The silver outweighs this Spanish Piece of Eight, but doubloons times two, and the clever fox never tries to be clever. Your password is You Sly Clever Fox."

Zach read the clue over and over, trying to put it in some sort of context, make some meaning from it, but the more he read it, the more it seemed nonsensical, nonlinear, non-nothing. Andrew did not share Zach's confusion or frustration.

"Okay, this is a piece of eight; the doubloons are gold. There's more silver than this one coin, but there's more gold than silver. Are you guys following me on this?" Andrew said, talking so fast he was almost tongue-tied.

Alice gave Andrew a slight smirk, knowing he knew what Jennifer had said about what if it was more money than you could spend. They were not sharing that tidbit with Zach, for the time being.

"It's got to be all coins; it only makes sense," Andrew continued. "What's this clever fox stuff? I'm stumped on that one."

41

Richard / Moorea

Bill Price opened the memoir and began reading.

Dawn was eminent, but still hiding in the early morning hours as we passed Tahiti heading for our anchorage at Cook's Bay on the eastern side of Moorea. Bruce put two of us on watch to navigate the heavy boat traffic around the busiest port in French Polynesia; commercial tankers as well as fishing boats bobbing up and down all night were obstacles we needed to avoid. At a six-knot speed, it felt like an eternity to traverse the eleven miles to our anticipated, thankful landing.

Long before we could identify Tahiti on our approach, the spire of Mount Tohivea pierced the horizon above Cook's Bay. Several peaks surrounded this four-thousand-foot giant, clearly making this the most unique and austere island of the trip. Supplies were spent and we needed almost everything. Water tanks were a few drops from empty and bottled drinking water dried up two days from port. Bruce knew that once the anchor was set, there would be a big let-down from the crew, everyone's energy would crater, so he motored us up to the service dock. With supplies, fuel, engine parts and lubricants, water, and general milling around, we thought it'd take a few hours to get things ship-shape. Jennifer made a list of supplies and we hailed a cab into Piha'ena, the largest settlement on the island. We had become accustomed to the limited stock, and semi-scant shelves in the island stores. Sorting through the store inventory, we found what we'd need for a week or so, jumped in a taxi and rode ten minutes back to the boat dock. Loading up our arms, we maneuvered down the steps of our boat, to the galley.

"How about you stay down here and get things organized and put away. I'll ferry the rest of it down," I said to Jennifer.

After delivering the last bags, I emerged onto the deck looking for Bruce or the other guys, but no one was in sight. Resting my hand on the lifeline, I looked over the side of the boat to about eight feet of water layering itself on flat, white sand, with ripples in the water reflecting the midday sunlight back up in an undulating, sparkling dance for my eyes. In short, it was an awesome sight.

Jennifer walked up behind me and put her hand on mine. "Gorgeous, all right," she said.

I knew she'd never been there before, so this sight was as breathtaking for her as it was for me.

"Richard, you know going home is not too far off. Have you thought much about it?" she said.

My attempt to forget anything but who we were, and where we were, had fallen into a dustbin of anxiety and guilt for the past week. Yes, I had thought about it. A new life, new beginning, wind in my sails, biscuits in the oven, buns in the bed; the dream was falling apart. Every scenario rolled around in my head, including a peck on the cheek and a hardy goodbye to Jennifer... the it-was-fun-while-it-lasted approach, to coming clean with Samantha and picking up where we left off in California.

"Okay, so I don't know what the best thing...I mean what the right thing...I was thinking maybe we think about it like...." My words trailed off into a shady, shallow cave with no floor or ceiling, Christ, a black hole.

"Look, Richard, it's occurred to me that I can't live without you, but actually I can. On the other hand, it struck me that a cordial handshake and sweet goodbye would take care of it. Or we could talk about the other question, as in do we have any business thinking about a life together?" she said.

I felt like a fist was in my throat when I tried to talk, but we got to the place that we needed to get to. I had to call Samantha, apologize for being almost a month overdue and attempt to catch up with the family. So, I stepped off the boat and walked to the dock master's office, where I was able to use a land line to dial Samantha. The housekeeper answered and in a sharp voice said they were all out. I asked when they were expected, and she was vague and couldn't tell me. It was Wednesday morning here, but Tuesday evening there because we crossed the date line in mid Pacific over a month ago. Hanging up, I thought I'd call tomorrow as early in the morning as I could to catch them home. It took three days to get Samantha on the phone.

"Hi Sam," I said in the cheeriest voice I could muster.

"Hi," was all she said, didn't say my name, didn't ask how I was. Nothing.

"Sorry things have dragged out, but Bruce underestimated the whole trip," I said, hearing only a muted crackle from four thousand miles of phone line, but no response from Sam.

"I can catch a flight next week from Papeete to Los Angeles, and I'll call you when I get it booked." I listened to no response. "That's in Tahiti. It's the airport in Tahiti," I said while feeling myself fall apart. "How are the kids?" I asked.

There was a silence that lasted too long, then she said, "A week will be just fine."

That phone call woke me up to the damage that was going to need repair. I knew I overstepped and the transition back was going to be messy.

Over the next few days, Jennifer and I dug down and decided that the only right move was for both of us to go home and sit with things as they were. When some time passed, we could talk and have choices with a clearer picture.

42

Wring Out the Static

Zach strolled into the open-air restaurant, picked a table, and as he began to lower himself onto the wrought-iron chair, his glance caught Jimmy sitting a few tables away staring right at him. A flash of anxiety rolled through Zach's limbs, but he was careful not to show it, and continued to sit. He could see the confident "I know what's going on" look on Jimmy's face as he walked over and pulled out a chair from the table. The silence was like a jackhammer on his nerves, and finally Zach broke the quiet.

"Any luck?" he asked.

Jimmy looked straight at Zach, nodding his head slightly with the smirk plastered on his face, never wavering, never giving ground, never giving in. Zach could see Jimmy contemplating questions that could have been asked or needed to be asked, like what are you doing here, why are you here, what do you expect to accomplish? Zach had his own questions that he didn't ask, like are you working with us or against us, are you by yourself, are you broke, are you in trouble financially?

Zach saw Jimmy swelling with rage and contempt at Zach's simple, stealth question. The response could have been a multi-volume tome, read by scholars and stored in its own library wing...the library of Jimmy. Zach knew it would be filled with every pain, inequity and rage Jimmy felt, for his family, his friends, his town, the system that holds him back, and pretty much the whole world. Zach leaned back in his chair, crossed his legs and waited for what he knew would be a lively and spirited train wreck.

"Just popped down for a little getaway for a few days. You know, wring out the static and recharge," Jimmy said.

Zach fielded this slow pitch with a nod, and no more. He knew how to stonewall bigger fish than Jimmy. *Let's just let this play out and see where it goes*, he thought.

"Good move," Zach replied. "You seeing the sights or just staying on Tortola?"

"Taking some day trips. The usual, Anegada, North Sound and the Bitter End; I took a self-guided tour of creepy little Marina Cay; maybe over to Jost today."

Both of them knew Jimmy was snooping around for the treasure. It didn't have to be mentioned. He didn't know what Jimmy had found, but he knew quite well what he hadn't found. Alice and Andrew had progressed through the clues, so the trail was long gone. Even if Jimmy figured out the first clue from the trust, the others were gone...actually not gone, but upstairs in Alice's room. Jimmy digressed into small talk about the islands while Zach weighed the ethics of telling Jimmy where they were with the clues versus the pain and disruption that would inevitably follow that disclosure. Of course, he knew that if Alice and Andrew strolled in for breakfast, the fireworks would surely start, the family circus would move to the Big Tent in full regalia, but right then Zach had things under control.

Zach noticed Jimmy's face contort a couple of times and thought he was about to downshift into a tantrum, but he watched a rare feat of self-control by his brother both times. When Jimmy's cell phone rang, he jumped up and walked away from the table, out to the boat pier so as not to be disruptive in the restaurant, but more to not be overheard. After a couple of minutes, he started walking toward the hotel and gave Zach a slight wave as in "goodbye."

"Did you tell him everything is under control; we're making progress?" Jimmy said into the phone.

"Mr. Dennison, your loan is getting bigger every day. The boss wants some assurances; he wants some form of collateral; he needs answers; he…." Blake was droning on and on, but Jimmy cut him off.

"Why are you calling me Mister Dennison? Why so formal all of a sudden? It's Jimmy, okay, just Jimmy," he said, fully aware that his voice was strained and squealing a little.

"Okay, Jimmy. He wants more than 'it's all under control.' He needs facts, he needs evidence, he needs gold and silver, or money, or a damn traveler's check. Jimmy, the boss always gets what he needs. Am I making myself clear? One way or the other, he gets what he needs," Blake said. "Patience is not a strong character trait in his family, as in he is losing patience with you."

"Well he can wait till we find it. What else can he do?" Jimmy said, but heard no response.

Jimmy went through the hotel lobby and onto Main Street, turned left and walked toward Wickham's Cay. Tourists, local bankers, and lawyers were milling around near the Government Administration Building, but he didn't even notice them. The air was converting from a cool and dry morning to warm and muggy. As he walked, he parsed scenarios and plots to manage this situation, which he admitted to himself was getting out of control. Could he disappear into the islands with a new passport and never be seen again? Not enough money, won't work. Maybe rent a boat and drive it to Cuba. No, he'd never make it that far. Get to Puerto Rico and blend in and disappear. It's a US territory, can you even disappear there? Nothing was jelling. Okay, okay, he told himself over and over. Okay, what? Find the treasure; that's what it was going to take. He paused his frenetic gyrations, and looked out over Road Harbour at the steady stream of boats, full sail, heading out into the Sir Francis Drake Channel. The wind was the usual fifteen knots from the southeast, nothing out of the ordinary.

Call the family. *See if any progress is being made*, he thought. Hey, a quarter of the treasure was better than nothing, or better than having to sell everything to pay the boss or worse being threatened or even assaulted. He'd make the first call to Maureen, just to get a flavor of the big picture. Since the islands are four hours ahead of the West Coast, he'd wait till early afternoon to call her. Maybe Alice next and see what tidbits he could gather before making the big move and onto Zach. Okay. He felt better now. A plan; he had a plan. *I can make this happen,* he thought.

He slowed his pace and his eyes started taking in the sights, stopping on a bench in the small courtyard in front of the government building. There were suits and dresses, but also casual slacks and open shirts. No patterned, so-called Hawaiian shirts, no shorts or sailors' hats adorned these businesspeople. He knew what an island look was, but his polo shirt and khaki shorts looked like he'd just strolled off the golf course. The British Virgin Islands was a sovereign country and fortuitously started a banking business which attracts players from all over the world. This was a laidback island community, but there was nothing relaxed about billions of dollars transacting there yearly.

Jimmy walked into the hotel, up to his room and threw himself on the bed, took a deep breath, and let it out with a sigh. He would shut his eyes for a few minutes and then call Blake and Jack. Then Maureen later.

A quiet knock on the door pulled Jimmy out of a light slumber. He opened the door halfway, expecting to see Zach. Jack was standing in the hall, but before Jimmy could invite him in, he stepped in and shoved Jimmy back, stumbling but staying on his feet. Before Jimmy could speak, Jack cocked his right arm and slapped Jimmy across his right cheek with the back of his hand. Jimmy reeled backward in shock.

"Sorry. No blood, no bruises. That's the orders," Jack said as his next blow was a right fist to the stomach.

It knocked the breath out of Jimmy and he crumbled onto the floor, where Jack kicked him a few times without much force, but enough to move him around the floor.

"The boss wants me to explain about the terms of your loan. Wanted to make sure he got your attention," Jack said in a muted but commanding voice.

Jimmy couldn't talk while he was gasping for breath. Jack sat at the table and just watched Jimmy try to regain composure. A few minutes passed and Jimmy tried to speak again, but nothing came out; no air passed by his vocal cords, and he settled for just lying there, all thoughts replaced by fear.

"The boss knows all about you; all your hangouts, all your friends. You can't hide. It's two million and counting. My suggestion is you get busy and pay up," Jack said.

Jack walked to the door, looked back at Jimmy whose eyes were as big as tennis balls, shook his head slightly and gently closed the door.

43

Richard / Portola Valley

Bill Price continued reading the diary.

The flight to Los Angeles was ten hours and I managed to sleep about half the time. Departing on Thursday morning, I arrived late Wednesday evening having gained a day in route. I found my gate for the short trip to San Jose, then found a pay phone in a quiet area of the terminal to call Samantha. Nobody picked up and the answering machine never clicked on. When I arrived, I jumped in a limo for the twenty-five-mile ride to Portola Valley. The house was dark as the driver pulled onto the circular driveway. My knocking on the front door brought no one, so I reached into the soil of the second planter box on the right and pulled out the "fake rock" with the door key in it. As I slid the key in and flipped on the light, I glared at an empty foyer; to the right was an empty formal dining room, and an empty kitchen. The driver walked in and said, "You better come out here and take a look at this." He walked me to the front yard facing Portola Drive and shined a flashlight on a realtor sign with a big diagonal banner across the front which read, SOLD.

I went into the house and tried Samantha's cell phone again. No answer. I called John Chakkera. No answer. The cab left and I sat in the empty den on the middle of the floor and thought about everything: meeting Samantha, the kids, the company, the pile of money I made; an endless loop of reminiscing swallowed me, while descending into the bowels of insecurity. I woke up about three in the morning and without a second thought dialed Jennifer.

"Hi sailor," she answered. "I was halfway expecting this call. How bad is it?"

I told her what had happened, and in my bewilderment, started repeating the thought-loop from earlier.

"Do you have a car?" she asked.

"I don't know," I said.

"Go look in the garage."

I flipped on the garage overhead light to see my navy-blue Roadster gleaming with its mirror finish in the florescent glow.

"Get in it and come over to Alameda," she instructed.

I arrived around 4:30 wrapped in a thin windbreaker, and collapsed on the bed, not waking till noon.

I got coffee, and about twenty minutes later dialed Chakkera. He was at the office in a meeting, put me on hold while he cleared the room.

"Are you back?" he asked.

"Last night. Do you know where she went?" I said.

"She went from perturbed to angry to resolved. She called three days ago to say goodbye. I didn't hear a clear destination from her, but it sounded to me like she was headed home. I think that's Mississippi, right?"

I couldn't muster a response except, "Right."

"I called the house earlier in the week, but got no answer, not even a message machine," John said.

Communicating around the world was not the easy, convenient, and expected thing it is today, even in the 1980s. In the 1960s and 1970s the only way to call back home from Europe, for example, was to go to the post office, wait in a long line, get an international operator, regurgitate a bunch of special numbers, all for a two-minute call. Or, call from a hotel and pay $50 to $75 for two minutes. I found out later that not only did John's calls never reach me, neither did ten or fifteen of Sam's make it through, even though they called cell phones, satellite phones and possible hotels. Not only did I think I was off the grid, I was off the grid and in another world…a world that left Sam and the kids stranded and alone.

"Are you coming to the office?" John asked.

"I'll be in tomorrow. I've got jet lag among other traumas."

Walking into the office was a bit disorienting. Feeling like I was in a dream, I even felt a little bit dizzy. My card key got me in the side door. I slowed down while passing the marketing department cubicles. One new face looked up, but did not recognize me. John was in his office on the phone. He waved me in and I pulled up a chair at the small, round conference table. Hanging up the phone, he walked over to the table without a word. Then said,

"How are you today?"

"Not much good to report. I feel like shit."

"Did you get hold of Sam?" he asked.

"I called her parents. Her mother answered and said she couldn't talk and would have Sam's dad call me back. We had a money market account at Crocker Bank. It's got a thousand in it," I said.

"How much was in it when you left?"

"Around five million," I replied.

"A drop in the bucket for you, old man. Besides, it may end up costing you a few bucks more than that," he said.

Not having seen each other in months, the polite pleasantries of a first meeting percolated down the circuitous tube to plop in the lap of "all about money"…what else?

Brushing aside that my life was falling apart, John brought me up to speed on the company. My temporary replacement, Neil Butcher, had concocted a marketing strategy for the new device and it was selling like gangbusters. The engineers were sure we outperformed the competing products, but were equally sure that the advantage wouldn't last, and the winner would be the company that stayed closest to the customers, anticipated changes, and had quick, real-time manufacturing fixes. Neil had already split off a team to concentrate on this project, and John's opinion was that we leave it in place and hire new people for the rest of the group.

As John rolled on about the company, I listened and offered suggestions, but felt distant and not interested. To John the whole world was right here in the technology capital of the world—everything revolved around the success of the company. But the whole world was bigger for me—the volcanic islands, the Tiki sculptures, the turquoise water, and people from the other side of the world. My palette was irreversibly altered.

44

Christine

Zach's cell phone rang, and as he picked it up, he saw no caller ID which was not unusual in the islands. Having international coverage didn't always guarantee the same level of service he got back home.

"Hello. Hi, Vivian. Well, I'm still in Road Town. Yes, the idea you had about the Soggy Dollar was a jackpot. There was a waitress there who had the clue. When we said the magic word, she walked to the back and brought it out. It was that simple. What? Yeah, well this is the craziest, most half-baked thing Dad ever did. If there's anything of value at the end of this trek, I'm going to be even more mad at him."

"Do you know where it is yet?" she asked.

"We're more confused than ever now. The next clue is something about 'sly clever fox,'" he said.

"Any reference to Jost Van Dyke?" she asked.

"No, nothing. Do you want to hear the whole clue?"

"Why not?" she said.

"'The silver outweighs this Spanish Piece of Eight, but doubloons times two, and the clever fox never tries to be clever. Your password is You Sly Clever Fox.' That's all I've got," Zach said.

"Okay, I'll call you if I think of anything."

A few minutes later a knock brought Zach to the door of his room. He opened it to see Andrew and just behind him in the hall, Alice. Without saying a word, Zach turned and walked back into the room, sat at the table and folded his hands in his lap. Andrew's svelte, six-foot frame led the way, stopping in front of Zach, while still standing.

"We're going to head over to Jost for a couple of days and look around," Andrew said. "There's something about this 'fox' thing in the clue that needs looking into."

"Foxy's Bar and the 'sly, clever fox may be something," Alice chimed in. "We rented that pink house on the hill at Great Harbour."

"The one on the right as you pull into Foxy's?" Zach asked.

"Yep. We had to rent it for a week and there are three bedrooms. Come over if you want," Andrew said.

"Maybe," Zach replied.

Vivian pulled the throttle back on both 300 horsepower Yamaha outboard engines as she pulled into Great Harbour. Boats with naked masts like stripped saplings swung on mooring balls throughout this protected bay. She navigated along the small channel to what they call the dinghy pier, cinched up the boat and took a 360 turn in place around the dock. A single car slowly rolled down the sand-covered road in front of the shops, and residents strolled in both directions. The tourist boats from St. Thomas were there, most likely gassing up and preparing to ferry the day's passengers back to their home port later in the day. After a deep breath, Vivian painted an island smile on her face, straightened her navy-blue windbreaker, and started down the pier toward the shore. She waved at several acquaintances, stopped and talked to a couple of old friends while making her way to Foxy's gift shop. Vivian and Tessa, Foxy's wife, were old friends. The gift shops each ran were targeted at the same boating visitors, so they tried to stock different things. Even though there was some overlap, they relied on talking regularly to keep things fresh.

She browsed around the shop, looking at hats, T-shirts and women's tops. They were the best sellers, so both shops carried a big inventory, many of which were the same, but sometimes the unique island logo was what the ladies bought the shirts for. One of the salesgirls told Vivian that Tessa would be back shortly. Vivian knew what "shortly" meant in the islands, so she strolled out of the shop, turned right on the sand-covered road. Just before the Customs and Immigration building, she turned right, stopping at the small-framed, converted house now called Christine's Bakery. She walked in and as usual it was like a school reunion. Everybody knew everybody. Like Vivian, Christine migrated from England, a little town just west of Leeds, each disheartened by pretty much everything in the old country, thought she'd give the islands a try, and for the past forty years, it appeared to have worked out.

Christine pulled up a chair and started the small talk routine. She was a faster and more persistent talker than Vivian, who nevertheless could keep up when she needed to. A few minutes went by and when Christine took a breath, Vivian took her turn.

"Did you hear Richard Dennison died?"

Christine looked up, her eyes resting on the opposite wall, and for once said nothing. Vivian anticipated the mixed feelings that Christine might have over this news. There were rumors she had a fling with Richard when he and Bruce were swashbuckling around a few decades ago. But it was no rumor because Vivian had talked her off the ledge for a year after it. Christine was a thin, tall brunette with English, fair skin, who liked going "native" around the islands. In those days she waited tables wherever she could and if the gang was heading south to the leeward islands at the spur of the moment, she was in.

"Jennifer stopped by a few days ago and told me. He'd been sick and finally lost the battle," Christine said. "I see Jennifer from time to time. She usually stays on Marina Cay."

"How did it go between you two?"

Her eyes gently moved back, engaged Vivian's, as she sat back in her chair, "Oh, we're fine. We talked the Richard thing over years ago. My time with him happened a long time ago and before she hooked up with him permanently," Christine said. "Hey, so does Jennifer have some interest in Marina Cay?"

Two old friends came through the front door and both the women stood up to greet and talk with them… obligatory small talk followed till the two sat down at an empty table across the room.

"I remember when Richard was trying to buy that island a long time ago, but I never knew how that came out, and if he did own it, where it stands now," Vivian said.

"She mentioned the island several times when she casually told me about some screwy adventure Richard left for all those children," Christine said.

"Really, what kind of adventure?"

"Back in the old days, Bruce was overboard about the Spanish galleons and all the wrecks around Anegada. They had a bag of coins they'd picked up diving around those shallow reefs. Gold and silver coins, and the whole bug rubbed off on Richard. It never sounded like they ever sold any of it. Maybe it has something to do with that. You know how Richard was," Christine said.

"Did she say anything else about this adventure?" Vivian asked.

"She was ruminating about the whole thing might have the opposite effect on the kids than Richard schemed. She thinks this thing went too far and is surprised Richard followed through on it. She is afraid the kids are splintering instead of working together," Christine said. "I have to give her credit, she's being stoic about it, as in *it'll be what it'll be*."

"Do you think she knows the details of this escapade, or is following clues one-by-one along with the kids?" Vivian asked.

"You know Jennifer, she's not as chatty as some people, so it's hard to tell," Christine replied.

Christine jumped back into work brewing up fresh coffee, as Vivian strolled back to Foxy's store. Off to her right down the beach, the ferry from Soper's Hole was just docking, a few boats were motoring past the buoys, and raising sails on a port tack toward Cane Garden Bay. She judged the wind at a tepid ten knots, a typical morning in paradise, she thought.

Tessa was standing at the register when Vivian walked in the store. She opened a big cardboard box to show Vivian the new ladies top that just arrived; a sheer, sleeveless stretchy fabric with an understated, small Foxy's logo on the back just under the collar. Foxy himself thought up the design, and all the shop staff was buzzing about it. They settled with a cup of tea on a small bench next to the changing room and started talking. When the conversation lulled, Vivian asked if she knew anything about Richard's treasure hunt.

"A treasure hunt? I thought he died," she said.

"It was in his trust and activated at his death."

"I used to marvel at Richard. The games, the tricks he came up with. You'd have to be drunk to want to go along with him, and of course, there were many takers all the time," Tessa said.

"You think Foxy knows anything about it?" Vivian asked.

"Walk over and ask him. He's in the bar," Tessa said.

Foxy, with his signature smile, was sitting on an open-air bench at the base of the three stairs that led to the dining deck. He built a thriving bar and restaurant business over the years with a guitar and a smile. Bourgeois sailors from all over the world pining away for the pirate days of old during their week's sailing vacation found Foxy by reputation and word-of-mouth. Big holidays like Fourth of July and Labor Day brought every would-be pirate to Great Harbour and Foxy's front door. The years had taken his voice, but his smile was permanently engraved on his face.

Vivian nonchalantly brought up Richard and then the treasure hunt with him. She didn't detect any nuance in his voice or body language that gave away any response other than the slight head shake right to left.

The two outboard engines roared and her boat lurched forward as Vivian cleared the buoy channel. She thought the Foxy connection was a long shot, but worth a try. The latest clue had to have something to do with Foxy's bar, she thought. Maybe that clever little guy Andrew would come up with the answer.

45

Richard / Hello Islands

Bill Price continued reading the diary.

I stayed at Jennifer's for a week, calling Sam every day. Then one afternoon I rang my travel agent and asked how soon she could book me to Tortola. Tomorrow through Dallas was the answer, nine AM. I called my chum, Tad Johnson, at the Moorings charter operation. He had a new thirty-five-foot Beneteau I could charter for as long as I wanted. That was perfect for single-hand sailing. Wheels up at nine. Hello islands.

A mid-afternoon breeze blew a light ripple in the water around my new sailing home. After tossing my small duffle bag in the front cabin, I jumped in a taxi and sped over to the Riteway market to pick up some of everything. My plan to stick around the boat for the evening was quashed when I popped a Carib pilsner and started walking around the finger of Road Harbour bay to the Village Cay Hotel. Meandering by the low rock wall that separated the bay waters from the traffic and tourists, I thought about the first time I arrived at Road Town Harbour, wondering what was next, taking a chance on Bruce, and Samantha taking a chance on me. It didn't seem like that long ago. Maybe I took all that instant money too seriously, or maybe Sam turned conventional and middle class after the kids were born, and it got boring for me. Just saying that felt shallow. I dug a big hole and climbing out of it was going to be painful.

The restaurant had a few groups segregated around tables; the after-work bankers and business crowd were separated from the tourists by their long pants and muted colors, while the scurvy, low-life would-be-pirates sat with bright colors, logo hats and flip-flops. I saw a lawyer I knew, and I felt fine about sliding in that group and was sure they'd like to talk about technology, Silicon Valley, rum, or Spanish gold coins, but my current mood was not amenable, so I diverted to the bar. The bartender was from South Africa and had odd-jobbed around the BVI for five or six years, sometime dive instructor, sometime bartender, and sometimes first mate on some bigger ships. A nice guy, but no real direction. A part of me felt like him in those days, and some of it these days too. I was aiming for flat-out being in the present and seeing how the future would unfold.

Jennifer was not comfortable with my sitting around and moping, and hinted I should go sailing… someplace that felt comfortable and familiar. Maybe she would join me later. The Tahiti trip was a long one, and she had a lot of loose ends to tie up. Chakkera didn't expect me back for another month. As some of the bar crowd filtered out, I reached for my cell phone to call Jennifer, but it wasn't connecting with the network so I let things lie.

At dawn the next morning, I pointed my bow upwind and hoisted the main sail, followed by the jib, and fell off the wind to a 285-degree heading, rounding the island at Soper's Hole, and then headed to the middle of Jost Van Dyke and Great Harbour. The Harbour is deep and protects boats from the sea swells that plague nearby White Bay, as well as across the channel in Cane Garden Bay. Sailing a boat alone, even a small one, has its challenges, and snagging a mooring ball is one of them. I snuggled up to the ball and by the time I could get to the bow, the wind pushed it out of reach. I would be embarrassed if I said it took me ten times to snag that sucker, so I won't say it. Bruce was a good teacher who explained one key rule of sailing, "It doesn't matter how many times you get it wrong, as long as you get it right in the end." I was proud of number ten, and one through nine got me to ten.

That cheeseburger at Foxy's is to die for. I motored my inflatable up to the dinghy dock, and walked along the pier to shore. Stepping into the bar, I ambled smack-dab into Foxy himself, who was climbing onto the small stage just to the left of the bar for an afternoon show. One guitar, two mics, and the biggest smile you've ever seen was how he kicked off the coolest island entertainment in the BVI. The "Welcome to Foxy's" sign, on the wall in back of the stage, was nearly covered up by a blue and red Auburn Tigers flag, a Clemson pennant, license plates from Montana and Illinois, and a T-shirt with "Nate and Natalie" scribbled on it in Magic Marker.

Tessa wandered into the back of the restaurant and I went over to say hi. We talked for a while when her eyes darted up. Foxy was blaring out a rum-drinking song, when a small hand banged on the table from behind me. The hand lifted and on the Plexi-covered tabletop was a coin. Without looking up to see who was the perpetrator, I said, "Spanish doubloon." Then another coin danced to a stop on the table. "Piece of eight," I said.

"You're either the king of Spain or Black Bart the pirate," a British voice chortled.

I looked up over my shoulder and saw a head of brunette hair on a petite figure.

"I'll go with the king of Spain," I said.

"Queen of Sheba for me, sailor," she said.

"Cut it out, Christine, you'll scare the poor boy," Tessa said.

"Where did you get these?" I asked.

"This South African guy I know found them in the reefs off Anegada. He thinks they're from a sister ship of the *Atocha* that was rumored to have been blown onto the reefs in 1715. It was full to the brim with freshly minted gold and silver coins," she said.

"How does he know that?" I asked.

Tessa chimed in, "He doesn't. Everybody thinks something about the treasures in the deep, but nobody knows nothing about nothing. Don't bore us with these stories, I've heard 'em all. Nobody has taken anything but trinkets from those reefs, trust me."

"Nobody you know, anyway," Christine said.

In lieu of a scowl Tessa shrugged, smiled, and gave a hearty giggle. We all laughed, but I was intrigued. Bruce had been talking about the shipwrecks and the treasure spilled by the Spanish over a three-hundred-year period. A lot of wrecks happened off the south Florida coast in shallow water, but the eleven-mile shallow reef surrounding Anegada snagged hundreds of boats over the years, and some had huge stashes of gold and silver that have been lying on the bottom of the ocean for hundreds of years, hidden and brooding in deep sand.

Tessa left the bar after Foxy's set and headed back to the shop, while Christine and I had another round of sailor elixir.

"She's right about the big-talking treasure stories that get thrown around down here, but I know there are a lot of coins on those reefs," Christine said. "One of the biggest wrecks ever recorded was an armada led by the *Nuestra Senora de Soledad* off the coast of North Carolina at Cape Hatteras around 1750. There were ingots of gold and silver as well as jewels and huge troves of gold and silver coins minted in Central America. The Spanish were all over the cleanup and recovery, supported by the American authorities. Putting a few coins in your pocket and sneaking out the back way would get you shot, and you can imagine it happened a bunch."

"So, what does that have to do with Anegada, and how is it you're so smart about this?" I said.

"First of all, I'm not so smart about it. There was a book passing around and mostly I read the chapters about the local wrecks, but here is the thing about Anegada. Most of the coins slid off the *Soledad* in Florida in shallow water and were easy to recover, while the bars and jewels were scattered over a mile and a half. A mid-size sloop was loaded up with the coins and sent south for safekeeping," she said.

"Wow, what a tale," I said.

"Here's the kicker. That boat hit a big squall just before it got to the protected waters of the Virgin Islands, and wrecked on the reefs at Anegada. Some crew were saved but the ship broke apart and the coins were lost."

"Anybody have any earthly idea where it went down?" I asked.

"That's the problem. Everybody has an idea and, like Tessa said, nobody knows."

The waitress kept bringing the elixir and we sloshed into the evening. I was happy to see a few old friends. My special South African friends, Graeme and Bridgett, stopped by and we reminisced about the early days when he was helping me fine-tune my sailing skills. But I kept thinking about the Spanish treasure on the sea floor waiting, sitting for first-come-first-served entrepreneurs. I was getting the buzz that Bruce had been churning about on the Tahiti trip.

I walked Christine to her little "island shack" apartment. The elixir had taken effect on both of us. The minute we got to the door, she turned and then, like a lioness to her cub, she pressed in, snuggled up close and raised her head, her mouth fell on mine and we kissed like mad lovers. She took my hand and pulled me inside, and again the passion filled the room like flames in a furnace. My hand found her bare back and I pulled her tighter, moving down to cradle her soft, round butt. When our clothes came off, we dropped to the floor, where the sure thing was going to happen.

Then, like a sharp bolt of Caribbean lightning, I stopped and rolled to the side. Was I ready for this? What a question! I was always ready for this. Get real, I told myself. We both lay there and no words were spoken. After a few minutes, she got up and came back with two plastic bottles of water. I sat up leaning against the back of an old, worn fabric chair and sipped water. We were both a little dazed, and finally I got up to leave. I shuffled out the door and onto the dinghy dock, flipped on the running lights and motored out to my boat.

I heard a squeak on the deck, opened my eyes and saw a faint ray of morning light through the window. Looking for my watch was like looking for a lost diamond ring in Tijuana…. Nowhere to be found. I rolled over and looked out the cabin door to see Christine holding a cup of steaming coffee and wearing a subtle smile. She set the coffee on a shelf and climbed over the one step to my berth, inserted herself under the sheet, pulling in prone to me. Her hands were like velvet and her lips were like burning coals. Small and petite, she moved like a cat all over the bed. The hot coffee sat abandoned on the shelf, and turned to a cold drink by the time the sun was high and we surfaced back on deck.

46

Jost Van Dyke

Alice opened the door to the pink house, and walked into the living room... a little musty but not too bad. The furniture was reminiscent of English antique, well made, but very worn, and easily recognizable as not vintage. The front bedroom featured a large picture window with a view, west overlooking Great Harbour. Andrew dropped the luggage in the corner. Alice emptied the small bag of groceries including coffee, milk, and mangos, and stashed them in the refrigerator.

"It's around two o'clock, let's walk down and get lunch, and we can start looking around," Andrew said.

Alice had been around Foxy and Tessa many times, but you couldn't exactly say she had been introduced or that she knew either of them. Dad snagged a mooring ball in Great Harbour on a regular basis when they were kids, and he and Mom would park the boat here for days at a time. Of course, in between that it was North Sound at Virgin Gorda, then Norman Island, and on and on.

They climbed the two steps up to the open-air dining room at Foxy's and ordered the lobster sandwich. Nothing eventful happened and the crowd was small, so they walked down the beach past the ferry dock, as far as they could go to around Dandy Point.

As the afternoon progressed, the sun moved lower in the western sky and the clouds transformed from white and puffy, to red and fiery, punctuated by gray, bulbous, backlit companion clouds floating like giant oceans in an endless sky. The warm rays of sun receded, but the air stayed warm and slightly muggy. The two treasure seekers stopped back at Foxy's for a rum punch and sat down while Foxy played the final set for the evening. The room was packed with mostly skippers and their crews. Alice made it a point to walk in front of the stage several times to see if she could catch Foxy's eye, but he gave no indication that he'd ever seen her before. Alice's resolve to find the treasure was melting away her endemic shyness and fear of being too bold and overstepping ... a trait not everyone in the family shared.

The next morning the phone rang and Andrew picked it up.

"Good morning. Are you guys at Jost?" Zach asked.

"Yep. Got here last night. Are you still in Road Town?"

"No. I'm back in California in the office. Any news on the next clue?" Zach said.

"Nothing yet. We're going to find Tessa and Foxy and say hi. If it goes smoothly, Alice is going to bring up the trust and mention the treasure hunt, and ask if they can help in any way," Andrew replied.

"My thought is to keep it open-ended and see what comes back at you. Sometimes people like to chat and can easily 'overshare' before they realize it," Zach said.

"Alice wants to know if there is any word from Jimmy," Andrew said. "She's on pins and needles about him throwing a monkey wrench into things."

"Nothing. Look, we need to get some resolution as to how this bounty is going to be shared. Are we all working together or competing? Christ, Andrew, you knew our dad, it could be a whole lot of nothing at the end of this rainbow," Zach continued.

"Yeah, well together, yes all together.... Anyway, we'll get back to you as soon as we know something."

Andrew looked over at Alice. "What does he mean, share? Jimmy is a loose-cannon-fool who couldn't find anything right in front of his face, and Maureen is sitting at home on her hands. Whatever we get is ours shared with Zach, damnit." Andrew paused and shook slightly with frustration. "I really mean it!"

Alice didn't say a word, but marveled at this side of Andrew that was rolling out in front of her eyes. She wondered whether it was built-up frustration or newfound greed … or both.

Around mid-morning, the duo strolled down from the pink house and walked into the gift shop. They looked at hats, T-shirts, and jewelry until Alice saw Tessa appear from the back room. She walked up to her and said, "Hi Tessa, I'm Alice and you knew my dad, Richard Dennison."

"Oh dear, it's so good to see you. I was so sad to hear the news. We will really miss your dad, but I hope we'll see more of you. I remember you and Zach year after year playing on the beach, and you knew right where my secret ice cream cones were hidden," Tessa said.

"Thanks, Tessa. We are all feeling a big loss. Mom is staying busy, and doing well," Alice said. "I wanted to ask a favor. Dad left us all a puzzle. It was in his trust, and we're not sure what it is or how to solve it. I was wondering if you might be able to help us. We're following clues and there is one about a clever fox. Is that anything that rings a bell for you?" Alice asked.

"Leave it to Richard. What a jokester! But I never heard anything about this puzzle idea. Sorry," Tessa said.

"Okay, well thanks. Could I ask Foxy if he's heard anything about it?" Alice said.

"Well, dear, he's right out in the courtyard. I'm sure he'd love to see you."

194

47

Boston

The American Air nonstop from St. Thomas landed on time at Boston's Logan Airport. Jimmy was the third passenger to emerge onto the jetway from first class. He threw the strap from his carry-on over his right shoulder, reached for his cell phone, and stared at it waiting for the signal to connect. He talked to Maureen the day before and even though he was cordial, nice and not pushy, he got no information from her. She was distracted with a project Randy was working on, who had a flow of guests from China that were potentially massive clients, and Maureen had to create entertainment, dinners, cocktail parties, and whatever else Randy perceived the need for at the drop of a hat. His calls to Alice went unanswered, causing some anxiety. Zach? Well, he thought better of calling him without an agenda. He had no information or news and nothing to offer. Small talk was out of the question. He'd call Zach later.

As he walked by the boarding gate, a heavy-set man strolled up beside him with a slight smile, more like a smirk. Jimmy turned his head to get a better look at this stranger, to see six feet, a dark complexion, and jet-black hair combed back with too much oil. Jimmy instinctively slowed his pace, but the man slowed along with him. Jimmy veered to the left to duck into the men's room, but the man casually locked his arm around Jimmy's and whispered, "Come on with me; you'll be okay." They took the escalator down and Jimmy pointed to the baggage claim carousel, and the man said,

"It's being taken care of." The automatic glass doors opened as they walked onto the curb, where Jimmy was "invited" into the back seat of a black Escalade, whose windows were dark, preventing him from any advanced warning of what might be in store for him. Jimmy was petrified and couldn't think of anything to say.

Finally, as the car pulled onto the freeway, the man said, "The Boss wants to talk to you."

Jimmy felt like he was melting into the seat. He started running scenarios in his head about how he was in control of the treasure hunt; it was just a matter of a short time, and he'd have the money; his interest in the family real estate holdings would definitely cover the debt; he just needed time to work out the details; his brother Zach was working with him, and was on board to clear this up; and on and on. Jimmy shook all over. He took a deep breath and slumped in his seat.

48

Richard / Sharp Glint of Gold

Bill Price woke at 5:30 a.m. The family was still asleep, so he made a latte and ambled into his office. The diary was still open from the night before. Without meaning to, he picked it up and began reading.

That afternoon I felt like a man without a country, or a man without a home, or one with no direction. I thought about Jennifer and Tahiti and the best experience of my life; and I thought about the short time it covered; the euphoric fling thing. Were Jennifer and I the real deal, or was I a floating free spirit making this Christine thing okay? Then I heard a friendly voice yell out, "fresh mangos." The grocery boat had arrived. I bought bananas, apples, arugula, and mangos. Making breakfast was the perfect distraction from trashing myself.

I pulled out of Great Harbour a couple of hours later on a port tack around West End, Tortola, passed Soper's Hole, then due east into Road Harbour. The radio crackled with traffic as I pulled into an assigned slip given to me by the dispatcher. I caught a ride with a guy I met around the bay to midtown, and headed to the government building which was open till five, so I had an hour to wiggle a coveted chart with footnotes of the suspected wrecks off Anegada from the clerk. To be honest, I knew her from the party circuit in the islands. She handed me a rolled up, large-format paper chart, and gave me a stern warning not to show it around to just anybody… top secret!

I made it back to my boat, where I rolled out the chart and took a long, meticulous overview of the wrecks, when my phone rang.

"Captain Richard, Captain Richard, Captain Richard. This is Christine of the Islands. Do you copy?"

Many times, a marina will monitor a common frequency, but prefer to talk on a more private channel. Christine was mimicking a VHF radio call just for fun, so I played along.

"This is Captain Richard. Switch to hot pants channel 46," I replied.

We started laughing, and then I told her about the chart.

"So, you're jumping on this sunken treasure thing. Everybody gets excited about it for a while. You'll spend a lot of time underwater and find a few coins, and then get tired of it. It's the way it happens for everybody," she said. "I can get the last ferry and be over there before dark. Sound good?"

The sky was fiery red again as the sun set over St. Thomas when Christine strolled up to the boat carrying a small duffel.

"Looks like you're staying for a while," I said.

"I got a call after we talked. It was from my mom in Baton Rouge. Dad had a stroke, and I'm booked on the late flight to Puerto Rico, staying overnight there, then an early flight to New Orleans tomorrow. Don't know how long I'll be gone," she said.

I sat looking at her, not knowing what to say, after knowing her for only a short time.

"I hope he's going to be all right," I finally said.

"They got him to the hospital quickly, so I'm hoping for the best."

After Christine left, I poured over the charts, tried to make notes of the names and dates of the wrecks. Some were thought to have gone down with treasure and others not, and others had no designation. The next morning, I walked into the Moorings office asking about reference materials on the wrecks from their random library of books that were left on charter boats over the years. Mashon, the desk clerk, showed me to the shelves in the back room, but with a quirky smile on her face, as in another wild-eyed guy with too much time on his hands. Most of the books were about fauna and flowers, and snorkeling in the Virgin Islands, no help for me, so I headed back to the boat.

A few hours later as if on cue, Bruce walked up behind me while I was on the bow straightening a dock line.

"Hey, hey, Captain," I said as we gave each other a man-hug. "How did you find me down here? I thought I was hiding."

"I called Jennifer, and she told me the news. Sorry to hear it. How are you feeling?" he asked.

"Unwinding a lot. I think it'll take a while," I said.

We talked about Sam and how Jennifer was feeling, and John Chakkera, and the company, and life in general. He told me he'd hired a crew to sail his boat back from Tahiti, but it would be several months before the winds were favorable for the trip. Then he caught a glimpse of the chart. I brought him up to speed on it and my need for more background and details.

"You're in luck!" he said and pulled out a three-inch-thick paperback tomb entitled, *Wrecks of the Virgin Islands.*

Bruce rented dive equipment, and the next morning we sailed past the Dog Islands to a latitude even with Virgin Gorda, then fell off due north to Anegada. A sailboat keel would be thrashed on the reefs if we tried to anchor out there, so we upgraded the rubber dinghy to bigger and better, and dragged it behind us to the "drowned island." A healthy dose of rum and lobster finished off the evening.

I was up at dawn drinking coffee the next morning as Bruce emerged from his cabin. We ate a light breakfast, packed a lunch, and slowly steered the dinghy to our first way point on the compass. For the next three days we explored different locations without a scrap of gold or silver... not a speck of anything except sand, reefs, and plenty of lobsters hiding on the bottom. Even though the diving was not deep, we felt some mild exhaustion. So, taking a couple days off was a health issue. I had time to think about the short tryst with Christine and was embarrassed and regretful of the whole thing. I didn't want to still be the kind of guy who would do that, as if I had no one I cared about. I had stopped trying to reach Samantha, assuming I had irrevocably ruined my old life with her.

We were four hours ahead of California, so around one p.m. I dialed Jennifer. After some small talk, I asked her to come down to join us. Three days later she arrived at the

Beef Island airport. Bruce and I sailed into Trellis Bay and waited in the dinghy as she walked across the road from the terminal. I booked a room looking out on Virgin Gorda on the adjacent island of Marina Cay. A few days alone with her was the thing I needed. On the third day, Bruce took a taxi out to Trellis Bay from Road Town and rode the ferry to meet us on the island. Jennifer caught the treasure-bug too and we sorely needed her help. The last night in the hotel was full of excitement about the shipwrecks and what treasures might be down below waiting to be liberated.

Two weeks went by while we blanketed the reefs with only a few artifacts to show, iron tools and fragments mostly. When you spot gold in the sunlight, it shines with a luster like it was just minted, even though it spent the last three hundred years washing around in salt water. Silver, however, tarnishes badly, turns black, and pieces fuse together.

The first time a sharp glint hit the corner of my eye, I turned, kicked slightly with my fins, reached down, and in my fingers drew back a gold doubloon. My hand instinctively reached down again into the sand, and clutched two more gold coins. Dropping a maker at the location, I ascended through four feet of water to the surface. I threw my mask off and shouted to Bruce, "the mother lode," and held the coins out for him to see. He took them and started laughing. After climbing into the boat, we examined the inscriptions. Coat of arms on one side, small pillars on the other, "Ferdinand VI" written around the rim on one side, and "1749" on the opposite side. They were all the same.

"These are all from one wreck," Bruce said. "Let's eat a sandwich and go back down." We went down for a short dive, swam around the reef area of the find, but didn't see any more coins.

The next morning Jennifer steered the dinghy out to the site. She located the floating marker we anchored the night before. We pulled up another handful of the identical doubloons, but each find was isolated, and no iron artifacts surrounded the coins.

"If we see other boat gear, like anchors or rails or something, we'd have some confidence that the ship went down right here, but this seems like random coins," Jennifer said. "Maybe they simply washed here in the surf."

"Or were spread out over hundreds of yards as the boat scraped along these reefs," I said.

We created a grid with floating buoys to organize our search, and motored back to our sailboat in the afternoon with a small sack of gold in our bow that we collected, one at a time. Pouring over the map that night made us more eager, and next morning we were back at it.

49

Foxy

Andrew, followed by Alice, went to the front porch and skipped down the two steps to the sandy soil. He turned to the left and immediately saw Foxy talking with two sailboat skippers. Stopping in his tracks, he waited for Alice to catch up. He knew about Foxy, but had never met him, nor did he have the family connections that were needed in such a delicate matter as this. Alice slowed her pace down and skillfully waited for the sailors to walk away, then strolled straight up to the reigning celebrity of the island.

"Hi Foxy. Richard Dennison is my father. I'm Alice Dennison," she said.

"Hi Alice. Haven't seen you in ages. Hope you're well. Sorry to hear about Richard. He was my favorite sailor. Never a dull moment around Richard Dennison!" he said as he chuckled.

"We already miss him, and it's only been a few months,"

"How's my other buddy, Jennifer?" he asked.

"She's doing fine. In spite of everything, she's always been an independent person, and loved my dad, but she's getting along fine."

A waiter brushed up against Andrew while shuffling from the bar to the gift shop.

"Foxy, I wonder if you can help us with a little puzzle that Dad left in his trust for us to solve?" Alice said.

"Your dad was always hiding something and taunting everybody about it. It got to be that nobody around here was paying any attention to the clues and prizes, or the whole game until a new kid followed the clues and discovered around five thousand dollars' worth of gold coins. Leave it to Richard, they were all from this one wreck in 1750… a Spanish galleon called the *Soledad*, we figured," he said.

The details of this wreck and the description of the coins bounced off Alice's forehead and vanished in the ether, because she was on a one-track mission. "Okay then. He left us some clues and that's why we're here. The next clue says something about a clever fox. Does that mean anything to you? Or can you think of where we might find an answer to it?" Alice said.

"He never made the clues easy and usually they were weird and obtuse," Foxy replied. "You guys get a table and I'll send Brad over to get you some lunch. We just got a load of lobster from Anegada this morning. You've got to try our lobster sandwich."

They smiled and thanked Foxy, but sitting down at the table they were despondent and disappointed. Alice talked about what they could do next, or who they could talk to, but Andrew didn't say a word as he stared at the bar, then the sound stage, then he turned to look out into Great Harbour, and then to his beer which arrived with Brad, compliments of Foxy. They picked at the lobster and Andrew ordered another beer … and then another. The afternoon was whiling away with no progress on their quest, while Andrew felt the mega-rich fantasy that had driven him to this point, sliding away into nothingness … the dark abyss.

An afternoon crowd began filling up the outside tables as a mild wave of humidity rolled into the open-air dining room. The noise level increased with conversation and an occasional whoop from an exuberant tourist. Suddenly Andrew jumped up, hurling his chair to the floor behind him. He weaved through the tables to the stage as Foxy was walking offstage from a short song set, backing up a new performer.

He marched up to the grinning songster and blurted, "You Sly Clever Fox."

Foxy stopped in his tracks. A huge grin came over him, as he turned to a small chest, opened the top drawer and removed a brown envelope.

He handed it to Andrew and said, "Good work, young man. Richard told me you were a clever one." He turned with his guitar in hand and walked down the steps and was gone.

Andrew stood practically dumbfounded. The excitement of solving the clue and restoring the hunt was lost in what he'd just heard. His father-in-law thought he was the clever one? Never had he gotten any hint that Richard Dennison thought he had any intrinsic talent or worth. He didn't look at the envelope while he took his time back to the table where Alice was aghast at his sudden move. He handed her the envelope and said nothing. As she looked at the dogged corners of the package, her first thought was to rip it open, but couldn't take her eyes off Andrew who was in a daze.

"Your dad thought I was the clever one in the family," he said.

"What are you talking about?" she asked.

"Your dad thought I was the clever one in the family. Foxy just said it," he said.

Alice said nothing.

"Did he ever say anything like that to you?"

Alice was tongue-tied for a few seconds, then said, "Dad liked you just fine ...I mean Dad thought you were a good guy."

Andrew stared at her as if waiting for something.

"Dad was glad I married you ... I mean he was happy about it," she almost stuttered. "Yes, Dad thought you were very clever!" she announced.

Andrew sat back in his chair and Alice could see his shoulders relax, then the muscles in his face settle, and a slight grin form. The envelope temporarily demanded no urgency in the wake of this revelation from Foxy.

When the phone rang on Zach's desk, he picked it up and saw Alice's number flash on the console.

"We found the next clue. Foxy had it and when Andrew said the words, 'you sly clever fox,' he handed an envelope to him," Alice said. "We opened it and it looks worse than all the rest of them. It says, 'Everybody's big brother is Tommy. Uncle Sam and everybody knows Thomas. The secret is at the Secret. Spanish pieces of eight at Davey Jones Locker await … off you go,' and that's it," she said.

"Dad's got some gold and silver somewhere. I hope this thing winds up someday soon," he said. "What's the Davey Jones locker reference? Did he put it back on the bottom of the ocean?"

"We have no idea. Andrew, and me too; we're a little tired. We may come home for a few days while we figure this one out," Alice said.

"Good idea," Zach said. "Call me next week. I'll think about the clue."

Foxy sat down with a spoon and began digging into the fresh mangos he'd just cut up when Tessa walked into the kitchen of their house.

"I'm glad you found those. They are really ripe and I doubt they could last another day," she said. "Did you talk to Alice Dennison today?"

"Yeah, she and her husband stopped by and I bought them lunch. She grew up to be a nice girl. Her husband seems okay too," he said.

"Did they ask you about the treasure hunt clue?"

"Yeah, it took them a couple of hours and a few beers to figure it out, but they did it," he said.

"So, you gave them the clue?"

"Yep, handed it over to the young man," he said.

"Did you tell him anything else?" she said.

"Not really. Well, I did tell the boy that Richard always said he was the clever one in the family," he said.

"Really. Did Richard tell you that?"

"No. Never mentioned it. I just thought from looking at him, he could use a little ego boost."

"Cool. Do you know what this treasure hunt is about?"

"Not really. Richard did say that it was a big one. I guess they'll find out," he said.

50

Cash Jimmy

The Escalade stopped at the black iron gate. No one in the car said a word as both doors slowly opened. Jimmy knew he was still in the city, but didn't recognize the neighborhood. The street was tree-lined and each lot appeared to be a few acres. He presumed the iron fence in front of the house encircled the entire lot. Knowing he was at least going to be roughed up, he hoped it wouldn't be worse than the last one. He tried to pull himself together and be an objective player in this game, but bridling his fear was proving a tough hurdle.

The car pulled up in front of a two-story house with ivy climbing weathered, dark-red brick. The ancient, thick, wooden front door was adorned with gnarled cast-iron fixtures. When the car door opened, Jimmy was escorted into the house and seated in a small library. The ten-minute wait seemed like an hour. He noticed the books were sets of volumes, black and brown with gold leaf. The few titles he could see were Greek and English classics, science, history, philosophy, and mythology. No books were open, in progress or looked freshly read. The desk and chairs looked classic, early-American antique. Jimmy started to calm down and he took a deep breath. He felt sure they had to leave him intact and functional if the boss wanted to get paid back.

A short, stocky man strolled in the room, pulled up a chair and scooted it directly in front of Jimmy. He wore a black mock turtleneck, gray slacks, and soft, black-leather shoes.

"The boss sent me in to refresh your memory about the urgency of seeing some money come his way," the man said.

Jimmy launched into his oration on the progress of the treasure hunt, then to his family real estate holdings, and on he went, each theme talking faster as his voice modulated to a higher pitch. The composure he'd hoped for was MIA. Finally, the man interrupted him.

"We know everything about your family real estate, the payments you get, and we know about this wild goose chase you're on looking for pots of gold and silver," the man said. "You borrowed two million and the tab is up to two and a half million with interest. The boss is patient but he needs progress, visibility and results. Am I coming across to you, Mr. Dennison? Bring us one million by next Friday. We don't care where you get it. Cash, Jimmy!"

The man walked out of the room and down the hall where he was greeted by a tall, young hulk of a man.

"How did it go, Boss?" the hulk asked.

"Okay. Yeah, it went okay."

51

Richard / The Grid

The diary was practically reading itself as Bill Price flipped page after page.

The wind was gusting fifteen to twenty knots, chopping up the surface. Waves crested over the dinghy gunnels, splashing salt water in our eyes. I put on my face mask while Bruce and Jennifer did the same. When we got to the floating marker, Bruce took a small version of a Danforth anchor down to the coral reefs, found a patch of sand, and dug it in. I did the same on the stern, and then Jennifer killed the engine. We started on the south end of the grid with plans to scour the bottom, moving north until we covered the area. Looking for shiny surfaces peeking out of the sand as well as iron artifacts, anything that would give a clue to the location of the wreck. Two hundred and sixty years to nuzzle into the sandy soil or hide under reefs that multiplied and grew, gave the drowned ship and all its parts a leg-up on our simple plan of eyeballing the grid.

Our discussion last night about what would we even do with a lot of gold and silver deteriorated into blurring fantasies and bold pronouncements about saving the planet. We knew that in 1985, all the gold lost in the sea would fund the US Government for a week at best. Jennifer, not-so-calmly, suggested that we not worry about what to do with a treasure we didn't have and were unlikely to ever have.

I was somewhere in the second quadrant of the grid, just as I swam up on a sharp pinnacle of coral almost punching through the water's surface. A small sea-surge catapulted me directly into the sharp reef. It ripped into my thin wetsuit near my right rib cage. I felt the sting of the cut, then looked down to see a slight red patch on the rubber surface. I looked up to see a deep and practically hidden hole, almost a small cavern on the north side of the coral spiral.

The red patch got no larger and the sting subsided, so I gave a sharp kick with both fins and propelled myself into this underwater hideaway. There was nothing to draw my attention, but another kick took me to the sandy floor where I saw a dull-brown piece of metal barely protruding from the sand. My hand grasped the iron remnant and pulled, moving it easily up about six inches before it caught and held tight. I drew a small digging shovel from my tool bag to give the stubborn piece a nudge. The shovel dug in about three inches and I pulled it toward me along with the sand. My eyes squinted involuntarily as a sharp glare passed over them, and while the sand fell away, the reflection of the morning sunlight on a hundred shiny gold coins was almost blinding. I dug a wider and wider patch and more coins continued to reveal their brilliant luster. An odd-looking black mound rested in the corner. It wasn't coral and it didn't appear to be iron. I looked back at the coins, and then swam out of the cavern and to the surface.

Rather than swim to the dinghy and risk losing my location, I signaled to Jennifer, with some frenzied waving and yelling, to bring the boat to me. Bruce had not surfaced, so Jennifer and I re-anchored, and I crawled in the boat and told her about my find. She stood up and started doing the twist and then the jerk and then she almost fell out. We laughed and hugged, and of course, kissed.

Bruce and I filled up small pouches and swam them to the surface, but it was slow and hard work. Jennifer's idea was to use the equipment bag, fill it up with coins and haul it out with one of the anchor lines. We dumped out the gear, and Bruce and I took turns filling up the bags. Bruce surfaced after one of his turns, with a handful of black something. He reached over the gunnel and placed it on the center bench of the dinghy. With the pliers he pulled a piece of the black off the lump, then smiled and said simply, "Silver."

"Spanish pieces of eight," Jennifer said. "The coins are fused together."

"There are hundreds of them in that hole," he said.

The soft floor of the dinghy was weighted down to the max by mid-afternoon, so we headed back to Anegada Harbor. The grid cones were yellow and we decided to leave them in place so as not to pinpoint our mother lode for anybody. Jennifer tied a red bandana to the base of our location for easy reference.

We considered renting a hard-bottom boat, but didn't want to attract attention, so we settled on making multiple trips to the site with our blow-up dinghy. It took three days to strip the sand of its bounty. The gold coins were a chore, but the silver was the biggest obstacle. After hauling one of the fused hunks of silver coins up through the coral and into the dinghy, I trumpeted that we could just leave the silver, because the gold doubloons were overflowing. The response from both Jennifer and Bruce was silence.

She shot a glance at Bruce as he emitted a conciliatory laugh before he quietly said, "There are more silver coins than gold. What the heck, let's get it all."

"We owe it to all the people who created them...and to history," Jennifer chimed in.

A plastic tarp kept the silver blobs from directly touching the rubber bottom, but we still had to be careful not to let the sharp, corroded edges puncture the rubber. We were already pushing the limits of the small craft, and were wary of the bottom rupturing, returning our stash to its watery grave.

We kept the sailboat tied to the mooring ball for the next week as we stacked and counted the gold coins. They were all dated 1749, minted in Central America, during the reign of Ferdinand VI, the youngest son of Phillip V. The dates were mixed on the pieces of eight, but none after 1749. Bruce's book outlined most of the big disasters occurring on the south Florida coast. The story Christine told about the *Soledad* wreck, and the rescue boat wrecking at Anegada, was unfolding in front of our eyes.

We wore through five or six pairs of gloves hammering and chiseling the silver apart, and they had to be cleaned to eliminate the salt-water corrosion. But once liberated, each piece of eight was exquisite in form and workmanship. The book had page after page of detailed facts, but one section informed us that the process of producing coins had evolved to using the screw press. That's the reason the early coins were odd shaped and mostly not round. Our coins were virtually identical.

We tried loading them in a hefty leather valise, but the leather collapsed around the coins from the weight. After filling up the starboard cabin with the treasure, we took a few days off to tool around the island on scooters, drink beer and eat lobsters. We all felt light-headed and giddy ... like it was Christmas morning, under the tree, every day.

52

Slipped It In

Andrew booked two seats to Tortola for next Thursday. He hadn't spent much time thinking about the new clue, but was loosely waiting on some inspiration from Zach. He felt like taking complete charge, to get it done and oh yeah, to get filthy rich too, but thought it was prudent to work with Zach. After all, he still held the purse strings on most of the assets, and their lifestyle to boot.

That afternoon Andrew typed the clue into his computer, printed it out in big letters, and read it over and over. "Everybody's big brother is Tommy." There was no brother named Tommy; there was no Tommy at all in the family. He emailed John Chakkera: "John, sorry to bother you, but I have a quick question. Was there ever anybody that Richard dealt with, in or out of the company, whose name was Tommy? Was there a supplier, or vendor that you might associate with the name Tommy?"

John emailed back from his compound in Bangor, Maine: "Still trying to solve the mystery, I see. But, no. Nothing comes to mind. If something pops up, I'll ping you. All the best, John."

"Uncle Sam and everybody knows Thomas." Tommy, Thomas.... where could this be going? Alice set a small sandwich and a glass of Coke in ice on the desk in front of Andrew. He didn't look up or acknowledge her ... lost in the pursuit of riches. She looked at the clue, read it once and said, "Book a flight to St. Thomas," turned and walked out.

The layover in Dallas was a short hour and a half. As Alice and Andrew waited in line for the nonstop to St. Thomas, her phone rang.

"Alice, it's Jimmy. How are you, dear?"

"Fine, Jimmy. Are you okay?" she said.

"Oh, you know. Just fine. Everything is all happening at once, as usual. I've been really busy and I thought I'd check in on this pesky treasure hunt business," he said.

"Oh yeah, the treasure hunt. Let me see."

"What does he want?" Andrew whispered.

Alice crimped her face at Andrew, and he knew what that meant. Be quiet.

"I mean it's no big deal, but I'm just circling back around," Jimmy said. "Dad wins the prize for being the biggest jokester on the planet. But really, we should try to clean this up and move on with our lives. Don't you think? I mean like let's have a frank talk with Bill Price, or your mom. Jennifer's got to be able to help us. I'm sure she'd like this whole business to be wrapped up," Jimmy continued.

"Right, Jimmy. What kind of plan are you thinking about? Mom has not said a word and I don't have any reason to think she knows something. She just says that Dad was a big puzzle guy, and he did it all his life. She said even though he drove everybody crazy with pranks and mysteries, at the end of the day most people got a kick out of it," Alice said.

"Come on, Alice. The only kick we're getting is a kick in the pants. I'd call your mom, but I think it's better if you do it," Jimmy said. "Anyway, we're stuck on this ridiculous Gordy's hat, and something about graves thing. This is a not what adults need to be spending time on."

Alice wondered facetiously if Jimmy was taking time away from his usual adult pursuits like creating world peace, or deflecting colliding asteroids from annihilating us.

"We've got to board a plane right now, so let me think about it," she said. "So, I'll talk to you later."

She pulled the phone away from her ear, and as she was punching the "end call" button she heard, "Where are you go…?" Click.

Alice settled into her seat, and fitted the seat belt around her waist when the phone rang again.

She handed the phone to Andrew. "You take this one, it's Maureen."

"Hi Maureen. Alice can't talk right now. What's up?"

"Nothing. Jimmy called me this morning fishing around about the clues and stuff. He's trying to not sound in a hurry, but I can tell he's hyped up," Maureen said. "He's my brother and I can tell."

"Did he have anything constructive to say?" Andrew said.

"Not really. But, I'm leaning his way on this stupid game."

"Have you been working on the clues, or anything like that?" Andrew asked.

"It's one drama event after the other with these kids, and Randy is working like mad on new deals. Some of the East Coast investors are like space aliens here in Silicon Valley. No clue how things are done. Some of them want balance sheets that make sense, and get this, they wear dark suits, and ties to meetings. Some people think they're the waiters. Anyway, have you guys found out anything, yet?" Maureen said.

"Oh, not much," he said. "Tell you what, I'll have Alice call you later."

"I'm having lunch brought in, Mom," Zach said. "I'm not up for the crowds today. Soup and half a chicken salad on toast."

"Perfect. How are you, dear?" Jennifer said.

"I'm happy that we sold those two buildings that kept draining our time, and really were performing subpar. Cash flow will be better on the new acquisitions," he said. "So, Alice has been solving some of these clues Dad left."

"Really? Alice is stepping into this?" she asked.

"Yes, but Andrew is working it pretty hard. They have it down to things like, everybody knows Thomas, and a secret of some kind, and Davey Jones Locker," he said. "It's all too obscure."

"Oh gosh, years ago we loved staying at this little isolated place on St. Thomas. Something about secret garden, or … secret harbor … Secret Harbour Beach Resort! That's it. Don't even know if it's still there," she said.

"You've got me. No idea," Zach said.

"Dad liked to fish back then. He got the bug on that trip to Tahiti. Can't remember what they called that funky old boat at the Secret Harbour Resort. Oh well, it probably sunk by now," Jennifer said.

After lunch Jennifer slid into the front seat of her black, two-door BMW coupe, with a cool, moist breeze off the bay blowing her hair. She could hardly fight the urge to laugh out loud. Looking through the windshield past the parking lot onto the blustery bay, she saw Richard's face in her mind's eye.

"Well, I can have a little fun with this, too," she said. "I know I wasn't supposed to help. But it was fun! I just slipped in the Secret Harbour tip; I didn't say the Davey Jones Locker part. I know I said the boat, but I didn't say the name." She paused and giggled a little. "I might help with the last one. It depends on how they're doing. I know, I know. This whole thing was your idea. Who else would do this to children?"

53

Frenchtown Deli

Alice and Andrew arrived at Point Pleasant Resort Hotel around six in the afternoon just in time for cocktails. The valet took charge of the rental car and after checking in, they skipped their room's ocean-view patio, and headed to the pool. The sun set over their shoulders, throwing the last rays of the day on Charlotte Amalie Bay. Alice had an intuition that the references to Tommy, Thomas, and Uncle Sam pointed to St. Thomas, but beyond that, she couldn't figure a thing out.

"Okay, we're here," Andrew said after ordering another rum runner. "Should we look in the phone book for Davey Jones, or under businesses for lockers?"

"Very funny. I don't know what to do next. Let's walk around Charlotte Amalie tomorrow and see if anything strikes us," Alice said.

"I'm beginning to think there is no needle in this haystack. Would your dad give us a dead-end clue, just leave everybody stranded?" Andrew asked.

"No, he wouldn't, and you shouldn't think that way. All Dad's puzzles were solved by somebody at some point," she said.

"All of them?"

"Well, almost all of them. Anyway, there will be a solution, and we will find whatever is waiting for us," Alice said.

"I'm checking later at the front desk to see if a cruise ship is landing tomorrow. That's a zoo. Thirty thousand of them stream off into these shops. They're frantic like they've never seen a shop with junky curios in it before," Andrew said.

"They're not all junk, Andrew. I happen to like the jewelry stores."

"You like jewelry. Well, that's a big surprise," he said with a snarky tone.

She tried glaring at him, but he looked away, and settled for a big huff.

The room service waiter knocked on the door around nine the next morning. Yogurt and fruit for Alice, and scrambled eggs and wheat toast for the chief inspector, Andrew, all washed down with coffee.

"Okay, where do you want to start looking for the needle in this haystack?" Andrew said.

"Let's head toward the cruise ship docks, then in to old town and the shopping area. I just want to land at the Frenchtown Deli for lunch. It reminds me of Dad." Alice paused. "Maybe something will pop up for us."

A Holland America ship carrying fifteen-thousand people left port headed for Puerto Rico last night and the next floating city was not due until tomorrow morning, so the strolling was civilized. They wandered into Captain's Corner Sundries a half a block from the marina. There were salespeople everywhere, mostly moving inventory around, staying busy, preparing for the throngs of trinket-starved tourists arriving fresh off the boat tomorrow. Alice perused the shelves while Andrew rifled through the small rack of island CDs for sale. The time was whiling away, but to Andrew the treasure was slip-sliding away, minute by minute. Through the front door onto the sidewalk, they escaped without trinkets or even CDs in hand. Back on the street, they took a left and headed to the serious shops, to fine jewelry, fine watches, oh yes, they'd been there before.

"Hey Andrew, let's talk about this treasure hunt," Alice said as they crossed at the light on Main Street. The roads became narrower, the buildings quainter, and the biggest smiles on the island greeted you if you stumbled into a high-end shop.

"Or the lack thereof," Andrew replied.

"That's what I'm talking about. Can you lighten up?" she said.

"About a possible fortune that's slipping out of our fingers."

"You didn't grow up solving puzzles. There were little ones and big ones all the time. Jimmy solved half of them, and I don't know, I guess Zach and I figured a few out," she said. "In fact, I'm surprised Jimmy hasn't made headway on this by now. Anyway, they don't get solved by worrying or giving up when you're stumped. And you can't unravel them becoming your own island in the ocean, isolated and greedy. You have to interact and network."

Andrew had no response as they hoofed it by the shops walking toward Frenchtown. Alice stopped in front of Fort Christian.

"It's the oldest building here, built in the early 1600s," she said.

"I guess you always need a fort around to protect your stuff," he said in a deadpan voice.

"It's a museum now. But anyway, we are going to find this thing, but we need to get clear on how to handle it when we do," Alice said.

"If you're talking about sharing it with your indigent and poverty-stricken family, no way! Jimmy's not finding anything … emotionally and socially disabled. Maureen is harmless, but come on, they aren't even interested."

"Andrew, take a deep breath. As kids we learned things about ourselves with these puzzles that can't be taught. Dad used to say, 'I can bring you face-to-face with the truth, but only you can grasp it … nobody can insert it into your heart.'"

Andrew shrugged, turned his head, and gazed across the street.

"Oh, please," he said.

"Bottom line, I want us to agree that we'll share what we find four ways," she said.

"What about Zach? Is he on board for splitting?"

"I think so. That's the way he wants it. All I have to do is say it, and he'll agree," she said.

"At this point there's nothing to share, so okay, I'll agree. But if Jimmy comes around and stirs the pot, I get to reconsider," he said. "Wait a minute. The agreement needs to include that we don't tell Jimmy about the clues, and where we are in this. That's a sure-fire recipe for stirring the pot. Agreed?"

"Yes. I agree totally. But we share it in the end, right?"

"Done deal. You tell Zach, and make sure he's on board," he said. "But I still don't like it."

Alice shot him a stern glance.

He rolled his head and looked out in space, then said, "Okay, okay. It's agreed."

The clock turned one o'clock as they were seated at the Frenchtown Deli. The sense of hopelessness and despair that Andrew was wearing all over his body didn't dampen his appetite. Alice picked at a salad.

"Let's get a taxi over to Red Hook after lunch," Alice said. "Dad liked it over there, and one time a clue was nailed to the back of the entrance sign. It's worth a look."

The late model Toyota Camry pulled away from the curb for the short ride to Red Hook Bay when Alice's phone rang.

"Hi Zach. Well, we came down yesterday. No, St. Thomas. That last clue had Tommy and Thomas all over it. No real plan at this point, just looking around. I thought we'd look around Red Hook. No, I'll wager it's not behind that sign again," she said.

"Look, I have an idea. You know that 'secret' thing in the clue? It's in there twice, and in one reference the word is capitalized," Zach said. "There's a Secret Harbour Hotel just around the tip of the island from Red Hook. I think that's the place to look."

"Okay, we can head there now," Alice replied.

"Look for anything about Davey Jones Locker, or just Davey Jones, or at the bottom of the sea kind of reference," he said. "I know it seems hard, but I think that one puzzle, when I was a junior in high school, was harder. Remember there were forty gold doubloons, and twelve pieces of eight in that box buried on the trail to the Robb White House on Marina Cay? You and I found it after looking all summer, and we gave Jimmy and Maureen half. Dad really liked that we split it."

"Oh, by-the-way, Zach, Andrew and I agree that whatever we find should be split. The usual four ways," she said.

"Yeah. I'm in on that," he said. "I got to hop. Let me know what you find out."

"Zach. We don't think Jimmy needs to be in the mix right now," she said. "You know, disruptive and anxious all the time."

"I agree. See you later."

54

Richard / Dirt Mausoleum

Bill Price resumed reading the diary.

Random coins were scattered around the sand and coral when we left the site, but the bulk of the find was in our chartered sailboat. We agreed to keep it quiet while deciding what to do with this king's fortune. Sitting in Anegada Harbor, Bruce decided to rent a house on Tortola to stash the coins and hang out for the time being. He picked a small house close to the water on Cane Garden Bay. There wasn't much traffic there, so we could load up a pickup truck in the evening and have a good chance of not being detected.

Jennifer and I flew back to Silicon Valley after the transfer was finished. I needed to check in with John Chakkera, and try to follow up on Samantha. One afternoon sitting in my cubicle at the office, I got a call that Marina Cay was for sale. No explanation was given why somebody wanted to sell it or why dumping the whole island was a smart idea. But the notion intrigued me. I thought about getting Bruce in on the purchase, but after some contemplation, made an offer on my own. It was well below the asking price, but I was questioning why I needed an island anyway, so I left it to the gods.

My boat was hanging on a mooring ball months later in the BVI, when a dinghy pulled up and handed me the closing papers for the island. A cold chill trickled down my back as the reality hit me ... *I own an island.* I set up a dummy corporation to own it, with Jennifer as backup owner if something ever happened to me. For the record, she was not excited about the whole island thing, but she humored me. I needed a lot of humoring, as she found out over the years.

Bruce's boat was back from Tahiti and the lease at Cane Garden Bay was almost over. Covering most of the island, looking for hiding places took a few months. Robb White had constructed his house at the top of the hill with a dugout basement for a refrigerator. It was dark and cold and the soil was hard and dry, but not much rock, so we hired a couple of world-wanderers from Australia who were floating through the islands, to dig an eight-foot-deep hole. A bar, a pick, and a shovel was all it took. Bruce wanted to pay them in gold coins, but I nixed that risky idea.

We moved the coins to his boat at night and then one at a time, put each box in a wood crate used for lettuce and pulled them to the top on a hand truck in the middle of the morning. Nobody cared about lettuce, so, nobody noticed. The boxes fit snuggly resting four feet down, and virtually disappeared as the shovel patted the loose dirt, level with the ground.

We each had taken a pile of coins out for amusement. Gold was $300 an ounce, making each doubloon worth about $600. The pieces of eight were worth less, as they were used like we use nickels, dimes, and quarters. Silver at $12 an ounce made a piece of eight worth about $2. My first idea was to give away mine as novelties to friends, but Jennifer pointed out the risk in that. They are too unusual and will invite questions that you don't want to answer, she'd say.

The children liked to present plays and skits in that basement, and sometimes Maureen and Alice played dress-up. All of that activity trampled down the dirt, and for all intents and purposes the coins vanished. When silver went to $30 an ounce and gold to $1000, our stash tripled in value. After liberating it from two hundred and sixty years of a salt-water grave, it sat humbled and undisturbed in a cold dirt mausoleum. No wine, song, women, or praise. Oh well!

55

Secret Harbour

The taxi dropped them off at the stone path leading to the guest check-in and the Blue Moon Café. Alice and Andrew were slow-moving, ambling down the path, one stone at a time. Andrew looked like Columbo studying every inch of the scene while mumbling to himself. Alice tried not to look conspicuous, eyeing eaves, gutters, and walls. In the restaurant she turned over one chair to investigate the bottom of it, and yes, she glanced under the table while she was at it. A waitress very respectfully asked her if she could help with anything. Alice was quick on the draw and said her dad dropped a family heirloom when last here, and if it was okay she was just poking around in hopes of locating it. When a customer caught the eye of the waitress, she went running, and Alice dodged the bullet of needing to explain what she was looking for.

Out back Andrew found the refrigeration units, the storage facilities, all the while looking for some reference to lockers. He had no expectation that a Davey Jones clue would present itself. That would be too easy. The beach had guests spread out on the sand, but no umbrella stands, and no elaborate lifeguard station; Alice strolled down there anyway. One thing her experience taught her was that you never know when or where the clue will pop up.

Andrew ran out of nooks and crannies to check out, so he stopped under a palm tree in the sand, and just looked around. A 360 turn gave him no hints, and no Alice in sight. He noticed a small pier with a few various size boats, and a turquoise-colored metal hut. Feeling unenthusiastic like the wind was knocked out of his sails, he walked slowly down the stone path. A boat was loading up with snorkelers for the afternoon trip. There were only three or four passengers that afternoon, who were sorting through the fins, masks, and snorkels. Andrew kept a little distance, but slowly moved toward the pier. The skipper freed the bow and stern lines, cranked up the diesel engine, and slowly steered out of the slip. By this time, Andrew was standing on the pier looking over the trip list for tomorrow. When he glanced out at the boat, it had just turned north, and the low western sun illuminated the port side of the hull. Andrew took a double take, blinked and looked again. The name of the boat put Andrew's body into a deep freeze. He turned his head and looked sideways, back to the other side, and looked again. From every angle, the name was the same: *Davey Jones Locker.*

"I bought snorkeling tickets for nine in the morning. I said you were a little skittish and may not snorkel, but you may try it if you get comfortable with things," Andrew said. "That'll give you a chance to look around the boat for the clue."

"You sound sure that it's there," Alice said.

"We found where it is. I'm totally sure. We just need to uncover it."

The muggy air from yesterday afternoon was hiding beneath a gentle Caribbean breeze at eight thirty in the morning as the treasure hunters walked up to the turquoise hut. The stern or rear of the boat was backed up to the dock for an easy step onto its deck. Trying to appear nonchalant and uninterested, they inched toward the boat, both scanning the exterior for tips that might lead to the clue. Alice wore a pair of yellow shorts and a light blue T-shirt over her swimsuit. Andrew's suit fell to just above his knees, his beige shirt straddling his waist.

"Nice and early. Just what we like our guests to do. Got coffee and donuts in the hut. Paper cups will have to do," the man said.

"Hi, I'm Andrew."

"Yes, and this is Alice, I'm sure. I'm Bob, and I own this little operation. I'm so glad to have you with us today," Bob said. "Have you snorkeled the reefs before?"

"As a kid I dove on a lot of the places here, the Indians, the caves on Norman Island, the wreck of the Rhone, but it's been a long time since those trips," Alice said.

"We've got a group of five joining us. They're all from Pennsylvania and staying here at the hotel. You'll get a kick out of seeing the Indians and the caves again. The ocean surge is slack right now, so it's the best time for the Indians," Bob said. "We'll start out at the caves."

"The Indians are more in open water, right?" Andrew asked.

"Yep, Norman blocks the currents from the south; that little rock, Pelican Island, blocks it some, but the eastern swells can bear down on them," Bob said.

Andrew let that sink in for half a minute, then asked, "Have you had this business for a while?"

Bob was looking out to the waterway and took a slow few seconds to turn back and respond.

"About fifteen years. Yep, fifteen years."

The other guests arrived in a group, and began choosing the equipment from a black Rubbermaid bin. Alice picked out a snorkel, mask, and fins, but was planning on feigning a nauseated stomach and stay on the boat. The boat pulled out of the dock around nine fifteen into flat water and motored past St. John and into the Sir Francis Drake Channel. After half an hour, Captain Bob pulled up to a permanent mooring ball and hooked on. Alice stayed in the corner and deferred to the others as they donned their masks and fins and listened to the safety rules that Bob delivered in an entertaining and funny expose. She finally suited up and joined the group in the large swim-in cave on the left, and then followed the group to a long, narrow passage. A few guests pulled themselves out of the water at the end of the cave, and crawled through the narrow passage leading to the open beach.

After a while they loaded back into the boat, heading for the next spot. Alice stared at the jagged rocks that formed the Indians as they approached. No place to land a boat on that, and besides the wind and chop made it impossible to tie up there. The others rushed around to prepare for the water, but Alice sat quietly to the side as Bob snagged a mooring ball.

"Are you feeling okay?" Bob asked Alice.

"A little queasy is all. Think I'll sit it out for a while," Alice said.

She felt like it was now or never to look for the clue. Not wanting to appear odd, she tried to think up something to chat about with Bob. She wondered if there was any connection Bob had with her dad, so she started there.

"How long have you had this boat?"

"I replaced the old one about a year after I bought the business," he replied.

"Interesting name. How did that come about?" she asked.

"Just took it from the old boat. Not too creative," he said.

A few minutes passed, when Alice stood up and stepped into the cockpit of the boat. It brought her out of the sun, and into the partially covered interior of the vessel. She studied each board and crevice, noticing each drawer and cabinet door. She ran her fingers over wood surfaces, feeling for anything unusual or suspicious. Bob was standing at the back of the boat watching the six swimmers, faces planted down, and fins slowly paddling around the reefs. He knew they'd be hovering over the "brain coral" as well as the multitude of colorful, tropical fish, but he liked to keep an eye on them.

He watched Alice out of the corner of his eye, and after a few minutes spoke up.

"So. You spent time down here with your parents, a while ago?"

Alice, lost in thought, driveled out, "Yeah. They loved it down here, especially my dad."

"Okay then. What was your dad's name?"

"Richard. Richard Dennison," she replied.

Bob turned his head and looked back at the swimming crew, took a couple of deep breaths, and looked across the channel at Tortola, tilted his head left and zeroed in on the forested coastline of St. John. The boat rocked from side to side as a maverick wave rolled through the water from the channel. He turned toward Alice.

"I think I heard around that your dad died a few months ago. Any truth to that?" he asked.

"Yes, he did."

"I'm sorry to hear it. I met him a few times and liked him. He was some character," Bob said. "Are you guys on vacation down here?"

"In a way. Dad left us some challenges, and we're just running down a few things."

Bob walked into the cockpit and stood next to Alice.

"Dear, you might be interested in the slat closest to the countertop. There. The one right there," he said.

Alice looked down, saw the board, but couldn't see anything different about it. She pushed it, and felt a slight wobble. She thumped it, and then rapped on the one above it. The sound was the same, no hollow noise. She looked at the edge for any signs of wear; she could not glean any inkling or trace of tampering.

"There's a screwdriver in the drawer," Bob said.

Alice looked at him and a strange feeling came over her. *He's leading me in a direction that is not obvious or logical, yet he's insistent*, she thought. She lifted the screwdriver from the drawer, stopped, and looked up, and stared directly into Bob's eyes. He returned her stare, but said nothing for a few seconds.

"I knew your dad very well. He helped me buy this business," he said.

Alice's mind blew up with thoughts. *What is going on, does everybody know something we don't know, are we being played, is this whole thing a joke, was Dad for real, is Mom in on this?* Finally, she put the screwdriver between the cracks in the slats, and carefully pried the lower board away from the wall. She could see something behind it, but couldn't make out an image. With the screwdriver holding the wood open, she grabbed the edge with her right hand, and pulled until she could see a small metal tube. Letting the screwdriver fall to the counter, she reached behind the board and pulled out the tube. It was nondescript aluminum about one-inch diameter with a threaded screw top. She looked up at Bob, and back down to the tube.

"The swimmers are coming back in; put it in your pocket and take it back to shore," he said. "This should put you on your way, I hope. Good luck."

During the half-hour trip back to Secret Harbour, Andrew sat next to Alice and made small talk about the coral and the fish, then he quietly asked under his breath, "Any luck?"

"Got it," was all she said.

56

Come Back After Three

On Wednesday, Jimmy showed up unannounced at Zach's office. He wore his best toothy signature smile, and looked composed. He sat in front of Zach's desk facing him.

"Well brother, what's new in the real estate business?" Without waiting for an answer, he said, "I've lost interest in Dad's treasure hunt. It's just too silly, and I have more important things to do."

Zach looked at Jimmy, saying nothing, but thinking that any important thing Jimmy had to do could surely be taken care of sometime between next week and never, most likely the latter. Zach sat, attentive, but silent.

"I've got an investment project with some permit deadlines, and vendor obligations, so I am going to need an advance on my normal trust payments," he said. "No big deal, but I'm sure it won't be a problem."

Zach had fielded these lobs from Maureen occasionally, but from Jimmy it was a regular occurrence. Before their dad died Zach would consult him about Jimmy's requests, and follow through on his decisions—that is up until a few years ago, when Richard would defer to Zach. He empowered Zach to feel confident about running the business, but also about managing the family. Jennifer was a good sounding board, but the buck stopped with Zach.

"I just need a million … shouldn't be a problem, right?" Jimmy said in a dismissive, detached voice.

Zach sat. No expectations for Jimmy was the right approach always. He never let himself think, "he'd heard it all." Always something new.

"We don't have a million dollars lying around. Sorry. What else can I do for you?" Zach said.

For the next half hour, Jimmy cajoled, whined, begged, insisted, and pleaded.

"I can maybe do half a million, but this is the last time. It's going to cost you interest, and you won't get payments till this loan is paid back. Are you clear on this?"

"But I need …"

Zach cut Jimmy off. "Half is all there is."

"I need it today," Jimmy said.

"Of course, you do. Come back after three this afternoon."

Jimmy arrived at the boss's home in Boston two days later. The gate swung open, and he followed the long circular driveway to the front of the house. The door opened as he climbed the steps, and he was ushered into the library. After twenty minutes the same, familiar man walked into the room. He wore the familiar gray slacks, and a black turtleneck. He looked relaxed and confident, and smiled.

"What have you got for me?" The man asked.

"We're all set. I have the money for you," Jimmy said.

"Good. Do you want to show it to me?" the man said.

"Of course, but I'll need a receipt. I typed one out to make it easier for you. Hope that's all right?"

"We'll see. Where is the money?"

Jimmy lifted his briefcase onto the desk, inserted a key, and opened it to show a full case of cash.

The man smiled and said, "Good job. Now let me see that paper you have."

He looked up after scanning the page. "What's this about half a million?"

Jimmy answered in a cool, confident voice, "No problem. I'll get the rest to you next week."

The man didn't seem to react, and after a minute, walked out of the room. Ten minutes later the hulk joined Jimmy in the library.

"The boss has invited you to be our guest for the evening," he said.

"That's very nice, but I can't possibly do that today," Jimmy said.

The man wrapped his arm around Jimmy's and walked him out of the room, up a flight of stairs, and into a suite of rooms.

"Make yourself comfortable, Mr. Dennison," the hulk said as he left.

As the door shut, Jimmy stepped forward and turned the knob, but it didn't move. He looked around for another door, and then he knew, things were going to deteriorate from there.

57

Davey Jones Locker

Andrew put the unopened cylinder on the side table in their room. He wanted to be calm and alert when he saw the clue for the first time. Alice sat at the table as Andrew slowly unscrewed the top. His fingers reached in and pulled out a rolled-up piece of parchment. Slowly unrolling the paper, he and Alice saw the clue at the same time. "*The red roofs show off well on this postage stamp that caps the reef. But when the curtain goes up and the jester gives a sign, look down humbly, and the treasure you'll find.*"

They both re-read the text, and Andrew began parsing the words, trying to see if the sound, the feel, or a mental image might jar a memory or signal a direction for the hunt, but nothing jumped out to point a direction. He read it out loud once, then two more times, but stayed silent between the readings. He hoped the spoken words would jar a memory from Alice, the rhythm, the juxtaposition of the words, something, anything. But Alice did not say a thing, while staring out the front window.

She turned to Andrew and said, "I'm going to make a cup of tea. Want one?"

Andrew sat back in his chair. The one thing he gleaned from this clue was that this might be the final one, the one that led to the "treasure," as the clue said. He took a deep breath and tried to let the excitement and trepidation run down his spine, and into the floor … staying calm and focused. He told himself, "the home stretch," just stay with it, sit with the clue. The answer will come.

Andrew thought about calling Zach. Yes, he might help, might conjure up an image or a recollection. But, did they really need him? Could he and Alice answer the questions, and find the treasure by themselves? This business of sharing with the siblings, those disinterested, deadbeat losers. Maybe leave Zach out of it for now. *Well, he has helped out; maybe we'll cut him in, let's wait and see,* Andrew thought.

"Yes, tea sounds good," he replied.

Alice placed a cup of steaming tea on the table beside Andrew. She quietly sat down, and swiveled her chair around to look out over the ocean, and the passageway between Jost and Tortola. The parchment lay flat in her lap, and between sips, she re-read it, slowly. Without anticipation or contemplation, she picked up her mobile phone and punched in a number.

"Are you sitting down?" she said.

Andrew's head jerked around when he heard her. What was she doing? he thought.

"We found the clue. It was on a snorkeling boat docked at Secret Harbour Resort. Well, listen to this. Dad knew the owner, a guy named Bob. It's like he was expecting us. He pointed me to a panel on the boat. Well, really, he just told me where the clue was," she said.

Alice read the clue to Zach over the phone a couple of times so he could write it down. Andrew looked away from Alice so he could pout unnoticed. *Okay, so I'm not calling all the shots,* he thought. Even so, he figured he'd probably be the first one to the treasure. He'd keep his focus and be ready to take any opportunities that arose.

Alice put the phone on the side table. "He'll be down here tomorrow," she said. "He sounds more interested, maybe even worked up over it. Who knows, it's just a feeling."

As Zach walked off the small prop plane at Beef Island Airport in Tortola, a text came through. He read it and grabbed the handrail to steady himself. Their office complex near Sacramento was losing its core tenant. They were moving to Austin, Texas to save huge money on taxes and business fees. "NO looking back, they're gone," the text read.

Zach made it down the outdoor stairs to the tarmac, and in a daze followed the others into the small one-story terminal. He walked with his small bag across the packed-sand road to the ferry dock and poured himself onto the shuttle to Marina Cay. Checking into the inn, he made no mention of his favorite room, and instead proceeded to the assigned bungalow. He dropped his bag on the floor, turned around and walked out the door, headed to Pusser's restaurant. As the trail crested the hill and began its descent to the water, he saw the bright-red roof of the restaurant of the famed sailor's hangout. Zach had been let in on the secret that Jennifer was in some sort of ownership position of the island, but the details were still unclear to him. He went straight to the bar and ordered a Rum Painkiller.

The sun set and the night was settling in, as Zach still sat nursing another glass of rum when Alice and Andrew walked in. They sat down after a quick greeting, then Alice shoved the parchment in front of Zach. Andrew sat, still sulking, but felt a glimmer of hope that the actual clue might trigger a recollection from Zach. Alice picked up their drinks and walked over to a four-top table with an open-air view of Trellis Bay, and the guys followed.

"Every roof on this island is red," Zach said.

"But almost every roof in Road Town is red," Andrew replied. "So where does that leave us?"

"It leaves us on Marina Cay, and this place has a big reef all around it," Zach said. "And, Marina Cay is a postage stamp."

"It could be anywhere, I know," Alice said. "But, just maybe it's here. What do we do?" she said, looking to her big brother for encouragement.

"The other clues were in public places," Zach said. "I think it could be right here at Pusser's."

"Let's get started," Andrew said.

"In the morning," Zach said.

Later that night Zach called his mom.

"We want to search around Pusser's on this treasure hunt. Can you grease any skids for us, just make it easier to look around?" Zach asked her.

She didn't say a word for a full minute, then said, "Ask for Zephyr in the morning. She'll help you out."

"Who is she?"

"She's the manager. She'll help with whatever you need."

"Mom, the businesses are going to go through a rough time in the next year. If you can help out with this clue thing, it might help us bridge the gap," he said.

"Good luck, dear."

58

Richard / Cutting Edge of the Future

Bill Price picked up the diary. He was hooked on it by now.

I wore a long-sleeve button-down shirt, and get this, I wore regular shoes and even socks, as I strolled through the hall at Intermediate Micro for my meeting with John Chakkera. It was ten in the morning, so the engineers were just rolling in. Half of this talent pool wore flip-flops and shorts, while a bunch of them donned ragged Dockers, or holey jeans, but every single one of them looked like they'd slept in those clothes for a week.

John stood up from behind his desk, and invited me into his cubicle. He asked about my travels, with a few random sailing questions before launching into the day's agenda.

"Richard, this is all about the Information Age. The only product is information. All the rest is tangential, secondary, and derivative. We have the opportunity to move this company to the cutting edge of the future," he said.

"Okay, I get that," I said.

But really, gold, silver, rum, and sailing were stuck in my head, and the cold reality of products, customers, and this future that everybody was ruminating about was finding it difficult to penetrate the fog.

"Computing power will double thirty times in the next two decades, and I need you on board, Richard," he said.

"What do you want me to do?"

"We are ten times better at information processing than anybody in town, and our R&D guys are at the cutting edge, but there's one big problem. These guys are intuitive geniuses, with no communications skills. They know what to do but can't describe it to anybody. You, my friend, know these guys. You know where they live inside those genius, bizarre minds, but you know how to translate that to manufacturing guys, marketing, and customers. I need you to work with us, but more to the point, the future demands it!" he said.

I limped to my cubicle after John made his case. The legal pad from months ago lay on the desk just the way I left it. A sweater-vest hung across the back of my desk chair, undisturbed, and a paper cup sat to the right of the phone holding only a brown stain in the bottom, dregs of long-ago, dried coffee. Logging on to the company network, I perused the financial numbers and sales figures, while simultaneously watching the flow of bodies in the hallway. The numbers corroborated John's assessments, and the people watching reminded me of the focus and dedication these people had to the company, clearly a reflection of John's leadership.

I agreed to get onboard three days a week, and I set up meetings with marketing and engineering. The new title of Vice President of Strategic Planning tacitly implied regular shoes, and a button-down shirt. Over the next year the stock climbed thirty percent. My holdings eclipsed $100 million.

My first land purchase was a failing winery in the Santa Cruz mountains, that small range that lies between Silicon Valley and the Pacific Ocean. I'm fairly sure that every mega-rich tech dude turns a blind eye to reason, and buys a winery. After I got that out of my system, I bought a light industrial building in Fremont, followed by two apartment buildings in Sunnyvale. Each one had negative cash flow, so they lost money for a couple of years, but after that, higher rents and appreciation were the name of the game.

59

Zephyr

As the sun was breaking over the eastern horizon, Zach placed his flashlight in his jacket front pocket. The grounds in back of Pusser's were an extension of the sand beach, so he scraped his foot over the surfaces, kicking and prodding just to see what might pop up. The phrase, "when the curtain goes up and the jester gives a sign," kept rolling through his mind. Looking for a curtain or something that could be construed as a curtain, an awning, something. The jester could be a joke, a pun, a funny twist of a phrase, something funny, unusual, anything that might have a flavor of Dad's quirky sense of humor. Nothing was all Zach had discovered, so before the staff began arriving, he trounced back to his room, and made a cup of coffee. The restaurant opened for breakfast at nine, so he planned to walk back around seven thirty to meet up with Zephyr.

As the sun rose, and a gentle eastern breeze began to bathe the coastline, Andrew gave a terse rap on the open door as he walked into Zach's room.

Without a greeting Andrew launched, "You got a plan?"

Zach's deadpan expression gave away no emotion. "Thought we'd cover every inch of the Pusser's site. It's got to be there," he said.

"Can we get away with snooping like that?" Andrew asked.

Zach kept the "Zephyr card" close to his chest, "Let me see what I can do."

Zach found out that Zephyr was in Road Town doing the banking and not expected till around eleven. He walked in the back of the building, looked in every door, nook and cranny on his way to the table where Alice and Andrew sipped coffee.

"There's a curtain in front of a dry-goods storage closet in the back. We need to search that room for anything jester-like, or funny, you know, Dad-kinda funny," he said.

"Hi Jennifer. It's Zephyr. Well, they're crawling over every square inch of this place, like you said they would. But, Zach wants to tear the walls off this little dry-goods storage closet, and may want to pull up the floorboards. It's going to be a mess, and I can't guarantee that the structure is all that solid. It could need major work to put it back together," she said.

"I hear that," Jennifer said. "Let them do it. It won't take too long. I'll cover it all. Oh, and by the way, bill me for your consulting services, make it five thousand dollars. I don't want you to feel put out."

"Okay, will do. What are they looking for?" Zephyr asked.

"Oh…. It's just a game. They'll be out of your way in a little while."

"Zach thinks that cartoon pinned to the wall in that closet is a jest, and this is the kind of clue Dad would leave. He got the manager to let us strip the walls and floorboards," Alice said.

"There's probably room for a bunch of coins down there. When do we start?" Andrew said.

"Zach is in Road Town buying a crowbar and a big hammer. We'll start when he gets back."

Andrew went for a walk while Alice relaxed on the deck outside of their room. He followed the trail up past the Robb White House and descended to the water's edge. Walking along the beach, he proceeded cautiously to the restaurant. His left hand held a five-foot-long broken-off piece of rebar that he saw sticking out of the sand near the trail. When he entered the dry-goods closet, one waitress flew by him, but made no notice. Pulling the loose curtain as snug as this old fabric would go, he found a wobbly board on the wall, stuck the rebar between the slats and began prying it loose. When he could get a handhold, he took the board and yanked. It pulled away with ease, and he looked in the dark hole, using the rebar to poke around. Nothing was behind that piece but muggy, moist air.... no insulation, no wiring. The surrounding boards pulled off with ease, a few bending and crumpling in his hands. He could see better into this mini-abyss as more light from the naked bulb overhead found the stripped studs. The empty walls, though a possible hiding place, seemed too small for the kind of treasure he was expecting. Three more walls remained, but he was now looking down at the floorboards as the more likely treasure trove. Getting to the floor necessitated moving bins, and stacked boxes out to the narrow hallway or all the way outside. He deferred that task, and stripped one more wall with the same empty-air outcome.

Taking a break, he slid through the narrow hall to the restaurant bar. A beer sounded like it would hit the spot, but duty called and he settled for a club soda. Taking the drink, he settled onto a chaise lounge on the beach. The sun was low in the western sky when Alice walked up and sat in the sand next to him. Andrew thought he was hiding his gluttonous ambition to find the treasure first, but Alice saw it written all over him.

So, when he told her he hadn't waited for Zach to return, she said nothing. Deciding to go with the flow, she had no illusions that he could find it first, or would be able to move it by himself, if he did. It was going to be split; she had decided. But all-in-all, Alice was astounded with the change in Andrew. Ever since college, he was easy-going, laidback, with modest ambitions. He cared about environmental and social issues, and even wrote poems that he hoped would encourage other people to spend their own money on his interests. Greed was a new look for him. She was not a fan of the change.

"Look, we agreed to split this up, but if it's small, not that many coins, which could happen, I think we need to adjust the split," Andrew said. "Sure, give them a cut, but we should get a bigger cut. Zach too. I mean a bigger cut for him, but the others, we just peel off some for the record."

Alice stared out over the bay.

"Come on, Alice, that's only fair."

Well, maybe he has a point, she thought. We've done all the work. Maureen will be happy with whatever we give her, and Jimmy? He'll just squander it.

"What kind of split are you thinking about?" she asked.

60

Fast Boat to Cuba

Jimmy cut through the red, lean meat and separated it from grizzly fat on the sirloin. The red wine perfectly matched the flavor of the steak and had to be a very old cabernet. Sautéed green beans in wine sauce with sliced almonds, and caprice salad rounded out the dinner on Jimmy's second night of captivity.

"Look here, I can't arrange for the rest of the money while locked in here," he told the hulk when he delivered the evening meal. He'd told him the same thing at breakfast and lunch. The hulk gave a slight smile, more like a smirk, then left. Jimmy sat more tired than upset. The frustration had drained away sometime between breakfast and lunch, and was replaced by impatience and boredom.

Around ten o'clock the deadbolt clicked and the short man walked in by himself. He walked silently to the dining table, pulled a chair out and motioned for Jimmy to sit across from him.

"Why did you show up here with your hands half full? The Boss has been generous with you, and he gave you the time you originally asked for, yet you failed to perform."

"I ran into a glitch, but I've got it handled now. I'll have the money to you right here, in this house, in three days," Jimmy pleaded.

Jimmy knew there was no cash to be had, and as he spoke he was running scenarios in his head to disappear, fade into the folds of time, pull out the invisibility cloak, gone, history.

"Compounding interest is a beautiful thing and a terrible thing, depending on the side of the table you're on," the man said.

Jimmy became fidgety; he felt the "other shoe" dropping like a lead weight.

"A million is due. In three days!" he said, got up and walked out.

Jimmy walked to the door as the deadbolt clicked. He moved to the window, looked down to see the short man step into a black sedan and speed away. Looking to both sides, he noted the copper downspouts only inches from the window, and the ivy climbing up the two stories of aged brick. A few minutes later, the hulk walked in with a big smile on his face.

"The Boss wants me to explain the seriousness of the situation," he said.

"No, no, I get...."

The hulk grabbed Jimmy by the throat and lifted him up, partially strangling him. His feet lifted off the carpet, and when they touched down, the hulk landed a fist in Jimmy's stomach. Gasping for breath, Jimmy tried to talk, but his lungs delivered no air to the vocal cords for talking, not even a squeal. A backhand to the jaw hurled Jimmy to the floor. The hulk stood over him and glared.

"I take it you get the point," the hulk said. "And don't try to disappear, we know everything about you."

Jimmy lay on the floor after the hulk left, then half crawling, he made his way to the window. They were double-pane, and locked, but no bars, and it was only two stories down. He made it to his feet, and combed the room for anything that might help. In a small cabinet he noticed a round object. Reaching into the dark crevice, he wrapped his fingers around the smooth, cold piece and pulled it into the light. His face could not subdue the smile that had no basis to replace the terror he felt. Grasping the onyx bookend, he turned to the window. It would take several strikes to break enough glass to make room for him to get through. He could do it, he knew he could. Climb down the gutter pipe and run for it.

He could make it to a phone, and call Samantha. She knew people and would get him to Florida, then a fast boat to Cuba or Argentina. He could get his payments from Zach eventually wired to wherever he was, and make this whole thing disappear. Live the simple life, forget about deals and making money; he would change; he was changing; now; at this moment. He knew he was… changing! What did he need to prove to anybody anymore? Dad was dead, and that was that. In the middle of the night, he would make his move to freedom … and his new life.

61

Charlotte

The first floorboard crumbled as the crowbar separated it from the floor joists. Zach leaned over the gap and glared below. Nothing was the only treasure that he could see. Each of the next two boards pulled up in one piece, but the flashlight revealed only packed sand. When Zach stood up to take a breath, Andrew squirmed past him, grabbed the crowbar and yanked up two more boards. These practically disintegrated as Andrew kicked the pieces under the curtain to the hall. He dropped to the floor like he was doing pushups, but instead stuck his head into the hole and scoured the sand below. He followed the beam of light to every corner, then reached down and grabbed a handful of sand, looked for uneven surfaces, anomalies, miracles, acts of god ... nothing made sense.

The bartender put three beers on the bar, along with rum shots.

"We're not defeated," Zach pronounced. "Let's down these shots and know ... we will solve this. Lost the battle, but not the war."

All they found was a dead-end, but Alice wasn't focused on the treasure. Her attention was trained on her brother. There was a man at the bar who looked just like her brother buying shots. Come on, buying shots? Mr. Glum. Captain Serious, zero-fun Zach? He can't be coming out of his shell, she thought. Pretty soon he'll be wearing a party hat, dancing around in a toga. The family structure and well-being is all structured around Zach being boring.

After two shots, Zach sauntered over to the opposite side of the bar and started talking to a couple of sailboat skippers probably about the weather, or an engine or whatever. A woman walked up to them at the bar and a few minutes later a short, petite blonde joined them. Zach attempted to be subtle, but couldn't keep his eyes off her.

"This is my wife, Janet, and this is her sister, Charlotte," one of the skippers said.

"Nice to meet you. I'm Zach. Are you ladies sailors?"

"Charlotte is staying here on Marina Cay for a few days while we cruise to Gorda and out to Anegada," Janet said. "Just some R and R for her. She's not much of a sailor."

"You'll be very comfortable here. I stayed here many times with my parents growing up," Zach said. "Have you been to the islands before?"

"No, my husband and I were golfers, and he liked the desert courses, so we mostly kept our trips in the States," Charlotte said.

"Is he here with you this trip?" Zach asked.

"No, he passed away last year," she said. "Janet and Rob invited me to join them for the week."

Alice watched this conversation from across the bar. While she couldn't hear them, she saw Zach's countenance light up and knew there were some sparks flying. Her brother was becoming a new person. When Zach's wife died, he turned inward, focused on business, and almost became somber. Even before she died, he was quiet and methodical. This was a different, new person. Then she thought about Dad dying. Was Zach under some pressure working "under" Dad? Was his true nature suppressed because Dad was so dominant, so in charge? Yeah, well in charge was a whole different animal with Dad, so quirky, like this crazy treasure hunt, my god! Two facts she couldn't deny, though. Dad made tons of money, and Zach was changing before her very eyes.

Zach looked up to see Alice and Andrew slip out for the evening. He was talking sailing with the guys, but slipped in a mention of all the golf courses in the desert he could remember. Charlotte had been to a few of them, but Zach was right on target and she was giving most of her attention to him. She asked Zach to meet her for lunch there at Pusser's, the next day, and the date was set.

62

Bill Price

Bill Price took a deep breath as he sat down at his desk in his home office. He resumed reading the diary and quickly paged through the company's successes and challenges, many of which he helped navigate. Richard included passages about the children growing up and parenting along with Jennifer and Samantha too. Bill Price was familiar with most of this era during which he became close to Richard and the family. He skimmed the pages looking for hints or clues to the treasure hunt, but it was as if Richard forgot about all the coins and the treasure, and Price never saw another mention of it.

63

Two Really Good Shovels

After failing in the dry-goods closet, the island-team meticulously scoured the building, occasionally loosening a floorboard or a wall slat. Alice and Andrew kicked up rocks, looking for any trace that could lead them in the direction of the single focus in their minds … the treasure. But … the big-but, they were empty-handed, tired, and discouraged.

Alice woke in the morning before Andrew, and slipped out the door for a walk. She took the path around the perimeter of the tiny island, then in front of the pier, veered up the hill on the path to the Robb White House. Visualizing herself as a child running up that same path paved in pebbles and sand, and then chasing Maureen or Zach right down again, gave her pause, and brought a slight smile to her tired face. When she reached the house, she stopped to catch her breath and sat on the three-foot-high, rough stone wall. The door to the house was cracked open, so she headed toward it in small, slow steps, like she was sneaking up on the house. A world of memories flooded her mind as she walked through the door and into the room. She stopped and could see Zach in her mind's eye, standing on a pedestal in the corner at fourteen years old in full oration mode, reciting the Gettysburg Address … "four score and seven years ago our forefathers…." Before she could think, she ascended the imaginary pedestal and in her deepest Zach-like voice recited, "four score and seven years…," before she broke out into a giggle. Then an all-out-gut-wrenching laugh filled the room, while Zach appeared from the far corner. Alice jumped off the stand and ran straight to Zach as they threw their arms around each other and hugged as only siblings can. It was comfort, and it was relief from this dubious mission that their dad had left them, a mission that was pulling everything apart, splintering the foundation of their lives.

Zach looked at Alice as deep as she ever remembered, and said, "I think I'm doing better, like a curtain is lifting from around me." He paused. "There is so much to live for, to explore, to be a part of. I'm feeling happy and confident."

"Dad died, Zach," Alice said.

"I know. I always thought I should stay resolved, steady, reliable, unnerved, and predictable, for Dad, for Mom, for you, and you know, for everybody," he said.

"You don't have to be propping everybody up," she said. "We're all okay. Mom is strong and Samantha is living her life. Maureen's Silicon-Valley soap opera will move along at its own pace, and Jimmy…"

"There's nothing to add about Jimmy. He is just Jimmy," Zach said.

"Take care of yourself, my big brother." She paused. "Do you like that woman from the bar last night?"

"She's a terrific person and get this, I'm having lunch with her."

"Cool," Alice said.

They both sat and laughed about all the fun they had as children in that funny little house.

"Hey, remember when we did all those plays down in the basement?" Alice said.

"I sure do. There were some doozies."

"Let's go down there and look," Alice said.

Together they shoved the wooden lid away from the hole in the floor.

Zach reached into the cavern and felt around on the tiny ledge just under the opening. His hand grasped the small flashlight, and he brought it up, flipped it on and shined the beam into the basement.

"Still cold down there," he said.

"It's a refrigerator," Alice replied.

They descended the ladder, and when on the ground, Alice spied their old kerosene lantern. From his pants pocket, Zach pulled out a book of matches. The lantern fired up, and the room seemed to come alive as the walls illuminated.

"Remember the Bird character in the 'Bird the Mouse and the Sausage'? I think I really nailed that part. Don't you think?" Alice said.

"Well, the speech in *Nicholas Nickleby* was my triumph," Zach said.

Alice paused, then said, "Hey, read the clue again. Do you have it with you?"

Zach pulled a folded piece of paper from his back pocket.

"The red roofs show off well on this postage stamp that caps the reef. But when the curtain goes up and the jester gives a sign, look down humbly, and the treasure you'll find," Zach read.

"The curtain goes up? Maybe the clue means down here. Where the curtain goes up," Alice screeched. "Remember when the stage was right there, in that corner?" she said.

Zach nodded.

"Maybe it's there. Should we dig it up?" she asked.

"It's hard packed, and we'll need a pick, and two really good shovels," Zach replied. "Go get Andrew and tell him to look for a pick around the dock area. If he can't find one, take the boat to Road Town and get one, and two digging shovels. I'll check around Pusser's and then I have a lunch date."

64

Just Feel It

Zach started off toward the restaurant, but thought better of getting seen by Charlotte looking disheveled. He diverted to his room, showered and cleaned up, then tried on three different shirts ... the Hawaiian print; no, too presumptuous; the rust-colored silk button-up he just bought in St. Thomas; no, too stiff-looking for lunch; the pullover golf shirt with subtle horizontal stripes...yep just the ticket.

At eleven thirty he started down the path to Pusser's, to look around for digging tools. As he descended the path and took a sharp right around a modest stand of trees, he saw Charlotte on the path in front of him.

"We're both early for lunch. What do you think that says about us?" he said.

"Maybe that we're both hungry," she replied with a catty smirk, and they both broke into a giggle.

Their light attitude continued through lunch. The waitress finally stopped by the table and said her shift was ending and could she bring them anything more. Zach looked at his watch, discovering that it was three o'clock. He shrugged his shoulders and looked up at Charlotte.

"Well, okay then," was the only thing she said as they both gave a smart little snicker.

"There's a hole-in-the-wall fish place in Road Town out on the point; the conch is their specialty," he said.

"I've never tried it, but it sounds good," she replied.

"If it's not too much in one day, I'd like to take you there tonight."

"Okay, Mr. Zach Dennison, I'm up for a trip to Road Town," she said.

Zach took the long way back to his room and circled up the hill. He arrived at the outdoor patio and saw Alice sitting in a recliner looking onto the ocean channel.

"Andrew is on his way to Road Town now to get a pick and shovels. He was running down to the pier like a jackrabbit. My guess is he'll be back in record time," she said.

"I think there's a good chance we're in the right place. What do you think?" he said.

"Remember the fun Dad got out of our plays and our acting? Even when we bickered about little things like 'Jimmy did this to me' and 'Maureen's not fair,' or who got which part. He looked like he was enjoying the turmoil," she said.

"I remember him watching us work those things out on our own, and getting satisfaction from the process," he said.

"And Mom in the background." Alice paused. "Do you think Mom deferred too much to Dad?" she asked.

Zach looked out onto the gentle rolling sea. The sun was beginning its descent to the western horizon, and the normal, gentle ten-knot wind washed over their sun-browned skin through the trees.

"I think they had a silent rapport; a tacit understanding. I think it worked really well for them and for us," he said.

"Maybe it didn't work for Jimmy, though," she said.

"I think about Jimmy a lot. He was the one I looked up to; the one I wanted to be like until that one summer," Zach said. "I've thought about it too much over the years. I can't put my finger on it."

"He was the oldest, and I think he was competitive with Dad. He always tried to show Dad how good he was at things, how smart he was," she said.

"Something must have happened during that school year back in Florida, because when he got to California for the summer, he was different. Like sharp and edgy. Beats me," Zach said.

Zach stood up and took a slow lap around the patio area; stopped in front of the small sound stage, and took a deep breath.

"Let's go down the ladder to the basement and look around while we're waiting for Andrew," he said.

"I'll meet you there. I'm getting a sweater for that icebox," she said.

"Grab one for me. My room is open," he said.

When Andrew rapped on the concrete floor surrounding the opening to the basement, Zach glanced up and saw Andrew holding an iron digging bar.

"Hey mate, I'll hand these down to you," Andrew said.

The bar went first followed by two shovels and then a large construction-type pick. Zach needed both hands and both feet planted on the ground to manage the weight of it. As he set it down, he wondered if this good-idea-heavy-duty pick was overkill for their abilities. When it hit the ground, this monster would crush the firm-packed dirt, but swinging it up over his head continuously was going to be a challenge.

Andrew stepped carefully down the ladder in the low light. Even with the new 150-watt light bulb burning and two florescent lanterns glowing, his eyes took a few minutes to adjust.

"We've decided to dig over there in the corner where our stage used to be. Alice thinks the reference to the curtain going up and looking down, is just what Dad was hinting," Zach said.

"We're going to find it. I can just feel it," Andrew replied.

Zach turned his head away from Andrew and rolled his eyes. Whenever he could "just feel it," Zach felt like Andrew was about to write a wispy poem about dizzy-dancing clouds, then tango around the room with a tie-dye scarf. But Andrew was a transformed poet; a digging machine, a titan of wealth, intent on success in the business of treasure. The "just feel it" was a regression to a has-been inhabitant of his body. The poet was now the baron of jet planes and private islands.

Andrew grabbed the pick, and lifting it over his head, he commanded his arms to mercilessly strike precisely at ground-zero. Zach watched the forward thrust of Andrew's body buckle, crumbling backward to follow the giant pick to the ground behind him; his hips and back falling flat on the ground while the back of his skull collapsed on the hard-pack two inches from the pick's business end. He lay there stunned and motionless. Zach looked up and saw Alice starting down the ladder, having narrowly missed the unfolding calamity befalling her husband.

"Andrew, are you all right? What happened to him? What is going on around here?" she asked.

Zach looked down at Andrew's motionless body, then up to Alice's crazed eyes.

"He fell over trying to use that pick," Zach said.

"Where did that come from?"

"Your husband bought it in Road Town."

She dropped to her knees and cupped Andrew's face in her hands.

"Andrew, Andrew. Can you hear me?" she uttered in almost a whisper.

She lifted his head, felt in back for blood, but detected none. Then her ear hovered over his heart, listening.

"He's still got a heartbeat. What do we do?" she asked.

"Getting a limp body up that ladder is impossible without hurting him.

He may have broken bones. We can't move him right now," Zach said.

Alice pulled her sweater off and laid it over his chest, then sat on the cold earth next to him.

Zach went down to the restaurant to find out from Zephyr about getting help for Andrew, while Alice paced around the basement. When the cold got to her, she climbed out and walked outside to stand in the sun. The big orange ball still had several hours before it bedded down for the night, but catching a few rays meant she needed to walk down the path a bit to an open spot between trees. A few minutes warmed her up and she was feeling better when Zach and Zephyr arrived. The medics had been called, but would take thirty or forty minutes to arrive.

At the house, Alice jumped onto the ladder and scampered down; Zach followed, and then Zephyr. The first thing Alice saw in the dim light was Andrew moving his right arm, then rolling his right shoulder. His eyes opened to a squint as he looked around the room. Alice touched his hand as he rolled his body to his side.

"Andrew, are you all right?" she screeched.

He made a feeble effort to clear his throat, then said, "I think so."

65

Glass Shards

The glass shattered as Jimmy pulled the bookend back from the window. The small blue towel protected his hand as the glass shards crumpled on the windowsill. His prison was open and without a second thought he pulled himself through and stood on the sill. Reaching for the downspout, he dragged himself toward it until both hands clutched the round, smooth column of copper. He drew his left foot from the sill as his entire weight settled on his precarious grip, and clutching harder, he was able to hold tight. Starting to wrap his feet around the pipe, he felt a jolt as the downspout groaned and pulled away slightly from the wall. Jimmy moved his right hand down the spout to start his descent. Assured he could drop to the ground once he reached the first-floor level, he inched downward. Then without warning, the brackets trembled, pulled away, and released the pipe from the wall. In a heartbeat, Jimmy straightened his arm, reaching to the wall to grasp anything he could hold, but the pipe fell like a drunken sailor to the shrubs below. The foliage barely broke his fall as he hurled to the ground. While tumbling headfirst could have broken his neck, he landed flat on his back.

Under the bushes, a coupling joint for the irrigation system protruded about eight inches above ground. The sixth lumbar of Jimmy's spine barely missed the coupling but the impact drove his head and chest into the trunk of an oak tree, knocking him out for a few minutes. As he began to move, a sharp pain shot through his body. Pulling himself to his feet, he was sure ribs were broken. He dragged himself the short distance to the wall surrounding the house and managed to kick open an old wooden door and run into the street.

66

The Jester

After the paramedics pulled Andrew up the ladder, they loosened one strap at a time from the skid. On-the-spot diagnosis didn't find any broken bones, and they agreed a mild concussion was the extent of his injuries. After being helped to his feet, and though a little dizzy, he could take a few steps. Alice eased him out the front door and slow-walked him down the hill to their room, where he was instructed to stay till morning. Zach watched the paramedics leave along with Zephyr, then pulled the cover over the basement entrance. Back in his room, he looked at his phone. Twenty texts and double that amount of emails all screaming problems with the buildings in the Valley. But the one arresting his attention was that building in Fremont. On its way to becoming vacant, the staff was finding leaky duct work, heating problems and a plethora of dry rot under the roof. He figured it was all fixable, but the cost of repairs and worse, the no-rent year-and-a-half he saw coming up would kill cash flow. A load of gold and silver would go a long way to bridging the gap ... he needed to find Dad's stash, and the sooner the better. But not now. He had a lady to entertain.

Charlotte's long dress accentuated her natural curves, and her hair was pulled back in an "island" bun, a casual roll of hair held together with a mother-of-pearl clip. They leisurely made their way from the shuttle boat to a taxi whisking them along the twenty-minute route to Road Town.

Zach was comfortable in the low-key restaurant, surprising himself with his social ease and finesse, even telling jokes at dinner. He put his arm around her on the boat ride back, and she fit right into his hold. Nervous when they got to her front door, he extended his hand for a shake, but they fell easily into a warm embrace.

Jumping high and clicking his heels was what he wanted to do, but he settled for an inconspicuous skip up the stairs and into his room.

At breakfast Zephyr approached his table and pointed to the hallway behind the bar.

"It's over there," she said.

Zach nodded and although he couldn't see it, knew it was the regular-size pick she had brought back from her banking trip to town that morning.

The cover to the basement was just as he left it. He laid the pick on the floor and slid the lid back. The damp, cold basement gave him a shiver, and he shook all over until he lifted up the pick and swung it at the dirt. Chunks of ground flew up and to the sides, settling back in the hole, mingling with the loose ground left from yesterday. When he heard a rattle on the ladder, he looked around to see Alice stepping off the last rung and onto the ground.

"That's a lot of dirt, and you're only three feet down," she said.

"Do you think it's the right location?" Zach asked.

"It looks right to me. Maybe the stage was a foot that way, but you're in the general vicinity," she said. "I can't think Dad would have buried this too much deeper. Maybe we'll hit pay-dirt soon."

Alice grabbed a shovel and scooped out the dry, black dirt, throwing it on the pile.

"Andrew is awake, and I told him to go slow and come up here only if he feels okay," she said.

Sweat rolled off both of them as they dug deeper, excited and expecting the shovel to clink into their inherited treasure trove at any minute. Another foot down, Zach tossed the pick onto the pile of dirt, sat on a small round stool, and let his face collapse into his open palms.

"I can't believe it's any deeper than this," Zach said. His voice low and almost in a whisper.

Alice stopped and looked at Zach. She opened her mouth and waited for the right words to fumble through her lips, but nothing but silence eked out. She grabbed the iron bar and practically threw it at the center of the hole. Chunks of dirt flew into the air as she grasped the bar and hurled it again and again into the would-be grave of their treasure.

"I guess Dad got us again," Zach said. "This seemed so logical, but it's wrong. All wrong. Maybe there's no treasure. Maybe we're the brunt of Dad's last joke. I need some air."

Alice followed Zach up the ladder and headed to her room to check on Andrew. He was sitting up and on the deck, looking out to sea. She pulled up a chair and told him the disappointing news. He slightly groaned like he wasn't that interested, and she attributed it to the concussion. She walked into the room and in a few minutes came back, opened the folded sheet of paper, and passed it over to Andrew.

"The red roofs show off well on this postage stamp that caps the reef. But when the curtain goes up and the jester gives a sign, look down humbly, and the treasure you'll find," Andrew read.

"Read it again," Alice said.

He read it aloud two more times as Alice stared out over the small, intermittent whitecaps punctuating a quiet sea.

"What about 'jester,' that word?" Alice whispered, like she was saying it to herself. "More specific than just a play or a skit. Dad was very clever and very precise."

"You tell me," Andrew replied. "You were there."

"Did Jimmy play a jester? I think he did," Alice said. "Yes, in that little play Samantha adapted for us, *King Arthur*. That's it, *King Arthur*. Jimmy was the jester. What was his name? On the tip of my tongue. 'Dra … something. The script had juggling, and he tried to learn, but never could, so he told stupid jokes. Dad loved that play. That's it, the jester, *King Arthur*. I know that's it. Dagonet, that's his name. That's the jester's name!"

"How does that help us find this treasure?" Andrew asked.

Alice thought a minute, while visualizing the scene and the play on that day years ago. Her mind's eye could see Dad laughing, Mom grinning, and Jimmy hamming it up on that stage.

"Okay, how's it going to help?" Andrew said. "I'm just saying, where's the treasure?"

Alice looked up in a start, then jumped out of the chair and ran out of the room straight to Zach's room. She burst through the door and called for Zach. No answer. Turning on a dime, she darted down the path to Pusser's, erupting into the open-air dining room. Spotting Zach, she beelined to his table.

"Hi, Alice. Let me introduce you to Charlotte," Zach said. "This is my sister, Alice."

"Zach! *King Arthur*, the jester. Jimmy was the jester. Dad liked the play," Alice cried.

Zach was uncomfortable and a little embarrassed. His eyes darted between Alice and Charlotte. He mumbled something and snickered out of nervousness. His eyes rested on Charlotte.

"Alice and I have a little family project going on. You see, we spent a bunch of summers on Marina Cay as kids…well you know, stuff like that," Zach fumbled with his words. "Well, then," he said. "That's interesting news; maybe we could go over all that later this afternoon."

Alice's eyes locked on Zach's eyes. "The stage was in the middle of the room. Not on the side. The middle!" she said.

Zach looked out in space, and then back to Alice.

"Get started and I'll join you later," he said.

67

Philip V

Andrew picked up the shovel and watched Alice wail into the tamped-down dirt directly in the middle of the basement floor. After a few whacks at it, she commented that the ground was a bit softer than before. Andrew shoveled out the loose dirt when she stopped to catch her breath. About a foot down, and three feet square, she'd moved a real pile of dirt, but her thrusts yielded nothing but more dirt. Cold sweat rolled into her eyes, and they agreed to take a break. Outside the mid-afternoon sun warmed them both, and their mood was equally excitement, disappointment, and trepidation.

"What are you thinking about?" she asked.

"About what if this is a bust, and we never find anything, and about what we do with it if we do find it, and do we share, and if we do, how to share," he said.

"Yeah, I know. I'm totally confused, too," she said. "How long are we going to dig up that basement? I mean, do we dig up the whole thing? Does the clue mean something totally different, and we are completely off target?"

They sat silently; the frustration, and fear of losing, and thought of going home empty-handed was crippling.

"What is your thought on sharing?" she said.

"It's hard to focus on right now, but I still don't think it's fair," he said.

She looked away and shrugged.

Andrew rose from his chair and started shuffling toward the basement, with Alice following. They looked down the ladder and got a glimpse of the pick swinging through the air. Another foot deep, and the hole had expanded to four-feet square. Zach turned his head and saw them from the corner of his eye, but made no gesture or acknowledgement; just kept flailing at the dirt.

Drenched in sweat, he stopped and leaned on the pick like it was a cane.

"Little Jimmy, the jester. Yep, I remember that play. I was King Arthur and you and Maureen were Knights of the Round Table."

"I was Lady Marion, too," she said.

"Double cast; that's the way we did it," Zach said. "Jimmy adlibbed the jokes and it was hilarious."

"Jimmy, Jimmy. What are we going to do with him?" Alice said.

"He gets his share, like everybody else, just like everybody," Zach said. "That's what we're going to do with him."

Alice walked over and took the pick from Zach, signaled him to move away, lifted it over her head, and slammed it into the dirt. After the pick hit, they all stopped dead in their tracks; no one moved; nobody said a word. The crack of the pick smashing into something solid echoed through the concrete room. Alice turned to look at Zach and then to Andrew, who grabbed the shovel and began scraping and scooping the dirt away. Zach knelt down and brushed the loose soil away from the small hole in a wooden crate. He stuck his hand down into the crevice, felt the cold hard contents, wrapped his fingers around something circular and pulled it up. Holding it up to the light, he read, "Phillip V 1733, Utraque Unum."

"Both worlds are one. That's what it means. It's Latin," Andrew said.

"It's a silver coin, a Spanish piece of eight."

"We found it. We found the treasure!" Alice shouted.

Then from the top of the ladder, they heard, "Found what?"

It was Jennifer making her way slowly down one rung at a time until she had both feet on the dirt floor.

"The treasure, that's what," Alice said.

"Wow, what a coincidental time to arrive," Jennifer said. "Is it down in that hole? What's in there?"

"So far we have one piece of eight, but I'm guessing there's more, maybe some gold too," Zach said.

"Fabulous," Jennifer said. "Are you going to share it?"

"Equally. Yep, it's going to be all evened out," Zach said, looking sternly at Andrew before flashing a quizzical look toward Jennifer.

"Finish digging up your treasure. I think you earned it," Jennifer said. "Let me take a look at that Spanish piece of eight."

THE END

CPSIA information can be obtained
at www.ICGtesting.com
Printed in the USA
LVHW011352140322
713063LV00002B/3